BLACK DEMANDS

A KELLY BLACK AFFAIR

CJ THOMAS

cj@cjthomasbooks.com

ABOUT THE AUTHOR

CJ lives in the Green Mountains of Vermont. You can find CJ skiing, hiking, and spending time with family when not typing away on the latest hottest read.

Connect with CJ:

cj@cjthomasbooks.com

BLACK DEMANDS, BOOK DESCRIPTION

He gave me a promise ring and I made the commitment to be his.

Submission was a game to criminal defense lawyer, Kelly Black, and he set the expectations high. I had to be flawless as he demanded I do better. There were guidelines that needed to be followed. Rules of engagement he insisted I learn. And just when I thought our relationship was progressing, it came crashing down hard.

My body temperature spiked before plummeting with fear. He was an enigma and I feared that I wasn't his only one. I could see it in his eyes, the secrets he had hidden inside. Panic and uncertainty rolled through my bones as I worked to uncover the truth.

But then everything changed when I saw him, the man who stole my innocence and haunted my dreams. My spirit was as broken as my past and I feared that Kelly would leave me because of it. I was determined to fight knowing that, together, Kelly and I were the most beautiful natural disaster waiting to happen.

1

Kendra

I stopped a short breath away from the door. Balling my hand into a fist, I lifted it, ready to rap my knuckles against the wooden door to announce my arrival.

Then I pulled back.

My lips rounded as I blew out a controlled sigh.

Kelly had my head spinning.

Thinking twice about entering, I looked up the hallway then back toward the elevator I'd just stepped out of. It was silent; no one around but me. Now that I'd agreed to his contract, I knew that he'd soon be taking our relationship to the next level—a new height I was anxiously waiting to learn more about.

The man was incredible. Strong, dominant, mysterious. He had it all. I loved how he kissed me with enough passion to make my lips feel bruised. And when I touched the tips of my fingers with the pad of my thumb, I could still feel his tight waist on them. Kelly Black had seared his way into my brain. Each time I closed my eyes I could see him staring back, searching deep into my eyes as he threaded his strong fingers through my hair, lightly tugging at the roots.

I bit my bottom lip and hung my head. Just thinking about him had my nipples tightened into hard little knots of the most delicious agony I'd ever experienced.

It was early morning and without knowing what waited for me on the other side of this door, I thought it best that I just use the key I was given and let myself in without turning my visit into some kind of huge production.

Digging in my purse, I found the set of keys and slid the match into the slot, unlocking the deadbolt that was always in place. I heard the shower running in the back as my heels clicked across the floor to the kitchen. My lips curved into a smile when I saw the coffee had already been brewed. Pouring myself a full mug, I proceeded to make myself at home, slicing a bagel in half and toasting it before smothering it in vegetable cream cheese.

There was a new set of flowers—a sunny splash of color made up of lilies and roses—perfectly assembled in a glass ginger vase. Setting my bagel down on the plate, I couldn't help but move to them, drawing in a breath to smell the lovely fragrance that drifted through the room.

I glanced over my shoulder when I heard the shower turn off.

Quickly, I reached for the note still tucked between two stems, unable to stop myself from snooping.

Alex, work just isn't nearly as fun without you by my side. Can't wait to get home and back into your arms. xx ~ Nash

My eyes rolled.

Never in a million years would I have thought Nash Brooks would be so cheesy. Though I could probably give Alex credit for breaking the man down. Without her, he'd still be holding on to his reputation of swinging his bat at everything that was tossed his way. She'd stopped that with a homerun-winning hit, and that filled my heart with pride. I was happy for her—for them.

Setting the note down on the countertop, I slid back into my chair, taking another bite of my bagel and washing it down with the hot black coffee. No matter what I said to her, or how pathetic I made their relationship out to be, I also couldn't deny that I wouldn't mind if Kelly started to give me flowers on a regular basis. Pursing my lips and tilting my head to the side, I couldn't recall ever having a man do that for me. Probably because I would never allow it to happen.

"I thought I heard someone rummaging through my kitchen." Alex's soft voice bounced off the walls and filled the vast cathedral ceilings of her open living room.

I turned to find her smiling. "Just me, the regular freeloader," I said, batting my lashes.

She wrapped her arm around my neck and kissed my forehead.

"You look good. Is that what you're wearing to work?" My eyes raked over her cute sundress. And though her hair was wet, her natural curls tightened into sexy spirals that bounced perfectly with each step she took.

Alex rounded the kitchen counter, stopped, and looked down her front. "Why? Something wrong with it?"

"It's perfect." I thought how lucky she was to be able to wear such comfortable dresses to work. Any other profession—besides my own—would have her sent home. My eyes glanced back to the flowers.

"They were sent over this morning." Her eyelids hooded in a sense of longing for her man to return.

"When's Nash coming back?" This was the longest they'd been apart since they got together.

"Not soon enough." She frowned.

I couldn't stop rocking back and forth on my tailbone, causing the chair to squeak.

"What is it?" Alex turned to me with a quizzical look on her face.

My spine pulled to the ceiling and I sprang forward, balancing on the tips of my toes. "Since you must ask…"

Alex deliberately lowered her head to study my expression.

In a split second, I pulled my hand out from under the counter and dangled my fingers in front of her face, showing her the ring Kelly gave me.

Alex's mouth rounded and her eyes popped out of her head. She stumbled backwards, bringing her hand up to cover her mouth.

I nodded, lifting a single eyebrow.

She swiftly stepped forward, taking my hand between her fingers. I watched her study the rock, glittering in the light above. It was beautiful and had my heart hammering for my man. I guess flowers weren't needed so long as Kelly gifted me jewelry like this.

"That was quick." Alex lowered my hand, then brought it back closer to her face. "When's the wedding?"

I pulled my hand free and clucked my tongue. "You know I'm not the marriage type."

"He just gave that to you?"

My gaze cast to the diamond, moving on my wiggling finger, shifting angles to see it from all sides. It was perfect in every sense. "It's a promise ring," I said.

The lines of Alex's forehead wrinkled. "And what exactly did you have to promise him?"

I could hear the skepticism in her voice. The tone made me believe that she thought I had to do something outrageous in order to receive a gift like this. "You make it sound like you've never heard of a promise ring before."

"I'm no fool. I know what a promise ring is, I just want to know what *he* thinks it means."

My tongue wet my lips as my gaze fell back to the silver ring reflecting light as if it was something magical. "It's his promise to me." Out of the corner of my eye, I saw Alex cock a hip and roll her eyes. "To live worry-free, promising that he'll take care of me."

"Ironic." Alex crossed her arms.

I lifted my gaze up to her. "Don't you think?"

Slowly, she turned her face to meet my gaze. "After all the shit you've given me about Nash being paternal—" her brows raised, "—he told you *that*?"

I gave her a firm nod, rounding my shoulders back and making sure to fold my hands on top of the counter with the ring proudly displayed for her to see.

"And you didn't make any promises to him?"

"No one said anything about not making any promises."

"So you did?"

"I did." I grinned.

"Care to share what those promises might be?"

I reached for my coffee mug and brought it to my lips. "One month, exclusive to him," I mumbled into the cup.

Alex tilted her head closer, cupping her hand behind her ear. "What was that? I couldn't quite understand you. It's like you didn't want me to hear what you just said."

My lips curled over the rim and I stole a quick sip, letting the roasted nutty flavor fill my senses before lifting my head and saying more clearly, "One month, exclusive to him."

Alex narrowed her eyes before letting her head fall into her hand. She shook her head and chuckled. That's when I noticed it. Around her soft wrist was a charm bracelet.

Slowly, I leaned forward as if being drawn in by some unexplainable magnetic force. I needed a closer look, needed to believe what it was I was seeing, what it was I was assuming. "What's this?" I asked, yanking her arm away from her head.

"Kendra!" Alex yelled as her body flung toward me. "It's nothing."

"Sure doesn't look like nothing." I brought it closer to my face, taking time to inspect a couple of the charms. "Nash gave it to you, didn't he?"

We locked eyes, neither of us willing to budge, before Alex said, "So what?"

"How is this any different?"

Alex peeled each of my fingers off her wrist and said, "For one, I didn't sell myself for a month."

My head nodded as I smiled like I'd caught her in a lie. "No, you just sold out completely."

"You really want to play this game?" Her eyes hardened as her face got serious. "Because, I can do this if you want."

"Go girl. Show me what you got." My muscles flexed.

She stomped her way around the counter and marched straight up to me, grabbing hold of my ear. "Let's talk about where you got these."

I winced when she pulled on them both, and it took me a second to remember what I had in my ears. But as soon as I did, I cursed, "Shit."

"Uh-huh." She released my lobes.

"Madam's going to kill me." I swatted her hand away, reaching up to make sure they were the earrings I thought they were. Alex looked on, patiently waiting for an explanation. "I forgot to give them back."

"You mean to tell me those are the Madam's?" Alex's words swirled in disbelief.

They were the rare, tanzanite stones she only gave to certain girls. "It's her way of visibly recognizing certain rights of passage."

Alex must have seen the look on my face because she backed off, knowing that I'd made a mistake—again—with the Madam. She leaned against the counter's edge and crossed her arms. "So, let me get this straight. Madam is cool with you being exclusive to Kelly for one month?"

I slid back onto my stool, taking a bite of my bagel, thinking how ready I was to get on with my one month with Kelly.

Remembering his promise to introduce me into his world of submission was both terrifying and exciting. After all, that was the exact reason I went to work for the Madam—to rid myself of the mundane path I was on. "She's all for it."

Alex looked at me, forgetting to blink. Her neck was stiff and I couldn't help but ask, "What is it?"

She pushed off the counter and moved to stand in front of the sink with her back turned to me. I watched as she filled an empty glass with water. "I'm not sure I like what's happening here."

"Nash will be home soon. Then you can get back to straddling him and forgetting about me."

Alex turned to face me. Her brows were drawn tight. "Aren't you afraid?"

"Baby doll, there is nothing to be afraid of."

She stared into her glass for a minute before saying, "Except there is."

"There's not." I smiled, my voice a soft, encouraging whisper.

"Kendra, don't you remember?" She cleared her throat. "Kelly is the one who set off your relapse."

I cast my gaze down at my hands. She was right, but I wasn't about to admit it. We'd been over this; it wasn't Kelly's fault he'd triggered memories of my rape. My cell dinged with a message.

"Just promise me that you'll step away if it happens again."

When I looked up at Alex, I could see it in her eyes—she still wanted me to seek professional help to deal with the trauma of my past. But I couldn't.

Ignoring all of the insecurities bubbling up inside me and pushing the fears to the side, I reached for my purse and pulled out my phone to check who had messaged.

"It's him, isn't it?" Alex looked on.

I nodded. "I have to go," I said, collecting my things and taking the last bit of my bagel along with me.

"Kendra." I turned to find Alex holding up the key to her apartment. "Don't forget this."

I stepped back to her with an open palm. Alex dropped the key into my hand and when I closed my fingers around the metal, I kissed her cheek. "Thanks, baby."

"You know I'm always here for you." She flashed a small smile, but her eyes didn't hide the true thoughts of what it was she was thinking. "No matter what."

2
_____

Kelly

The deadbolt on the door clicked over and I was met with wide, unblinking eyes.

"Hey." Sylvia turned and went back inside.

I stepped through the threshold and did the honors of checking the house out before I got too comfortable. It was an open floor plan with white and yellow walls framing large bay windows, bringing the outside in. "Why did you want to meet way out here?" I asked.

Laguna Beach lay south of Los Angeles and was known for mild year-round temperatures, stunning beach coves, and a thriving artist community. It was the artist community that I suspected brought Sylvia Neil to the area—if only for a brief escape from the chaos of the city.

"Can I make you one?" she asked, busy behind the espresso machine to the right of the sink.

She had her long hair pulled back into a tight ponytail. It was the same casual appearance she had most of the time, the only difference now was that she was still wearing the shorts she'd slept in, covered by a long loose-fitting tee. "That would be great," I said.

A minute later, Sylvia slid a fresh hot espresso across the marbled island counter and said, "Thanks for coming on such short notice."

"It's a nice place." I nodded looking around. "Is it yours?"

"Like I could afford such luxury on a journalist's salary." She smirked.

I took a sip and licked the foam from my lip.

"It's my publisher's place." She lifted her own mug to her lips, pausing to cast her gaze down. "After he learned about my week of threats, I was given a new assignment."

My brows raised, curious to know what her new assignment entailed.

"A few days here for a little R-and-R." She lifted her hand up loosely, palm up in a *who cares* gesture.

"You seem relaxed," I commented as my eyes drifted over her lowered shoulders.

"It's been a while since I've taken some time off." She set her espresso mug down on the counter in front of her. "Besides, here it's more laid back than the office and my stuffy apartment."

I turned my attention outside. Ocean swells lazily came to shore in their normal ebb and flow. With the windows open, I breathed in the salty air, appreciating what a short drive to the beach could do for a man's soul. Even with my short time here, I could already feel my own head clearing. I turned my attention back to Sylvia who was lost inside her own thoughts. "So, have the threats stopped?"

She held her breath and her posture stiffened before she nodded. "Just as I suspected they would."

The investigation into Maria Greer's death was an interesting case that was still evolving. Whoever was behind the threats had to be close, aware of whatever it was Sylvia was working to uncover. And it was those secrets that seemed to have someone very paranoid.

"I met with Wesley Reid." I looked up at her from under my brow.

She let out the breath she was holding inside her chest and shifted her weight to her opposite leg. Suddenly her eyes woke up, eager to know what I had learned. "And did you find out anything?"

I cast my gaze back to my fingers lightly drumming on the counter. She had told me to go to Wes, knowing that he knew more about Nash Brooks's involvement with Maria, suspecting that there may be more to her death than what the police had collected and put into evidence.

Sylvia stepped forward. "Was I right?" Her tone was sharp.

I hooked my finger through the mug handle, lifting it to my mouth before slowly nodding. "Wes knew about Nash and Maria's time together." There was a glimmer of hope flashing across Sylvia's eyes when I met her gaze. "And his attraction to his own interns."

Then her face twisted as her eyebrows drew together.

"What is it?" I asked, knowing something had gone off inside her head.

"Nash—" Her eyes darted across my face as she tried to keep up with her own thoughts. "He's dating an intern now."

I gave her a questioning look. "Alex Grace?"

"Yeah." Her tone was soft. "She's also an intern."

"Not anymore." My tongue darted out of my mouth, wetting my lips. "Promoted to Assistant Director."

"But they're still dating?"

"As far as I know. Why? Did you hear something that would cause concern for Alex's safety?"

Sylvia let out a heavy sigh and rubbed her face. "No."

"Then what is it?"

"It's just that his relationship with Alex began in the same manner as it did with Maria." She turned, ran her hand over her hair, and cursed. "Kelly, don't you see?"

My eyes narrowed.

She turned back around to face me. "If Nash begins to take her to Mint, then who knows what will happen next."

I could see her concern but without first talking to Nash myself, I wasn't going to make the leap to saying Nash was the one who murdered Maria. "How do you know Nash is a member of Mint?"

Her mouth slackened as she shook her head. "C'mon. Don't you know me by now? It's what I do. Report on celebrities and the lives they lead. Once word spread about Wes's new nightclub, it was impossible for me—and others in the industry—to not want to know more about what went on once the doors were closed. If it wasn't for the secrecy behind it all, I probably would have pursued another story. But," her adoration for the story hit her eyes, "I couldn't let it go. I needed to know who was visiting, what they were doing, and why the rest of the world wasn't invited to the hottest new party in town."

I didn't know if she knew my own involvement with Mint or that I, too, partook in the lifestyle that remained exclusively underground and out of sight. And for what it was worth, it didn't matter. This was about connecting the dots and seeing if Sylvia was as a reliable source as I hoped she was. "But my understanding was that Nash stopped coming." I redirected our conversation back on point.

Her lips parted slightly. "That's my understanding too."

"But there is something that I'm unclear on."

"Lay it on me." She folded her arms across her chest. "Maybe I can help."

"I'm just not sure if Nash stopped attending the club before or after Maria's death."

We locked eyes, looking into the depths of each other's

thoughts for the answers we sought, like two chess players strategizing the next move in hopes of achieving a checkmate. If Sylvia wanted to make me believe that Nash Brooks could be the killer —when I already suspected Mario Jimenez of being framed— then her answer to my question could forever change the direction of the investigation into the murder of Maria Greer and my defense of Mario Jimenez. "Do you know?" I asked.

"After," she said firmly. "Definitely after."

"That's what I was afraid of," I murmured, feeling a knot twist in my gut.

I fought to hide the regret I felt threatening to pull my face into a frown. Dropping my gaze away from her, I picked up my espresso from the counter and brought it to my lips. Deep inside I hoped that she was wrong, that her answer was only a slip in memory from the events that led us to where we were today. Because I distinctly remembered Wes telling me that Nash stopped visiting his club before Maria's death.

Now I didn't know who to believe.

After a few minutes of silence, Sylvia finally asked, "So, whatever happened with that girl you were chasing the other day? You know, the one I ran into when leaving your penthouse."

Warmth spread up my chest at the mere thought of Kendra. I would be seeing her right after I was done here and with her contract signed and the Madam giving me permission to have her exclusively for a month, I had a lot to look forward to. "You said she looked familiar—"

Sylvia nodded. "She's a friend of Alex Grace. Did you know that?"

I couldn't help but notice the irony of the web of connections between the same people whose characters we now questioned. "It's funny, isn't it?"

Sylvia pursed her lips and tilted her head to the side.

"How we're all connected."

She swallowed and narrowed her eyes.

"There was something else Wes told me."

"Sounds like you want to tell me what that is."

"Only if you want to hear it."

"Should I?"

"Might clear some things up for both of us."

"Then by all means, do tell." Her brows raised.

"I just wonder why you failed to mention it to me first." I looked her in the eye, but she refused to look back. "Sylvia, why didn't you mention that you also had a one-night stand with Nash?"

She stepped away and moved to the window.

I flattened my feet and stood, stuffing my hands in my pants pockets. "Do you know how this looks, keeping a secret like that?"

"I do," she whispered. "But I wasn't the one to murder Maria." Sylvia spun around and let her words fly fast off her tongue.

My shoulders shrugged as I moved to the front door, ready to make my exit. With one hand on the knob, I glanced over my shoulder and said, "It makes me wonder if the death threats you received were even real."

Her face ticked at the accusation. "I didn't make that up! Kelly, you must believe me."

"Look at it from my angle. How can I not speculate?" I opened the door. "Then again, if you did make it all up, it's not a bad diversion to keep me from looking into your own relationship with the very same man you're convinced killed Maria."

Sylvia dropped her hands to her sides, balling them into tiny fists as her face fumed red. "I think you better leave."

"Thanks for the coffee." I smiled. "I'm sure we'll be in touch."

3

Kendra

"What took you so long?" I questioned Kelly the moment I opened the door.

After leaving Alex's in a hurry, thinking that he would be arriving to my place soon, I didn't think much about anything other than making sure I was home by the time he arrived.

Kelly leaned in for a kiss and apologized. "The meeting took longer than I anticipated."

My hands reached out and clamped around his tight waistline before sliding up the ripple of his abs, hiding perfectly behind the thin white cotton button-up he was wearing. I tugged him inside and immediately wrapped my limbs around him, needing him to know just how much I'd missed him.

His thick lips came crashing over mine once again and I parted my mouth, sucking his tongue. Kelly was so sexy in his three-piece suit, having the look of the professional lawyer—ready to save the world—and I couldn't help but squeeze him tighter. He swirled his tongue against mine, tasting of creamy espresso. "God, I've missed you," he murmured against my lips.

My feet left the ground and I wrapped my legs around him, his hands quickly finding the globes of my ass. His fingers spread, then curled, beginning to massage the deep tissue I knew he loved so much. "How much have you missed me?"

He chuckled. "As much as you missed me."

"Impossible." I hadn't bothered dressing in anything other than something I knew to be comfortable *and* accessible. With Kelly one thing was certain, I could always expect the unexpected. "So, Mr. Black," I purred, "tell me when the thirty days of your ownership officially begins."

He smiled, leaning in close to kiss the tip of my nose. "*Bella*, I don't want you to think of this arrangement as anything other than mutual, between two consenting adults."

I hung off of him, sliding my body down far enough to rub my aching clit over his hardness. "Please, save the formality for someone else."

The vibration from his deep chuckle spread to my limbs, only intensifying the aching pain he inflicted upon my raging desire.

"And, besides, the Madam remains the middleman in this transaction. Let's not be fooled into thinking that this is anything other than what it really is."

"And how would you describe what *this* is?" His husky voice dropped a note deeper.

"The most beautiful natural disaster." I grinned.

He tipped his head back and laughed.

When his eyes came to rest on mine, he adjusted me to feel more of his steeled rod throbbing behind his zipper. I was eager for him to bed me. "Take me to my bedroom."

"I didn't take you to be an early riser."

"There's nothing better than hot sex in the morning." I pressed my juicy lips against his. "Now, take me to my bedroom," I demanded.

His smile crinkled his eyes. "Begging isn't a good quality unless solicited."

"Then give me permission, Counselor." I unhooked my ankles and dropped the balls of my feet back to the floor, tugging on Kelly's hand, silently pleading with him to follow me to the back room.

I wanted nothing more than to rid my flesh of my clothes and have his hot tongue work its way over my body until he slammed his thick girth inside me. I'd been on fire, eagerly awaiting his arrival, my thoughts filled with memories of what exactly he was capable of doing to me—how he could unwind me so easily. I couldn't take it anymore. Waiting was for the birds. "Tell me to beg. I want to beg."

He clucked his tongue, kissed me one more time, this time with a little more tongue, and said, "That's not how this works."

When he let go of my hand, I was left feeling lost. I wanted to say something but I couldn't. My thoughts were scrambled, my feelings all over the place. But when I watched him skirt past me and head straight to the back—toward my bedroom—a sense of hope filled me, making me think that maybe he *was* listening to my needs.

I padded lightly on bare feet, following three steps behind him. Not once did he turn to look back, and I was left questioning whether or not I should follow. I knew what I wanted —*needed*. For Kelly to sex me up. But other than his hard on, his actions spoke otherwise. With Kelly, he was full of surprises and I wondered if this was his way of giving me what I wanted while remaining in control. The agony of lust burned deep inside me and I just didn't have time to be playing games like this.

He disappeared out of sight and I heard my closet doors open a second later. By the time I stepped foot inside my bedroom, Kelly was already fingering his way through my clothes. This was nearly a repeat of the last time he visited, the only difference now was that he was delving into the more personal areas of my life instead of the kitchen. "What are you looking for?" I asked.

Kelly didn't respond and I watched as he dug through my closet.

Clothes were everything to me. Fashion let others know the type of person I was. What mood I was in, how I felt, the type of social circles I wanted to be associated with. Without my personal style, I wouldn't be the person I was. I strived daily to be perfect, but when Kelly didn't say anything during his deep dive into my closet, my heart raced and my palms grew sweaty. "I was hoping that clothes wouldn't be part of the equation," I said, hoping to get some kind of reaction out of him.

He moved some hangers to the side, turned his head, and looked at me. "Don't worry. We'll get there soon enough."

He pecked my cheek as he moved past me on his way to the bathroom. Again, he floated his way through the room, opening cabinets, checking product labels, smelling soaps, and hooking his finger through necklaces dangling under the mirror. There wasn't an item he didn't inspect. I was thinking he just wanted to make sure I was the person he thought I was.

"Find everything you need?" I said in my most sarcastic tone, leaning against the doorframe with my arms folded and legs crossed at the ankles.

He lifted his gaze, meeting his own reflection staring back at him in the mirror. "I have a request."

My tongue slid to the corner of my mouth. "And what would that be?"

"As long as you're with me," he turned his head to look at me, "I want you to shower as soon as you wake up, and again in the evening after the day is done."

I shrugged, thinking that on most days I already did that. "No problem. Anything else, Chief?"

He sauntered over to me with a sexy glimmer in his eye that left me breathless. Kelly clamped his fingers over both my arms, sliding his hands down my arms, past my elbows, over my wrists, until finding my fingers dancing with his. He squeezed each one of them, then dropped his gaze to my nails. "This is unacceptable," he said, pointing out a nail where the paint had chipped. "Fix it."

"Been meaning to do it." My lids hooded over when I caught his dark eyes searing into mine. "On. The. List."

He reached around my waist, pulling me tight against his solid chest, and kissed me. "And don't let it happen again."

Naturally, I reached for him when he let me go, turning his back and walking toward the shower. "I need you to be perfect." He twisted to look over his shoulder.

I swallowed down the fear that constricted my throat. A genuine distress prickled my skin, afraid to let him down.

But I'd never tell him that. It was the last thing I wanted to do. I wanted this—us—to be perfect—just like he wanted of me. "Am I not already?"

He ignored my comment and said, "That includes the way you eat."

I thought about my empty fridge, how I'd been basically living with Alex, eating whatever she had available.

"Sour milk and stale cereal won't cut it." His tone commanded my attention.

"Kelly, that wasn't normal for me." I shook my head, reaching behind to rub my neck. "I've been staying most nights with a friend." When he didn't react, it was like I was talking to deaf ears. *Was this man serious?*

But I knew he was. And at this point, I'd say anything to take his mind off of his silly demands and get back to concentrating on making me wet and him hard. I was so worked up— still making up for the period of abstinence the Madam forced me to go through—that all I could think about was getting fucked.

Kelly stopped in front of the mirror again, leaning his face close to it. I watched him lick the pad of his thumb and smooth out each of his eyebrows before saying, "And one more thing."

I held my breath. He strode over to me with his hands inside his pockets. Then I watched with a fluttering heart as one hand lifted to my lips. He tugged on my bottom lip with his tongue, dropped his head a whisper away, and murmured, "I'll require you to have sex with me a minimum of three times a week."

I reached up to dig my nails into the nape of his neck. "Make it five and we have a deal."

He chuckled and slid his tongue past the seam of my lips, thrusting it hard against mine. "Then I guess I don't have to tell you, you'll have to submit to my desire whenever I'm in need."

Kelly caged me with his large, strong arms and I reached for his zipper, pulling it down. "Most likely not," I said, reaching inside and wrapping my fingers around his hot shaft. Anything to get laid, I thought.

Frankly, I saw this whole thirty days of ownership to be nothing more than a stupid game Kelly needed in order to take his mind off of the awful realities of his job. I was happy to play along, knowing that my future rested in both his and the Madam's hands. And as long as I continued getting what I wanted, then everyone won. There was little reason not to go along with it.

"Are you in need now, Counselor?" I pumped his shaft.

Kelly threaded his hand through my hair, yanked, and stepped away.

My brows knitted, giving him a look of disappointment. "Fine. If my place doesn't do it for you, how about we go to yours? I'd love to see your main residence now that my lips are sealed shut."

He stood there with his dick hanging out. "My main residence is private."

"Even for your *Bella*?"

He strode over to me and took my shoulders in his tight grip. "You'll need to earn it."

"Can I ask you something?"

Kelly nodded, pushing me back into the bedroom and toward my bed.

"Why is Sylvia's life being threatened?" His eyes widened and I knew he was surprised to hear that I knew. "Madam told me."

"It doesn't matter," Kelly said, pushing me back until the backs of my legs hit the edge of the bed, sending me floating down on top of the comforter. My legs draped over the edge and he fell to his knees, letting his hands run up the length of my legs before wedging the tips of his fingers into the waistline of my underwear. Slowly, he pulled them completely off, revealing my glistening pussy. "This," he said, playing with the short hair that was growing since Alex and I last got waxed, "needs to go."

I bit my lip, nodding.

Alex was right. I did find my own version of Nash.

Then Kelly's mouth fell over my clit, sucking it between his teeth, sending my eyes to the back of my head in orgasmic bliss. *Whatever you say, Counselor.*

4

Kelly

When Giselle didn't have her head down, buried in her phone, she kept glancing at me. "I have a bad feeling about this, Kelly."

"It's fine," I said, turning my attention out the window.

We'd been over this before, and rarely did Giselle fight me on something once we'd made our decision. It wasn't like I didn't invite debate; I did. But it was the second-guessing on our agreed upon plan that I didn't like.

My driver, Maxwell, was behind the wheel weaving the vehicle through the city on our way to county to visit Mario. Though I refused to look, I could still feel her gaze boring into the back of my head. "We should really be talking to Nash first," she said, clearly annoyed.

"We've been over this." My fingers drummed on my thigh. "Nash is out of town."

"Yes, but he's the one person who we *really* need to hear from."

Giselle wasn't going to let this go. My muscles tensed a second before I snapped, "Don't you think we learned enough from Alex? Sylvia? Hell, even Wes?"

Giselle clenched her jaw, holding her chin high, refusing to cower to my anger. God, she was irritating today. But I'd find even more reason to be annoyed with her if she backed down to my raised voice. Weakness was one quality in a human that I found repulsive, especially in our profession.

"It will be fine." I sighed, taking a deep breath to calm myself down. "Besides, what's the difference if you still believe Mario is innocent?"

I never did share with her that Wes mentioned Nash having a one-night stand with Sylvia. Sure, that gave reason for Sylvia to want to get back at Nash but without evidence to support any accusations, I wasn't about to complicate things.

"I can't stop thinking how long Mario has been sitting in a cell," Giselle's voice cracked, "waiting until a little luck comes his way."

"Luck has nothing to do with it."

"I know that." She reached up to touch her hair, noticing that Maxwell had slowed the vehicle just before turning into the parking lot. "Except, to him, we are his luck."

I eyed the entrance and watched two detectives follow a cop outside. "And there is nothing Nash can say at this point to make us think Mario is anything but innocent."

"Maybe you're right, but wouldn't you like to know for certain?" Giselle undid her buckle and gathered her things.

As soon as the engine shut off, Maxwell jumped out and opened my door. I instructed him to stay close and moved around the back of the vehicle to open Giselle's door. "Let's forget this," I said, taking her by her hand, letting her feet find solid ground. "We've both been under tremendous amounts of pressure."

"You have no idea," she muttered as if there was more to it than what I knew. But now wasn't the time to ask. And if it wasn't business related, I didn't want to hear it.

"It isn't fair to Mario if we leave any doubt we aren't capable of doing our jobs."

Giselle nodded in agreement and smoothed her hand down the front of her skirt as we marched into the building with our heads held high. We passed security without an issue and found Mario already waiting in a visitation room. "Make my client comfortable," I snapped my fingers at the guard, "and please, for God's sake, take those cuffs off of him."

Mario rubbed his wrists once the cuffs were removed, and Giselle situated herself next to me on the opposite side of the metal table. "How are you doing, Mario?" I asked.

"Good." He glanced up at me. "Considering."

He seemed a bit more down than the last time I'd seen him, and I'd been around the block long enough to recognize when a man was losing hope. It went through a series of stages. First, anger. Second, fear. Third—worst of them all—depression.

"Anything we can do to make your stay more comfortable?"

Mario gave me an arched look. "You can get me out of here."

"We're working on it," Giselle said.

Mario turned his head to her. "Did you speak with Nash?"

My fingers worked to undo the buttons of my jacket before taking a seat. Giselle's tailbone sat gingerly on the edge of hers and she was already reading the paperwork she'd spread out in front of her. "Unfortunately," she flicked her eyes up to meet Mario's, "Mr. Jimenez, Nash Brooks is out of town."

"So you didn't get to speak with him?" Mario gave a stony expression.

I leaned forward, resting my elbows on top of the table. "What was it you wanted us to hear Nash say, exactly?"

"Are you fucking kidding me?" Mario flipped his palms up to the ceiling, rolling his eyes over to me. "That he did this." He swallowed hard, like he had something stuck in his throat. "I didn't kill her. *He* did."

I shared a glance with Giselle. It was what Sylvia wanted us to believe, too.

"What makes you believe Nash is guilty?" Giselle calmly asked.

Mario put his hands beneath the table and leaned forward until his chest dug into its edge. "He was after the missing money, and he was the one who knew Maria. Until I was arrested and shown a picture of her," the crease between his brows deepened, "I had never seen her face in my life." Mario shifted his gaze over to me. "I thought you were the best there was."

"Mr. Black is *the* best," Giselle said firmly, leaving no room for argument. "But if you're having doubts," she paused, "you're free to take your chances with a public defender."

All the air in the room was sucked out as the two of them stared into each other's eyes.

"Fuck," Mario huffed, "I might as well just plead guilty if I go down that road."

"Then we'll be staying." Giselle nodded.

Mario looked at me and narrowed his gaze. "Then we better move on to the next order of business."

My brows raised. "That's why I'm here."

"Blake Stone." Mario titled his head to the side. "Are you still interested to learn what I know about him?"

I pressed my lips together, my thoughts smoothing themselves out, holding his stare. Then it hit me. I shut the folder I had open out in front of me and said, "I'm sorry, Mr. Jimenez, but I can't represent you."

Mario's face pinched. "Are you serious?"

"Kelly—" Giselle angled her body toward me, disbelief etched across her face.

I held up my index finger to her and fixed my gaze firmly on Mario's brown eyes. "You heard me." I pushed my chair back and stood. "And, yes, I'm serious. Representing you would be a mistake."

Giselle's mouth fell open as I turned and left the room. I told the guards that I was finished and heard Giselle's heels *clacking* quickly behind me to catch up. "What was that about?" she asked.

"We'll talk about it in the car." I quickened my pace.

"Kelly," Giselle widened her stride to keep up, "we can't do that to Mario."

The second we rounded the corner, I nearly stumbled into Oscar Buchanan, District Attorney. "Kelly Black." He smirked, his hands hiding in his pockets.

"Not now, Oscar." I purposely plowed my shoulder into his as I passed.

"What's wrong, Kelly, lose another case? Did justice prevail?" His laugh followed me all the way outside.

I didn't have time for Oscar's bullshit, and especially not with Giselle on my ass about to explode on me for the decision I just made in choosing to not represent Mario.

As soon as Maxwell saw me storming for the vehicle, he pulled forward, hopped out, and opened my door for me to slide inside without a hitch. Giselle followed my lead a second later with words flying. "What the hell just happened in there? And why couldn't you have given me a heads up?" As soon as she shut her door, Maxwell set the wheels in motion. "Fuck, Kelly. You have some explaining to do. I hope you know what it is you're doing, because it's not fair of you to blindside me like that."

I remained quiet, choosing to let her get all she had to say off her chest before I explained to her our new plan.

"I thought we were in agreement on this one." She arched a brow and refused to take her eyes off of me. "Aren't you going to say anything?"

"Are you done?" My voice was calm, quiet.

"I'm ready to listen." She leaned back and squared her shoulders.

"Weren't you the one who didn't like us going in to speak with Mario before first talking with Nash?"

"That's what this is about?"

"Not quite."

"Kelly, if we don't help Mario, no one will." She shoved her hand through her hair and turned her head away. "You know Oscar is gunning for him to go down for this." Her head snapped back to me.

"I realized something in there," I said, picking a piece of lint off my thigh. "Representing Mario would be impossible if we're going to also take on Blake Stone as a client."

Her eyes popped wide-open.

I nodded. "That's right. Stone is our new priority."

"Look, Kelly. You know I'm up for the challenge, but we can't just let Mario hope for the best. Oscar will eat his case alive. You and I both know that."

I stroked my chin, appreciating the smoothness of a freshly shaven face. It was mornings like these that I lived for. Surprises. Turns of events. A reason for my blood to pump through my heart as if my life depended on it. Giselle might not be seeing the bigger picture as clearly as I was, but she'd come around. That much was certain.

"If we're going to represent Stone, I can't also represent a client who is going to offer up information that would put him away," my eyebrows raised as I nodded once, "because that's what seems like was about to happen in there. Wasn't it?"

Giselle's blue eyes darted across my face. "What the hell are you up to, Kelly Black?"

The corners of my lips curled up into a grin.

"And who are you going to have represent Mario?"

Reaching inside my jacket pocket, I pulled out a business card. "Call him," I said, handing Giselle the card.

"And what is it you would like me to discuss with him?"

"That's who will represent Mario." Her face tightened. "Tell him I told you to call." She pinched the card in the corner and glanced down, reading it. "And Giselle?"

She looked up from under her bangs.

"Let him know that my request is urgent."

5

Kendra

"Either your hair grows much faster than mine, or your man has made a request." Alex smirked when she found me in the spa lounge sipping a mimosa.

I crossed my leg over my knee and swung my foot. "Hun," I said speaking to the six-foot hunk behind the counter, "could you be a doll and please bring my friend here a drink?"

"That's all right." Alex turned to the man and waved him off. "Too early for me."

The man looked to me for a definitive answer.

"No, really." I nodded. "Her tight ass needs to loosen up. Make the woman a drink." I winked.

He glanced at Alex, nodding as if seeing what I saw. Alex was stiff, and I knew the reason why, but it wasn't worth saying anything in front of the handsome man now stirring up a drink for her. I'd been chatting him up from the moment I arrived, and since Alex was running late, she only deserved to obey the demands I made for her. Besides, having one drink wasn't like I was asking the world of her.

Alex glared at me.

"Or shall I say," my brows raised, "your tight ass needs to *be* loosened up?"

The man handed her a tall glass of orange juice bubbly. "You're disgusting."

I swung my foot to the floor and stood. "C'mon, let's go," I said, hooking my arm in the crook of hers while slamming back what remained of my second drink. "No time to waste. I've got a little trimmin' up to do."

"So, what is it?" Alex looked over at me as we headed back to our usual room. "Does your hair grow exceptionally fast or is there some other reason you're here today?"

"Okay, fine." I stopped, turned and faced her, and let out a long, low sigh. "Since you won't shut up about it." My gaze shifted to look down the hall just as Mr. Handsome Drink Man passed. If Nash never came back, I would hook him up with Alex. He looked like a fun toy to play with. "Kelly wants me to keep a landing strip."

Alex covered her mouth, and though I couldn't see her lips, I could see it in her eyes—the way they began to water—that she was stifling a burst of laughter.

"You can laugh." My hands rooted on my hips. "It's okay. I can take it."

She hurled over and busted up laughing. I stood there and took it just as I said I would. And when she came back up with a purple face, she said, "He's a lawyer, not a pilot. What the hell does he need a landing strip for?"

I tugged on her arm, needing to find my place of exile before anybody walked by and overheard our conversation. "It's better than the love triangle I gave him."

Alex giggled her ass off the entire way into the room. But when she didn't make a move for a robe, or make any indication she was going to remove her clothes, I pinched my brow and gave her a look.

"What?" She shrugged. "We were just here."

"And you're telling me nothing has poked through? No roots to pluck?"

Alex plopped her butt down in an empty chair. "Nash is away, so what's the point? It's not like I'll be getting any anytime soon."

"That's the spirit." I rolled my eyes, my words laced with sarcasm, as I began to undress.

"Besides, I only came because I needed a break from work. I can't stay long." She looked down at the drink she was still holding and finally decided that drinking in the morning was the way to go. "Nash is sending tons of work my way and expects it all to be done come tomorrow morning."

"That guy is an asshole." I snickered, unclasping my bra, letting my twins hang free.

"And I'm already behind on work." She took another sip. "This isn't so bad," she said peering down into her glass.

"Like I'd suggest you drink something bad?" The side of my face scrunched up like an accordion. "How is Nash, anyway? You still wearing that little number while video chatting?"

"He's busy. We haven't been talking as much as we did when he first left."

"But he still sends you flowers."

"Yeah," she sang.

I stepped out of my panties and moved to the wall where the robes where hanging. I plucked one off the hook and turned to Alex. "Do you ever worry he's not being loyal?"

"Why would you say that?" Alex's nostrils flared.

"It's just a question." My eyes rounded as I pulled the robe over my shoulders. "Once a playboy, always a playboy," I muttered under my breath.

"I knew I shouldn't have come." Alex reached for her drink

and swallowed down a healthy gulp. "Are you asking because you're doubting Kelly's loyalty?"

"Our arrangement is different," I said, lying back on the cushioned table.

We all had our doubts and nagging insecurities, but I wasn't about to admit mine. Even to Alex. Maybe there would be a time that would make sense, but I was feeling rather spirited today and I didn't intend to ruin what was setting up to be a perfectly good day.

"I know Nash is totally into you."

"Thanks. That makes me feel a whole lot better." Alex's tone was sarcastic. Then she picked up a magazine from the table and snickered. "Have you read this?" She held up the cover of the tabloid for me to see.

"Isn't that William Wade?"

"AKA Big Willy." She burst out laughing.

"Huh?"

"So you haven't read the article?" She turned the magazine around so I could see the cover. "It's been out for ages." She glanced up at me.

I shook my head.

Alex pulled the magazine back into her lap and flipped to the story she was referring to. "Here. Read this."

I took the magazine from her and began skimming the story. "What is it with this town? Does every man have a dick the size of an elephant?"

"So what if they do?"

My eyes scanned more of the article and I felt my lips tug to my ears. "You're right. This is funny. Big Willy." I rolled my head over to Alex. "How much do you think he paid to have this article written about him?"

"Big bucks I'm sure." Alex shrugged her shoulders.

When the room fell quiet, I broke the awkward silence by

saying, "I never did tell you what happened with Kelly yesterday, did I?"

"You mean after you refused to talk about...well, you know."

She was referring to my rape, but I wasn't in the mood to talk about it. Because I knew she would only worry about me, question Kelly's intentions, and be concerned about Kelly setting off another trigger. "Anyway, the dude totally went detective on my place."

"Detective? What do you mean?"

"I mean, he was snooping through my closet, digging through my clothes and shoes," I sat up and propped myself up on one elbow, "he even went through my entire bathroom." My forehead wrinkled. "That's, like, extremely personal stuff, man."

"*Wo*-man," Alex said, pointing at herself. "And, by the way, that's totally weird. Are you sure he's worth it?"

"Aren't you the one who pushed for me to sign his silly contract?"

Alex tapped her finger on her bottom lip and looked up and to the left. "Are you even allowed to be in a relationship?"

My brows knitted. "Of course I'm allowed to be in a relationship."

"I mean, since the Madam is technically still involved in the decision making—is what you and Kelly have even considered a relationship?"

I dropped my feet over the side of the bed. "She doesn't make my decisions for me."

"Except she allowed Kelly to pay an undisclosed amount to have you—"

I shoved my hand in her face, dangling the ring Kelly gave me under her nose, close enough for her to remember that piece of him that made Kelly worth all the risk in the world.

"It's nice." Alex lowered my hand away from her face. "I'll give you that. But what other requests has he made?"

Over the next several minutes, I laid out the demands Kelly

made. How I was to eat healthy, shower twice a day, keep my makeup and appearance in place, and have sex with him at least three times a week. "Or whenever the mood strikes."

"Him or you?" she asked, biting the inside of her cheek.

"Either." My shoulders rose then fell. What did it matter? "He just wants me to stay in tip-top shape. Don't you want that for me, too?"

"I could use some motivation in that department." Alex sighed before finishing her drink.

My hands slapped down on her shoulders. "We can do it together."

Alex pressed her lips together. She didn't look as thrilled as I'd hoped she would. "Maybe I spoke too soon."

"C'mon. It will be fun!" I shook her as the excitement rolled through me.

"We'll see." She smiled, causing me to plant a wet one smack dab in the middle of her beautiful forehead.

My aesthetician knocked on the door and peeked her head inside. "Kendra?"

I turned and smiled. "Hey, baby."

"Ready?"

I looked back at Alex. "I have to get back to work," she said, standing.

"Now, if you'll excuse us, Ms. Grace—" I snickered, "—we have some primping to do."

Alex stuck her tongue out at me just as she was leaving, and I knew that Kelly's demands would do both of us some good.

6

Kelly

My thumb scrolled over the screen of my phone, searching.

I couldn't recall the last time I'd spoken with Colin Cobbs. Message after message, I looked to find when the exact day—even year—was. Except there was nothing. Clearly, we were in need of reconnecting. And though I'd instructed Giselle to contact him suggesting he help us with Mario's case, I knew that once he heard I put in the request myself, he'd want to phone me, if only to see how I was doing.

I stopped my scrolling when Kendra's name appeared.

My dick twitched at the mere thought of her—how her curves glowed, radiating perfectly to accentuate all that made her beautiful.

The sun beat down on the crown of my head, getting me to angle my chin to the sky. It was bright and intense as I squinted under the heat before moving to the shade.

A woman passed in front of me, sending familiar, intoxicating scents of Kendra straight to my brain. If it wasn't for the smell, reminding me of what I had to look forward to, then I wouldn't have bothered watching the woman continue on down the street. I would have let her go. Forgetting her completely.

Instead, I stared, imagining that it was Kendra swaying her hips from side to side as I got lost in her magnificence.

I leaned my shoulders back against the building's wall and the woman glanced over her shoulder as if she could feel me staring. She even moved like Kendra. Graceful and fluid, like she didn't have a care in the world.

Kendra had cast her spell on me. I saw her everywhere. Even when I licked my lips, I could still taste her tight pussy on my tongue. The way it went from tart to sweet after she came. Closing my eyes, I could feel her squirming beneath my weight as I thrust my tongue deep into her hot cavern, driving her to ecstasy. She was a vixen that I couldn't get enough of.

And that was why I demanded she be perfect. I knew she thought my requests were ridiculous, but she didn't have a choice. And neither did I.

I glanced up from my phone when a loud trash truck drove by. Still, there was no sight of the Madam. God, I hated waiting. She was catching on. Knowing my own tactic of purposely arriving late so as not to be the one left waiting. I'd have to remember this for next time I scheduled a meeting with her. Unless she had a worthy excuse, her tardiness was uncalled for and I'd be sure to pay it back sometime in the future.

Turning my head back down the street, I caught sight of the woman I'd been watching just before she rounded a corner and disappeared completely.

My cock thickened at the memories of how Kendra made me feel.

The demands I made of her were simple enough and served two very important purposes. First, to see if she could obey my command. It was important that she could—without hesitation —when moving her into the submissive role I wanted her to take.

And, second, to make sure she looked the part I needed her to fill. She might not know it now, but I was grooming her for a life next to me. And that meant a life in the spotlight—a life under both scrutiny and praise. Together, we had to be flawless.

And it wasn't like I requested her to do things without first thinking of my own needs. I placed the same rigid lifestyle upon myself. Eating right, exercising, and taking time out of my busy schedule to relieve the dark desires I had boiling inside my groin. There wasn't room to slip up. We needed that time to get lost in each other.

Finally, unable to take it any longer, I typed a quick message to her.

Clear your schedule. I'll be by to pick you up in 30.

A couple minutes passed and I kept my eye out for the Madam before Kendra responded.

What do you have planned?

My thumb worked over the touch-screen, responding to my sweet *Bella.*

Surprise. Just be ready. See you soon.

I smirked.

P.S. And wear a short skirt.

Madam's jet-black limo arrived just as I tucked my phone away. I moved out of the comfort of the shade and into the blazing sun just as Jerome stepped out to hold the door open for me. "Morning, Mr. Black."

"Jerome." I nodded. "Always a pleasure." Ducking my head and sliding my body inside the vehicle, I found the Madam waiting on the opposite bench with her usual smug smile plastered across her face.

"I must admit, Kelly," she grinned, "I'm a bit surprised to be hearing from you so soon."

Jerome settled back into his seat and weighted down the back wheel-well. I leaned back in my seat, unbuttoning my jacket so it wasn't so tight around my mid-section. "And why is that?"

"After agreeing to give you access to Kendra for a month, I thought you two would disappear without a trace." She straightened out the white gloves she was wearing and tilted her head to the side, pausing.

"Work doesn't stop." I lifted my arm and rested it across the back of the seat.

"So that's the reason you requested to see me?"

I glanced at Jerome. He looked cramped as he sat on the far side of the bench from Madam. He was such a large man, I wondered why the Madam didn't custom-fit her rides to accommodate him. I knew she had the money, and Jerome had been with her long enough for her to know he wasn't going anywhere fast.

"I've decided to take on Stone's case," I said as soon as we started to drive.

She didn't act surprised. Not even relieved to hear the news. And after all her impatient moments, I couldn't even get her to smile. "Who will be covering for Mario?" she asked simply.

"I've got that handled."

"Kelly, Maria Greer deserves justice." Her chest expanded just before she let out a heavy sigh.

Her sudden interest in Maria had me skeptical. I couldn't help but wonder what her play was. Why she suddenly cared more for a strange dead girl than she did about her own motives was beyond me. It wasn't like her to forget her own interests, and so I assumed that she hadn't. But what was her angle?

"She'll get the justice she deserves," I assured her. "And Mario will be properly represented. Giselle is setting that up now."

"If you're stepping away from Mario, then I assume he told you everything you needed to know about Stone?"

My tongue worked over the front of my teeth as I glanced out the window over her shoulder.

"What Mario told you," Madam continued, pressing for information when I remained tight-lipped, "is it enough to put Stone away for good?"

We passed a corner deli that served up delicious blueberry muffins worth dying for. Suddenly my stomach grumbled, realizing that I hadn't had much to eat today. I tried my best to hide the fact that I was on to her, that I knew what she was up to and why she wanted to see Stone locked away for good. There wasn't enough evidence to convict—or even accuse her today of my suspicions—but I knew Adrianna and I were onto something worth fighting for. We were close to uncovering her dirt.

My eyes drifted back to Madam's. We held our gazes and I stared back into her tiny pupils, questioning if I even knew who she was anymore. "Mario didn't tell me anything."

She squinted as I watched her posture go stiff. Madam was the best at hiding her frustration, and if it weren't for the years of getting to know her—watching the way she operated—I would have missed the subtlety of her resentment toward me. "Kelly," she tsked, "why would you make such an amateur move?"

My brows pinched. "Are you questioning my strategy?"

"Kelly, darling. That wasn't the plan we discussed. I specifically instructed you that I'd like to know what Mario knew about Stone." She angled her head over to Jerome and cackled. "If only to make your job easier." She turned back to me and smiled. "That is all, sweetheart."

I thumbed my ear, thinking. "How do you even know Mario knows anything about Stone?"

"Honey," she dropped her chin and looked at me beneath sunken brows, "you and I both know that he knows something."

Of course I knew that. But I wanted to know how she knew. "Then tell me. How can you be so certain?"

The driver made a turn, heading back toward my office. "My girls. They tell me everything. Isn't that right, Jerome?"

"That's right," Jerome said in his deep baritone.

I cast my gaze at Jerome, watching him sweat in his suit. His hands were perfectly stretched out on his large thighs as he stared straight ahead, never once taking his eye off of me.

"Kelly," Madam lifted her brow, "you need to get what Mario knows on record."

My tongue wet my lips.

Her other brow rose. "It's imperative."

"It shouldn't be a problem," I said as the limo stopped at the curb outside my office building.

"That's good." Her shoulders relaxed. "I hope it's not."

"I'll be overseeing the case. Every step of the way I'll be reported to." My eyes narrowed. "But it's important I also mention that none of this can get leaked. No one can know that I'm secretly running the show on both Mario and Stone."

"My lips are sealed." Madam grinned.

"It will all be done in private to keep the conflict of interest hidden and out of sight." I leaned forward, preparing to exit the vehicle. "Madam, it needs to be done this way if we are going to get Stone convicted. Trust me when I say that I haven't lost sight of our original intention."

Madam held her chin high with a satisfied gleam in her eye. "Report back to me, Kelly," she said as I opened the door to leave. "We can't let this drag on forever. This city and its interests move much too fast to be dicking around."

7

Kendra

The moment I stepped into my empty apartment I knew I didn't have much time.

If I knew anything about Kelly, it was that he hated to wait.

I glanced at the kitchen to check the time. It had already been ten minutes since he'd texted telling me to wear a short skirt. I wondered if he wanted me to wear anything beneath. I snickered at the thought.

Tossing my handbag on the couch, I scampered to the back of my apartment, swung my closet doors open, and began digging for a skirt I knew he'd love to see me in. With as good as he had been treating me, I had no reason to purposely upset him. And depending on what I chose to wear, I could easily dictate how today went.

Sliding the hangers to the side, digging and fingering my way through the bundle of clothes bunched up on either side of the closet, I debated my options. It was impossible not to see Kelly here going through my clothes, telling me that they weren't good enough. I didn't get it. Didn't understand why everyone was so down on my sense of fashion. I had a great sense of style. Why couldn't anyone see that?

Renewed with a sense of determination to prove Kelly wrong, my fingers pinched the fabric of what could be a worthy option for me to wear. I thought how Kelly never did say what it was he had planned. Just for me to be ready. Which reminded me—time was ticking.

I could pair my tight-fitting leather mini-skirt with extremely tall heels and a white button-up to give him the sexy professional look. Or I could go with something less risqué. My closet was packed full of options; sometimes it made for tough decisions.

When I hung the clothes back on the pole, I wondered out loud, "Did he need a quickie before finishing his afternoon work? Or was this more about us, taking me out for lunch to socialize?"

Working my way to the back, that was when I saw it. Forgetting I had it, my eyes widened, sparkling with joy, knowing that this was it. It was beautiful and had an edge of danger unlike anything else I owned. I *had* to wear this.

Pulling it free and holding it out in front of my face, I smiled.

It was a contemporary style with a curved hem to show all my most tempting features, and the snake skin patterned mini-skirt had all the elements Kelly had requested. It was figure flaunting and I knew that if I paired it with a deep V-neck blouse—dangling a necklace to draw attention to my bra-less girls—and fitting strappy heels over my feet, Kelly wouldn't be able to keep his hands to himself.

My nipples puckered at the thought of driving him mad.

With no time to waste, I began shedding the clothes I was wearing and exchanging them for my new outfit. I was thankful that I had showered before visiting the spa and that I still smelled of citrus oils and hot wax. A shower now was most definitely out of the question.

I was dressed and downstairs in no time flat. With my heels clacking through the lobby, Mr. Anderson, my doorman, lifted his head with a smile. "You seem to be in a particularly good mood."

I slowed my gait in order to respond. "Am I not always?"

"Today, you have more bounce in your step."

"Must be the heels." I smiled.

"Must be." He winked.

"Or...it could be this." I stepped forward and dangled the diamond ring Kelly had gifted me in front of his face.

He angled his head to the side and gave me a questioning look.

"It's what was in the box the other day." I nodded, staring at the exquisite jewel. "I should be thanking you—"

His brows pinched. "Thanking me for what?"

"For keeping Kelly Black around."

He bowed his head. "Anything for you, Ms. Williams."

"You know, I really like him," I said, holding my chin high.

"Mr. Black is a true gentleman." Mr. Anderson nodded to the resident who entered the building.

"Well, I'm glad you think so, because that's who I'm on my way to see now."

"May you enjoy your afternoon." He nodded his head, this time to me, and smiled.

As I made my way out of the building, I thought how I liked how cordial Mr. Anderson was. He was a gentleman, the man who never had anything bad to say about anyone or anything. And I liked that I could share my life with him. After watching me come and go, I was certain he knew more about me than I'd ever allow most people to learn.

The outside hit my face like a breath of fresh air. Kelly was already waiting, standing next to his jet-black Escalade SUV, his infamous sexy smirk dimpling his cheeks.

Heat spread through my core, keeping my nipples the sharp little bullets they always were when I was around him.

His driver was behind the wheel with his focus forward and Kelly pushed off the vehicle and strode toward me, meeting me halfway. "Look at you." He pulled his hands from his pockets and quickly wrapped his fingers around my waist, pulling me in for a deep, lingering kiss.

I melted into him, my heart fluttering out of control.

He swirled his tongue against mine before dipping me.

I couldn't recall ever being dipped, and it got me to laugh. "What has you in such a great mood?"

His lips brushed against mine. "Get inside," he pulled me back upright and tugged on my fingers, leading me toward his car, "and you'll find out."

Kelly's broad shoulders sheltered me from the squelching sun as he opened the door, assisting me into the backseat. The windows were darkly tinted and a privacy partition kept his driver free from whatever happened in the back. As soon as Kelly shut the door, the vehicle pulled away from the curb and we were off. "Mr. Anderson says you're quite the gentleman."

Kelly smirked, reaching for my hand, gently tugging on my fingers. "He said that about me?"

I nodded.

"Then Mr. Anderson doesn't know me at all." Kelly's voice was deep, sultry.

"Are you saying you're not a gentleman?" My core temperature spiked as the sight of his eyes darkening went straight to my pulsing sex.

"Would a gentleman do this?" He smoothed his rough hand up over my knee before reaching under my skirt and between my thighs.

"Perhaps you're right," I breathed as my eyelids grew heavy at the feel of his finger grazing my damp mound. "A gentleman would first ask to touch a woman there."

Kelly chuckled close to my ear. "*Bella,* did you do as I say?"

His moist lips tickled my ear, prickling my skin. "Depends what it is you're asking."

He hooked his finger beneath my jaw, turning my head to face him, and kissed me.

I sucked his tongue deep into my mouth, thrusting against his. Then I reached my hand to his lap, finding him already pitched. "Find out for yourself," I purred.

Kelly moved to the floor, settling his torso between my knees. Smoothing his hands up and down my thighs, I nibbled on a fingernail, daydreaming about what I'd like to see him do next. There were so many possibilities, so many different ways I could see this going.

Then he hooked his fingers through my laced thong and began pulling it off my hips, down my thighs, letting it fall until I was cuffed at the ankles. He widened my knees and I watched his gaze fall to my treasure. "That's a good girl," he said, sliding the tip of his finger between my wet folds, appreciating my new look.

"It was time for a change." My heart thrashed as I bore my hips down on his finger, pleading for him to enter me. My body was on fire and needed to be cooled. Only he could relieve this heat and find a way to unwind all the tension he was creating inside of me.

"Yes, it was," he said, grazing my swollen clit.

Then he pushed his finger inside me. My back arched off the back of the seat and I mewed with relief.

"You feel amazing." He twisted his finger and touched my smooth bare skin with another. "Don't you like the way it feels?"

"I do." I licked my lips, needing more of what he was giving me.

He leaned close, lunging his finger deeper, speeding up his thrusts. I tightened around him, seeing stars flash across my vision. My body told me I was close to coming, and I knew he could feel it, too. Kelly curled his finger, hitting the exact spot that curled my toes, and leaned close to blow cool air over my slick clit.

My muscles tensed as I unfolded my elbows, shoving my fingers in his hair, and shuddered through my release just as I felt the vehicle roll to a stop.

Kelly kept his finger inside me, feeling me pulse against him, swirling around my juices before pulling free and bringing it to my mouth. "Taste yourself," he said, pushing his finger between my lips.

I had never tasted my own orgasm before, and though he didn't give me a choice, I sucked his finger like I would have given him head. Swirling my tongue over the tip of it, I sucked my own juices away, cleaning it completely until my orgasm was wiped off his finger.

"How do you taste?"

"Not as good as you would have." I smirked as I played with the collar of his shirt.

"You keep doing as you're told and I'll continue to award you for good behavior." He straightened his spine and leaned forward to press his firm lips against mine. "Now, let's find you some new clothes."

I blinked in the bright sunlight as I stepped out onto the sidewalk. It took a minute for my eyes to adjust—having been living in the darkness of his car, and having been cross-eyed from the orgasm Kelly showered down upon me—but once I focused I said, "Rodeo Drive?"

"The only place to shop."

Kelly reached down and threaded his fingers with mine. "I know plenty of other places to shop," I said as I fluffed up my hair with my opposite hand.

"But when you shop here," Kelly looked around, "you become someone."

I was familiar with Rodeo Drive. I'd been here before. Not for shopping, but browsing. I also knew just how pretentious and out of my league I was when walking the area. But maybe Kelly could show me what it was really like—what it really meant to be here purchasing expensive items for my own consumption. "I've had a drink at Mojito," I said.

Kelly stopped walking, turned to face me, and peered down with questioning eyes. "Is that right?"

"That's right. I even met the owner, Wesley—"

"—Reid." Kelly finished my sentence.

"He was having drinks with Nash Brooks." I flung my hair over my shoulder and tugged on his hand to get his feet moving again. "And I know you know Nash."

"He's dating your friend, Alex."

"It's creepy that you know all this." Then a thought struck me. My heels dug in and I pulled my hand away from his. "Is that why you wanted to be with me for a month?"

Kelly titled his head to the side.

"Tell me now or lose me forever."

He reached up and wrapped his fingers around my shoulder, ironing his hands up and down my clothed upper arm.

"Is the only reason we're together because you need me to dish out information on Alex?"

He offered me a bemused smile and I hated how he thought I was anything other than dead serious right now.

When he didn't answer, I asked, "Is this about the case you're working on?"

His eyes crinkled and the corners of his lips curled upward.

"Because, if it is, I'll leave you now."

He stuck his finger in my mouth, shutting me up completely. "Are you willing to walk away from this?"

I rolled my tongue over his finger, letting the last remnants of my orgasm spill over my taste buds and I felt my knees give out. My head shook.

"I don't want to talk about work. I'll tell you this once." He thrust his finger in and out of my mouth, nice and slow, jarring my memory of what it felt like to be fucked by him. "And after I tell you this, I don't want you to ever ask me again. Do you understand?"

I nodded with hollowed cheeks.

"I'm with you because I find you attractive." He lowered his chin and looked at me beneath a sunken brow. "I'm curious about you. My decision to have you for a month has nothing to do with who we both know—what we both might know—and has everything to do with the way we make each other feel. Is that clear?" He slipped his finger out of my mouth.

I swallowed down the salty taste and said, "Clear."

"Clear, sir."

My brows knitted.

He nodded. "Say it."

"Clear, sir," I said.

"Good." He took me by my hand again, tipped his head back, and led me down the street.

I suppose he was right in not wanting to discuss work. Talking shop was boring. And though I was certain he loved what he did, I also assumed that if he was anything like me, he needed a break from the stress and I was his one chance at clearing his head.

We window shopped a few stores, discussing women's fashion and how we both agreed that it was women's clothing that dictated what a man should wear, not the other way around. I was certain Kelly purposely avoided passing Mojito, but that was fine with me. He was on a mission, knew just the store he wanted to take me to, and when we arrived I walked inside with my head spinning. "What did I do to deserve this?"

"You signed my contract." He smiled as he rocked back and forth on his heels with his hands buried inside his pockets.

I browsed racks of clothes, making sure to touch everything, needing to feel it all for myself. Nothing had price tags, which only meant one thing—it was all more expensive than even I would be willing to pay. "Is that all?"

"And because I only want you to have the best."

"Mr. Black." A woman came out from the back and greeted Kelly.

"Kristin." He smiled and air-kissed her cheek.

"Long time no see." Kristin met my gaze and smiled. "What brings you in today?"

Kelly held his arm out to me. "My girl, Kendra, needs to fill her wardrobe."

My cheeks blushed in embarrassment. He said it like I didn't own any clothes or that I needed him to take care of me.

"This your normal style?" Kristin moved closer to me, circling around to check me out.

"I have clothes." I folded my arms over my chest, eyeing Kelly. "Mr. Black, here, insists that I—" I searched for the right word.

"Don't worry, hun," Kristin whispered in my ear, "he's totally worth it."

I kept one eye on Kelly, not sure exactly how to take Kristin's comment. Was she simply suggesting I put up with Kelly's demands and let him pay for all that he wanted to buy me? Or did she actually *know* that Kelly was worth it.

Jealousy won in the end and I hated to think Kelly had been with any other woman besides me. "Kelly, darling, remind me again. What is the occasion we are shopping for?" I added a little mockery to my voice to grab his attention.

His eyes darkened as he raked them over me and I couldn't help but notice how his bulge swelled against his zipper. "Dinner."

"Dinner?" I turned to Kristin. "I guess I'm going to dinner."

He sauntered over to me with sex in his eye. "Tonight."

"I know where to start." Kristin squeezed my shoulder as she hurried to the far end of the store.

Kelly clamped his fingers around my tender mid-section and tugged me against his hardness. "And I want everyone to lust after you."

"Shouldn't be too hard." I shrugged.

Kelly chuckled, sending pleasing vibrations to my flexed stomach.

"Kendra, over here." Kristin waved for me to meet her on the other side of the store. "I want you to see what I have pulled out."

I took one step before Kelly caught me by the wrist and twirled me into his arms. He smashed his lips over mine, as if he could feel my insecurity threatening to doubt my own abilities. What he was asking of me—I knew I could do it—but with him actually saying it, somehow the pressure escalated to a point I knew I would overthink things until I ruined it all. *I want everyone to lust after you.* Kelly's words echoed between my ears. When he finally released me, Kelly pushed me toward Kristin who'd watched it all.

"See, what did I tell you?" Kristin leaned her shoulder against mine and talked quiet enough so that Kelly wouldn't hear. "The man is amazing."

Kristin had several outfits laid out but before I could make a decision, I needed to ask Kelly where we were going. "Surprise," he said.

"Really? You know that doesn't help me make a decision." Don't get me wrong, I liked surprises, a little bit of mystery, too, though without knowing for sure what he had planned, it was proving impossible to make a decision on what to wear.

"Then we better play it safe and go with something like this," Kristin said, holding up a sexy, skin-tight lace up dress.

I loved it immediately. Knew that I would kill it in black. And when I held it up to my body and looked in the mirror, Kelly's face stamped his own approval on the outfit. "Kelly, I don't need this. I have my own things I can choose from." I turned around to face him. "Are my clothes really that awful?"

"Our relationship is new." His hands landed on my shoulders, gently massaging them as he stood behind me, both of us staring into each other's eyes through the reflection of the mirror. "And so must it be with your clothes."

My gaze traveled the length of the dress. It was gorgeous. I loved it. Knew I'd look stunning in it. And I also knew that I needed to have it.

"The last thing I need is for you to have already worn something, something you've worn when being seen with another man." He kissed the crown of my head. "This is a new beginning. It's important we start on a fresh note."

"If you insist." I reached out to smooth my hand down his muscular arm.

"I do." His fingers dug into my skin. "I'll also be giving you your own credit card to use so you can purchase anything you want even when I'm not here."

My head snapped up to look up at him. His eyes were sharp and sincere. There was nothing more beautiful than the way he was looking at me now. "Kelly, I have my own money. Really, you don't need to do this."

He smiled and lifted his head to Kristin. "Is there a room she can try this on?"

"Through there." She pointed to the back corner. "The door is unlocked."

"Thank you, Kristin. Give us a moment, will you?"

"I'll be in the front when you're ready." She smiled and walked away.

Kelly laid his hand on the small of my back and pushed me toward the changing room. "What do you have planned, Kelly?"

"Take me with you, and you'll find out."

I reached behind my back and felt his dick straining hard against his pants. If I wasn't mistaken, I knew exactly where Kelly was taking me—and what it was he wanted to do.

8

Kelly

Kendra glanced over her shoulder with hooded lids as I followed her inside the changing room. There was sex in her eye. She was on to me.

My fingers splayed on the door and without looking, I pressed it closed until I heard it snap shut. "Hang up the dress," I demanded, raking her curvy figure over with my eyes.

"I know what you're up to," she murmured, hanging the dress on the empty hook, following my orders.

I stepped forward, grazing her face with the fingers of one hand while smoothing the palm of my other down her side before settling on the curve of her ass.

"Keep your hands off me." Kendra peeled my fingers away from her body. "People will hear us. We can't do this here."

I put my hands back on her, tightening my grip, taking a firm hold of her in case she tried to push me away again. "Oh, yes we can." My lips kissed the side of her soft face. "And we are going to do this here."

"I'll do anything you want." She turned to me with pleading eyes. "Just not here."

My hand grazed over her breast before clamping around her throat, gently stroking her trachea with my thumb. "Remember your role." My eyes moved across her delicate features. "What you agreed to do. Who *you* agreed to be. Do you remember what I asked of you?"

"To submit," she breathed out.

"Exactly."

"I thought that was only for when we were in the bedroom."

I took her hand and placed it on my cock. "Oh, no, sweetheart. You must submit whenever I'm hard."

Kendra's breath hitched, her pulse fluttering intensely in her stiff neck. She licked her lips and swallowed hard. "Then do it."

In one swift motion, I cupped her lovely face with both of my hands. Her dazzling green eyes danced with mine. Taking me by surprise she lunged for my mouth, kissing me hard.

Her arms wrapped around my neck as her knee bent and clawed at the side of my leg as if looking for some kind of foothold to latch on to. I tugged her tightly against my body, needing to feel her heat against my own. We kissed fiercely, stealing breaths between the swirls of our tongues. Her taste had me harder than before and I took my fingers directly to the back of her skirt where I feverishly worked to unzip it.

"Kelly," she mewed against my lips.

I craved her. Couldn't take my mind off of her—what I wanted to do to her, how I wanted to make her feel. She was intoxicating and completely on fire, making me want her even more.

Kendra wedged her slender hands inside my suit jacket and pushed the fabric off my shoulders, letting it fall to the floor behind me. I worked to unbutton her blouse. A second later, I found myself squeezing her firm orb, letting her razor-sharp nipple slice through my palm. "Shit, woman," I growled. "You have no idea what I have in store for you."

"Maybe not." She threaded her hand through my hair and tugged at the roots. "But now that you've turned me on, I can't wait to find out."

I crashed my lips down on hers, thrust my tongue deep into her mouth, and spun her around quick enough to make her yelp. "Quiet—" I chuckled, "—you wouldn't want anyone to hear us."

"You're an asshole." She giggled.

"That I am." I grinned, snapping her hands above her head and pinning them against the wall.

"You're lucky I like assholes." She arched her back, pushing her ass higher into the air.

She looked absolutely incredible with splayed hands, high on the wall, perfectly placed on both sides of the large rectangular mirror. I hadn't thought about that feature when I followed her inside, but it proved to be a nice visual effect, allowing me to see both sides of all that she was. God, she was gorgeous.

Smoothing my hands up her sides, I grabbed a dangling breast over her bra and leaned close. Licking her ear, I said, "This is your one chance to escape what I'm about to do to you."

Kendra lifted her head and stared at herself in the mirror as if needing a moment to decide her fate. When she didn't respond, I took her silence as an invitation to continue my pursuit.

Pulling down her skirt, I tapped her leg and she stepped out. Then I kissed her legs, beginning with the calf and licking my way up her thigh. Her long laced heels were sexy on her thin legs and gave her several more inches of height—making it perfect for me to take her from behind.

"Now take off your shirt." My voice was low and deep.

"How far are you taking this?" Kendra peered under her arm, looking down at me still on my knees. "Because Kristin will be wondering—"

I could only smile. She was so damn cute, and with each of

her little protests of concern for getting caught, my need only grew with the challenge to make her scream. "As long as you stay quiet, there is nothing to worry about." I slid my fingers between her thighs, rubbing them against her damp folds still covered by her sexy thong I had seen on the drive here.

Her breath hitched and as she took her plump bottom lip between her teeth, my cock twitched. A second later she pulled her arms free from her shirt and turned to face me. There was a look in her eye that told me she was up to something. And when she looped her shirt around my neck, pulling me to her, I knew exactly what it was she wanted me to do.

I closed my eyes and inhaled her sweet scent. Letting my hands roam wild across her small body, I took in her beautiful shape. Perfectly sized, small perky breasts, firm and free with a tight mid-section that fluttered under the onslaught of my tongue.

Clamping my fingers around her waist, my thumbs dug deep into her belly before sliding one hand up and palming her other tit. I peppered open-mouthed kisses across her belly, tastes of citrus fruit coating my tongue.

Kendra's breathing labored and her stomach fluttered. And when I pulled down her thong, I took it upon myself to lift each leg to make it easy for her to step free before putting my mouth to her clit.

She whimpered a soft lullaby, letting the weight of her body fall back against the wall with a hollow thud. She clamped my skull between her hands to stabilize her balance that teetered on the edge of collapse, and began breathing harder.

I licked her until my cock strained with pain. Reaching for a pebbled nipple, I reminded her to keep quiet. "We don't want to get kicked out, do we?"

She shook her head and put my face back on her pussy.

I lunged my tongue deep between her pink lips, circled her swollen clit, using my talent to drive her mad. She fought to keep silent, swallowing down the moans I could hear she wanted to sing. They swelled deep inside her lungs, humming across her skin. She writhed her hips against my face and lifted one leg, letting it drape over my shoulder, opening herself even wider.

Kendra had my balls so tight I clenched my stomach in pleasurable agony. The way she was so willing to submit—even here, confined to the small box of a changing room made to fit one—was intoxicating in and of itself. She wasn't a normal muse. She was a mistress worth keeping around. And if she kept this up, that was exactly what I planned to do.

My tongue swirled over her smooth protruding clit, and I slurped it between my teeth, hearing Kendra suck in her last breath before her entire body tensed in orgasm. I kept my mouth on her sex, letting her release the flood over my tongue with her most intimate tastes, and once she could breathe again she whimpered quietly, "Fuck, that was good."

I lapped her folds one last time, sending her into a fit of laughter, before standing.

She looked at me with sedated, unblinking eyes. Feeling her sweaty skin against my touch, I clamped her face between my hands and pushed my pussy-soaked tongue into her mouth. Her lips were cold from the heavy breathing, and her chest still heaved with a fast beating heart. "You liked that, did you?"

"Very much." She hooked her leg around my thigh, pulling my hardness against her.

"Good." I spun her around and pressed her up against the mirror, kicking her feet wide. "Because I'm not done with you."

I undid my belt, then unzipped myself. Freeing my steeled rod, I let my pants drop to my knees.

Kendra reached behind squeezing my shaft, my cockhead swelling to its maximum size, and she placed it at her entrance. "Go ahead. Cross-examine me, Counselor."

I wet my shaft with her moistness, grazing her pussy lips against my veiny skin. "I'm going to make you scream."

"You better not." Her mouth pinched together, deadpan.

"That's up to you." I spread her cunt with my fingers, continuing to lubricate my dick with the leftovers of her orgasm. Her pussy was hot and slick, making it easy to wedge my cockhead past her lips and into her hot cavern for the first time.

With her standing tall in her heels, she was just tall enough for me to comfortably bend at the knees and work myself deep into her core. I teased her, pushing in before pulling out. She shook her head as if mildly frustrated with the way I was slowly taking her, and Kendra pushed her ass further back into me as if telling me exactly where to hit it.

With each stroke, I slid further than before, and when my balls tightened with pleasure, I slapped her ass loud enough for anyone close by to hear.

"That's not fair." Her head sprang up, her eyes wide as she found me in the mirror.

My hips lunged deep to her core, taking her mind off of the sting of my hand. I cast my gaze down to my cock thrusting in and out of her tight pussy. The perfectly round globes of her ass kept me so painfully hard, jiggling with each lunge, I couldn't see wanting this fuck to end anytime soon.

I reached around, finding her dangling tit, and took her peaked nipple between my fingers, rolling it. Kendra grinded harder against my pelvis, dropping her head down as if to stifle the sounds she desperately wanted to make. She was a wild animal, and being caged and muzzled was completely foreign to her. But I liked seeing her struggle.

I quickened my thrusts just as I heard someone step into the room next to ours. My lips curved with a challenging smile. I didn't care if we were caught. Didn't care if others knew what Kendra and I were doing. But I knew Kendra cared. "Now, quiet. We wouldn't want anyone to know what we're doing." I bent over her, nipping at her ear.

Kendra reached for the wall. Pulling an empty hanger off the hook, she bit down on the wood, clamping it firmly between her teeth.

My lips curved with satisfaction. She was tenacious, resourceful, and able to put it all on the line to do whatever it took to obey my command. Except it didn't matter what she did to try to stifle her own cries. I knew just the combination that would make her moan.

Clamping my fingers on one of her shoulders, I continued to rock my hips in long, deep strokes. From tip to base I worked her, feeling her cunt tightening on my length with each lunge I gifted. Soon my balls tightened and the ball of fire spread from the base of my spine, up to my shoulders, shooting my core temperature up another degree. She was close to spilling over, and if I allowed myself I would be right there with her. "You're going to come when I come," I said through gritted teeth, slamming my hips against her ass.

She nodded, the hanger still firmly clamped between her teeth.

I angled her hips up and cast my gaze down to her tight anus. Licking my thumb, I dug my fingertips into her fleshy cheeks. Everything about her ass tempted me like nothing before. Slowly, I slid my thumb down her crack, guiding it to her hole. I circled my hips, hitting her deep against her cervix, and whispered close to her ear, "Nod if you want to come."

Sweat pellets formed on her brow as she nodded.

My face twisted as I pounded in to her, our skin slapping loud enough for the person next to us to hear, and just as I felt her tighten around my cock, I pushed my thumb into her asshole. Kendra's mouth flew open, dropping the hanger, and crying out loud into the air.

In that moment it was just us. With the room spinning around us, nothing else mattered. It didn't concern me that someone was trying on new clothes while listening to us get off. If anything, I hoped what they heard inspired them in some way.

Once my dick went limp, I took a step back. Reaching down for my jacket, I took a silk cloth from the pocket. First I cleaned Kendra, then myself. We exchanged smiles, but neither of us spoke a single word. Then, out of the blue, a woman's voice said, "I'd love to know what you're trying on over there."

We both looked at each other and burst out laughing, wondering how we were ever going to be able to deny what just happened with a straight face.

9

Kelly

"I'm not sure I like you looking so damn sexy." Kendra smirked the moment I stepped into my penthouse living room wearing a tuxedo.

My eyes traveled the length of her, marveling at the gown we had purchased from Kristin. She looked even better now than when I first saw her try it on at the store.

I chuckled, feeling flattered by her comment.

Tonight, she had her hair flowing in lose waves over her shoulders and down the center of her back. Her dark hair was a perfect match to her dress. She looked delicate, yet strong. Mysterious, yet insanely sexy.

Sauntering over to her with my hands buried deep in my pockets, I couldn't escape the way she was looking at me with a knowing glimmer twinkling in her eye. She was pure gold. Black gold. My gold.

"Don't worry," I snaked my hands around to her ass, "I'll keep you close."

She angled her head up to look me in the eye. "And why would you need to do that?"

"To fight off the other kittens who will be clawing at me throughout the night."

Her breath caught and I felt her muscles tighten in my grip. "Can you please tell me where we're going?"

Her pleas only caused my stomach to flex harder, loving the way her sounds of desperation passed over her lips. It was similar to how she sounded when orgasming, and I'd do anything to hear her beg the way she was right now. Taking her forgiving face inside my hand, her soft eyes pleaded with me, showing only a hint of the concern I knew she was feeling. "Did she specifically tell you to wear these?"

Kendra reached up with one hand, touching the tanzanite earrings Madam had given her. "Yes. But not tonight. I forgot to give them back."

My fingers splayed as I smoothed the tips across her neck to take a closer look at the blue jewels pinned to her ears. "They don't go with your dress."

"But the Madam insists I wear them."

Slowly, my hands fell to her shoulders. Twisting her around, I faced her in front of the large wood-framed mirror hanging on the wall. Together we stared at our image—the image of us—and I could tell by the way she was standing, with her shoulders rolled back, chin held high, that she liked the image we portrayed as a couple. And I did, too. We looked strong. Like we could take the world on without repercussion.

"But they must go," I said, tucking her hair behind her ear.

Kendra remained silent, never protesting my moves to remove the studs from her ears. She knew it had to be this way. There was no way around it. Kendra was my girl now. She'd wear my things. Not Madam's.

One by one I removed Madam's earrings, setting them on the cherry oak dresser beneath the mirror. In a soft murmur I said, "Tonight, you're my girl. And with that, you must also wear my jewelry."

Side-stepping Kendra, I reached past her and opened the top drawer. Kendra watched as I carefully pulled a black velvet box out, placing it inside her opened hands. "Kelly—"

"Don't thank me. Just open the box." Her eyes watered as she smiled. When she opened the box I said, "You deserve it."

After we had picked out her dinner gown for tonight, I'd secretly had Maxwell make another purchase for me. Inside the small box laid a pair of black diamond studs encased in 14 karat white gold, with a necklace to match. "Thank you, Kelly. They're incredible."

"Here, let me assist." I hooked the necklace around her neck, balancing the stone evenly above her cleavage, while she put the stones in her ears. "Stunning." I smiled, admiring her beauty.

"You didn't have to do this," she whispered.

"But I did," I said, spinning her around, holding her in my arms. Our eyes danced just before I leaned down to kiss her. She sucked my tongue, purring against my hard chest. "Now everyone will know that you're mine; and not to lay their paws on you."

"I'd like that." She nipped at my lips before turning back to the mirror. "And wearing all this black will let them know that I'm dangerous and should not be messed with."

Kendra swiped her claws through the air like a cat and I laughed.

Then she turned to me, looping her arms around my neck. "We must be going somewhere *really* important."

"Depends who you ask." My hands fell to the globes of her ass.

"I'm asking you." She tipped her head further back, exposing the pulsing veins in her slender neck.

"And why would you suggest that?"

"Because you clearly want to show me off."

My fingers dug into her soft, fleshy backside as I kissed her. "A woman with your beauty deserves to be placed on a pedestal."

"And is that what you're going to do? Place me on a pedestal?"

I grinned, feeling my amusement hit my eyes. My lips pressed firmly into hers before my knees gave and I purposely slid my body down her front.

Kendra's forehead wrinkled. "What are you doing, Kelly?"

My lips pulled to the corners of my mouth, smiling as I reached up under her dress and gripped the thong she was wearing.

"Kelly!" She looked around as if someone was in my house with us. But we were alone. There was no one here but us.

"Put your hands up." My voice was firm, commanding her full attention.

She tilted her head to the side and gave me a skeptical look.

"Put. Your. Hands. Up." This time I said it with more authority than before. Slowly, she took her hands off of mine—still buried under her dress—and lifted her hands up, over her shoulders with palms facing out.

Gently, I tugged the elastic waistband of her thong off the bones of her hips. Kendra's hand fluttered to her neck as I worked the laced fabric further down the length of her thigh before letting it fall to the floor. A warmth spread across my chest when I saw the white, angelic color she'd chosen. I thought it ironic she chose that color when I had the rest of her covered in black. "You won't be needing these tonight," I said, working the loosely wrapped band away from her ankles.

Kendra looked away and rolled her eyes, letting out a sigh.

I balled her panties inside my fist as I stood. "How does it feel?"

"I feel exposed."

The pad of my thumb brushed her flamed cheek. "Excellent. It's the only way I'll survive the night."

"I hate not knowing where we're going." She pressed her thighs together as if she didn't like the feeling of air freely flowing up against her sex.

"It's not worthy of discussion." She watched me stuff her underwear inside my tuxedo jacket pocket before letting her hands fall onto my shoulders. "Knowing you're commando will keep me entertained when the environment gets stuffy, which it's sure to do."

"And what about you?" Kendra's tongue slid over her lip. "Are you also going commando?"

Flicking my wrist, I checked the time. "Maxwell is ready. I'd hate to keep him waiting." I winked.

But before I could step away, Kendra was on me. She reached between my legs and squeezed my package. "You're wearing underwear, aren't you?"

I refused to answer. Pushing her hand away, I moved to the door, collecting my things along the way. That's what I liked about her. Things had to be even. She demanded an even playing field, even if she knew she had a disadvantage. The game didn't stop the entire ride down the elevator. Kendra made multiple attempts to cop a feel, and even tried one last time before stepping outside the building to a waiting, running vehicle. We both said our quick hellos to Maxwell, and as soon as we were buckled into our seats we headed to the heart of the city.

Kendra reached over and touched my thigh. "Downtown, huh?"

"Don't you just love surprises?" I teased.

"Normally, yes. But tonight you're just pissing me off." Her eyes glittered like stars on a moonless night. "Must be an important function you're taking me to. Can you at least tell me if we'll be eating? I'm starved."

Without looking at her I said, "The Mayor always serves up a feast."

Kendra's gasp was loud enough for me to know her eyes just

popped out of her face. "We're going to the Mayor's mansion?"

I rolled my head back to her with a knowing grin on my face. Raising my brows, I said, "Is there a problem?"

Kendra nervously twisted her fingers over her lap. "Yeah. There is a problem."

My brow arched. "And what would that be?"

"I like to know these kinds of things before I make a commitment." Her gaze hardened.

"What's the point?" I leaned closer to her. Her intoxicating scent traveled straight to my brain. "You'd be coming with me regardless."

"That may be. But still," she swallowed, "I like to have time to wrap my head around what the evening will entail and who I'll be talking with."

She was so damn cute when nervous. A part of me hoped that she'd be out of her element tonight, if only to give her another reason to stay close and remain by my side. Reaching over, I took her hands into mine. "You'll do fine," I said, letting my gaze fall to the ring I'd given her. She looked good in silver and black. There was no doubt about it. It was her combination, the mixture that gave her a new edge. "Just like everything else, we're in this together," I lifted my eyes to meet her gaze, "no matter what."

"I'm not cut out for these people." Her breaths quickened.

"Me, neither." I hooked her jaw with my finger, turning her head toward me. "I'll be there for you." She nodded. "If there is anything I've learned over the years, it's how to interact in the high society we're about to walk into. Follow my lead and you'll be fine."

Kendra nodded and I kissed her plump lips. Our tongues gently pressed into each other as I gave her time to process the knowledge of where we were going. Closing my eyes, I was dizzy with feelings for her—overwhelming and intense, but welcoming at the same time. I'd do anything to comfort her, protect her, and ensure she had a great time. There was nothing for her to worry about. Kendra was going to do fine. And the longer we kissed, I felt her nerves melt away, shedding the layers of fear, beginning to uncover the strength I knew she had locked away, hidden inside her.

By the time we pulled up front, Maxwell stopping in front of the beautiful Tudor mansion, there were already hundreds of people here. It was an annual event that brought in LA's wealthiest and most influential citizens. Maxwell opened my door and I took the liberty of guiding Kendra to her feet. Threading my fingers through hers, I held onto her tight enough to reassure her of the promises I'd made of keeping her close.

Kendra looked around, touching her hair with an almost ghostly look on her face.

"Remember. These are just people," I said softly, kissing her pulsing temple. "Just like you and me. Treat them no differently as you would anyone else, and I know they'll appreciate you as much as I do."

We shared a quick glance and she squeezed my hand as we proceeded inside. I nodded to friendly familiar faces and greeted several acquaintances as we weaved our way through the front doors and across the foyer. Kendra probably didn't feel it, but I'd been around long enough to sense the politics buzzing in the air. This was as much a party as it was an event to cut deals with the city's top influencers. Bureaucracy was part of any job description, but here at the mansion of the Mayor, it stank of dirty money, blood, and political favors. Perhaps that was why a criminal defense attorney like myself always seemed to be one of the first to get invited.

"Mr. Black," the Mayor said, smiling as he approached.

"Mayor Bentley." I extended my hand to shake his, remaining fully aware to keep one hand constantly on Kendra. "Great turnout."

We both looked around at the many heads bobbing up and down as they swam past.

"You remember my wife, Mary, don't you?" His toothy smile filled his face.

"Always a pleasure." I stepped forward, bent my spine, and kissed his wife on the cheek.

"And this is my date, Kendra Williams," I said, leaning back and nudging Kendra forward.

Mayor Bentley's cheeks turned to apples as he lifted Kendra's hand to his lips. "Marvelous. You're simply marvelous."

"Thank you." Kendra nodded as she smiled.

"Mr. Black, I'm glad that you're here." Mary's face beamed with appreciation. "I wanted to thank you in person for your generous donation to the underprivileged community school."

"Anything to help." I smoothed my hand around the small of Kendra's back to curl my fingers around her waist.

"I'm sorry we couldn't express our gratitude that night, but too many others wanted the Mayor's ear." She turned her head toward her husband.

Mayor Bentley let out a booming laugh. "Not a moment to rest."

"Well, I hope to be making more contributions soon." My lips flattened as I nodded.

Mary's face brightened. "There is another program that I'm sure will catch your attention. I'll be sure to send over the information to your office sometime tomorrow."

"Just let me know." I leaned forward, dropping my face closer to Mary. "Always happy to help the Mayor."

More guests soon shuffled in behind us and I excused ourselves, not wanting to keep them from greeting others. It was their party, after all, and I hadn't forgotten about the secret intentions I had waiting around the corner for Kendra, either.

We watched them move on. Beginning to feel a little overwhelmed myself—by the sheer volume flooding into the room—I turned to Kendra and said, "Care to join me on a little adventure?"

"As long as there is room to breathe."

My lips curled. "Plenty."

With Kendra in tow, I skirted through the crowd, leading her to the back stairs I remembered from a previous visit with the Mayor. It was just us that day, the mansion absent of partygoers which made it easy to move from one side of the building to the other, unlike tonight.

"Where are you taking me?" Kendra asked as we climbed to the second floor. "Are you sure we should be going up here?"

I'd made my face seen, spoken with the one person who mattered, so stepping away from the festivities unfolding below —if only for a few minutes—was just what I needed in order to speed up the night. "Aren't you at least a little curious to see where the Mayor comes up with all his great ideas?"

Kendra locked her gaze on me. "Is that where you're taking me? To his office?"

I quickened my pace. Kendra easily followed behind and I could feel the tension she was holding in her shoulders loosen with renewed excitement. In no time at all, we found the door leading to Bentley's office and when we stopped, I turned to whisper, "Ready?"

Kendra nodded quickly with a wide grin.

I held my breath and reached for the doorknob. Slowly, I turned until the latch clicked over. Giving it a slight nudge, I peeked through the open crack to see if the room was clear. When I was sure that no one was inside, I rushed into the room, pulling Kendra along with me. She shut the door and I said, "Better lock it. I'd hate to have the Mayor walk in on me fucking you."

Her hair flung over her shoulder as she spun her head around to look at me, seeing if I was serious.

I nodded, stepping up behind her, taking the flesh of her hips between my fingers. "Lock it."

Without further hesitation, Kendra did as she was told. She

twirled her body around inside my arms and kissed me with feverish passion.

I curled my tongue over hers, clawing and digging my hands into her body. With each swipe of her tongue, I led her closer to the Mayor's desk. Lifting her dress up above her waist, I set her down on the edge and immediately brought my hand to her sex.

"You knew all along that this was what you wanted, didn't you?" Kendra clawed at my chest.

"I suppose I gave too much away."

She nipped at my bottom lip. "I'm on to you, Kelly Black. You're more of an open book than you may think."

I touched her quivering softness, sliding my finger between her slick folds. "God, feel you. You're so wet."

Her tongue slid over my lips. "Have been since you took my panties away."

My lips crashed over hers. Kissing her fiercely, I thrust my finger between her cleft. A soft whimper rolled over her tongue, steeling my cock. The harder it pressed against my zipper, the deeper I thrust my finger into her. The pain was unbearable, but totally worth it. "Your tight little cunt feels so good against my finger."

She moaned, tossing her head back. I licked the length of her neck, loving the way she writhed against my hand.

"Don't you come yet," I said, taking her ear between my teeth.

"But—" she cried, "—I'm almost there."

I pulled my hand away.

"Kelly!" she growled, pulling my face to hers. "That's not fair."

My finger was back inside her the next second and I reminded her, "I say when you can come. Understand?"

"Whatever." She nodded, bucking her hips harder. "Just give it to me."

Sliding a second finger inside her, her head came crashing down against my shoulder. "If I feel you about to come, I'll take it all away."

She grunted and I knew she wasn't listening. Kendra was busy working herself into oblivion, forgetting that I held the power to her orgasms. If I wanted to let her come, I would let her. But I didn't. Not until I had her begging for it.

Pressing my thumb down over her swollen nub, I felt her walls tighten around my knuckles. Her breathing sped up and she panted. "Oh, shit."

And just when I knew she was about to explode, I pulled my hand away, retreating.

"Kelly, please," she begged, slapping her palms down on my shoulders.

"I told you the rules." I reached up to her face and touched her quivering lips. "But you're not listening."

"I'm listening." Her eyes pleaded with me to continue.

I shook my head and pushed my pussy-soaked fingers into her mouth. "You're not."

Her tongue worked frantically over my fingers, causing my cock to swell painfully large. "Are you ready to listen?"

She pulled my hand out of her mouth by the wrist. Flattening her tongue, she licked my fingers, reminding me what it was like when she gave me head. The woman was an animal, and I liked her aggressive sexual nature. Then she placed my hand back to her pussy herself, directing me back inside.

God, this woman was something else. So amazing, and completely worth moving heaven and earth to keep by my side. She was proving to be worthy of becoming my submissive and if she kept this up, I would have her tied up before she knew it.

Sliding my knuckles deep and hard over her pubic bone, I circled her clit, firmly pressing it harder as she clawed her nails into me. She was about to explode, but through clenched teeth and sweat I could see that she was holding back, waiting for my command.

My forehead fell to hers and we stared deep into each other's irises until neither of us could hold back any longer. "Come for me, baby."

Kendra's hips bucked hard off the desk's surface. Her fingers spread over the back of my skull as she cupped it, pressing my head hard against hers. Then her lips rounded and her eyes fluttered closed.

"That's it. Make my investment worthwhile," I said, pumping my wrist so fast it hurt.

The next second, her entire body tensed and she held her breath just before she tossed her head back and wailed into the mansion's ceiling.

My fingers played with her pulsing pussy as I kissed her between gasps of air. "Now, I may be wrong," I murmured, "but something tells me that Mary hasn't had an orgasm as good as the one you just had in a very long time."

Kendra giggled, unable to stop kissing me. "That's because she doesn't have you."

Realizing that we had been away from the party for longer than I'd initially intended, I walked off my raging hard on while Kendra smoothed down her dress and fixed her hair. "There's nothing that makes me as hungry as I am now other than amazing sex." She laughed.

Without a care to our names, we left the office and took our time browsing the hallways until we found ourselves back in the middle of the party. Everything was going perfectly. Kendra was much more relaxed having found hors d'oeuvres and a drink. She radiated a glow that I was learning to love—wanting what she had in my life 24/7. Men's heads turned when she passed, and they couldn't keep from wondering who she was and what she was doing with me.

"Excuse me," I heard a familiar voice come up from behind, "but I can't help but wonder where it is I know you from."

I turned to find Wes touching Kendra at the elbow.

Kendra glanced at me for direction. "Maybe I should remind

you then?" I said.

A glimmer of amusement flashed across Wes's eyes as he lifted his gaze to me.

"Does Mojito ring a bell?"

Kami Burke, Wes's fiancé, hung off his shoulder smiling. Her baby bump was starting to show and looked absolutely incredible. "That's right," Wes said, staring into Kendra's eyes. "You were there with a friend."

"I was. Good memory." Kendra wrapped her arm around my waist.

"I never forget beautiful faces." He winked.

"They call me, Kendra."

"Is that right?"

"That's right." Kendra smiled.

Wes shifted his gaze to me and raised his brows. "Assertive."

"That, she is," I said. "Didn't expect to see you here tonight."

Wes lifted his drink to his lips. "Are you kidding? I'd never miss my chance to throw around my influence in hopes of passing favorable legislation."

I laughed and greeted Kami. "How are you feeling?"

"Don't be fooled. Being pregnant isn't as fun as I thought it would be."

"Kami, baby," Wes pointed to the bar, "why don't you do us a solid and get drinks for everyone."

Kami stood on her tip-toes and kissed his cheek. "Sure thing, baby."

"And maybe you can take Kendra along with you?"

"Of course."

"C'mon, honey." Kami reached out for Kendra's hand. "Walk with me. I'd love to know more about you."

I squeezed Kendra's hand, nodding, giving her my approval. Knowing Wes, he wanted to talk business. And with the women away, we were free to bring our secrets out into the open. "She's really something," Wes said as he admired his fiancé.

"We're two lucky bastards," I said.

"Kendra's Madam's girl, huh?"

I nodded, keeping my eyes on Kendra.

He folded his arms, lost in thought, and I couldn't help but wonder what it was he was thinking. I knew how much he resented Madam. Then, as if lightning struck him, he snapped his head up and said, "What's the latest on Stone?"

I took the next several minutes to let him know where I was, how I was in the process of handing Mario over to a friend, and having convinced Madam that this was what needed to be done. Wes turned to me, covered his mouth, and said, "And the Madam, is she business as usual?"

"She doesn't suspect a thing," I assured him just as the women joined us, their hands full of drinks.

Kendra handed me a sparkling water and I took a sip as Kami announced, "There was an old friend I saw that I'd like to talk to. It was great seeing you, Kelly. And Kendra, remember what I said." She winked at Kendra.

"Be in touch, Kelly." Wes slapped my back. "Oh, and heads up," he lowered his voice and moved his lips closer to my ear. "It looks like the DA is heading this way. Coming right for you."

Together, Kendra turned with me to find Oscar Buchanan lowering his brow, smirking. "Relax, Kelly. I'm not going to bite."

"I might."

Oscar was with Angelina Davis, the same woman he'd been with ever since I stole Kendra away. She smiled at me and scowled at Kendra when she thought I wasn't looking. "By the way you're looking at me now, I'd think you were about to ram your shoulder into me here, too." He laughed.

Kendra pressed more of her body into me as I responded. "In front of the Mayor? You know I wouldn't humiliate you like that."

The DA laughed. Stepping away from Angel, he hung his head and dropped his voice. "I heard what happened the other day." His forehead lifted when he glanced in my direction.

"It's no secret," I said, inching my way closer to him.

Oscar turned his back to the women and nudged my shoulder to follow. "Frankly, I was surprised. I thought you believed Mario was innocent?" His brows squished together.

"I do." I stole a sip of water from my glass. "He is."

Oscar chuckled. "He's going to need a good lawyer, like yourself," he pointed his finger at my heart, "because my office is coming for him. And we've built a strong case against him."

I glanced over my shoulder to Kendra. Angel was busy talking into her ear. I couldn't help but wonder what it was she was saying to her now. Then the DA started nodding. "Ahh…" He laughed. "How can I be so blind?"

My brows pinched as I turned my attention back to him.

"You son of a bitch." He slapped my back.

"Excuse me?"

"Stone!" He laughed. "That's why you dropped your defense for Mario."

Curling my lips over the rim of my glass I sucked back a piece of ice, not wanting to continue talking shop here of all places. When I glanced back to Kendra, she was pressing her clutch hard against her chest, meeting my gaze with a pleading look as if she needed to be saved.

"You just made my night, Black." Oscar turned back to face our women. "That is one battle I am truly looking forward to." He turned to look me in the eye. "It should be a show the country will follow."

I felt my nostrils flare when I watched Kendra's eyes widen at something Angel said. By the look on her face, I knew she was upset. "Have a nice night, Oscar," I said, excusing myself.

Hurrying over to Kendra, Angel stepped away, retreating back onto Oscar's arm. Once I had Kendra in my hands, I could feel her trembling. "Are you okay?"

She shook her head. "Just get me out of here, will you?"

10

Kendra

"What happened in there?"

I curled up into Kelly, unsure how I could possibly tell him the lies Angel wanted me to believe about him. I hated that I let her get inside my head so easily, but she had a way of convincing me that what she said was true.

"*Bella,* if you don't tell me what happened in there, I can't help you."

The world flashed under the street lights, and the faster Maxwell drove, the more it all seemed to blur together. I closed my eyes, trying to push her words out of my mind. But the harder I tried, the louder her voice rang inside my head.

Kelly's hand petted my hair—with my head resting against his chest, I resented the even beat of his heart. While his was calm, mine thrashed between my ears. He wasn't a liar. Kelly was committed to me. I was his only girl. There wasn't a reason I should doubt him.

Yet, because of Angel, I did.

"I'm not even sure if it was your conversation with Angel or your brief visit with Kami that spooked you." Kelly was mostly talking to himself, as if he couldn't let this go until he pinpointed exactly when the fun expired, spoiling both of our nights.

"It wasn't Kami." My voice cracked. It was the first time I spoke since crumbling inside the back of Kelly's SUV and my body shook as I inhaled my next deep breath.

"What did Kami tell you?" Kelly looked straight ahead. The privacy partition was down, giving us a clear view of the back of Maxwell's head, but I was sure that he was trained to ignore what he heard. "She told you not to forget what she said. What did she mean by that?"

Kelly's hand stopped stroking my hair and I felt his gaze angle down to my face. I swallowed down the sandpaper scratching the back of my throat and refused to look at him. "It was nothing. Just girl talk."

"Fuck, Kendra." He shoved his hand through his hair as he turned away.

I glanced down at the promise ring Kelly had given me. Twisting it around my finger, I couldn't stop thinking about what it symbolized, how it propelled us to take that next step. Against my body, I could feel Kelly's muscles twitching with frustration. I appreciated his desire to help, but when it was all said and done, what did it matter? "It doesn't matter," I murmured through dry lips.

"It does fucking matter." Kelly balled his hand on top of his thigh. "If someone is treating you badly, then I need to know about it."

"Why? What will you do?"

His head whipped around to me. "I'll end it."

Lifting my head off his chest, I asked, "Who is she, anyway?"

"Who are we talking about? Kami? Angel? Someone else I missed tonight?"

I pushed off of Kelly's solid chest and sat upright. "Angel. Who is she?"

"Oscar's girlfriend."

"But do you know who she works for?" My speech stammered as I rushed through the many questions I had when it came to who Angelina Davis really was.

"What do you mean? I don't know the woman."

"She's clearly an escort, but I haven't seen her around Madam's."

Kelly met my stare, his eyes darting across my face. "You think Angel is one of Madam's girls?"

"You don't think it's possible?"

He tipped his chin back and let out a heavy sigh.

"Tell me you don't find her presence as strange as I do." I paused to gauge Kelly's reaction. "Especially knowing Madam's tendency to want to squash her competition."

"What do you know about Madam's business interests?" The lines of Kelly's forehead deepened.

I rolled my eyes to the window, stealing a glance outside. "Probably more than I should."

Kelly dropped his shaking head into his hand. "Dammit, Kendra. You shouldn't go looking for trouble."

A sharp pain spread across my chest, leaving me with the inability to speak. I thought back to the files I'd stolen on the Madam before I ever worked for her, and though they weren't all that revealing, Kelly's reaction had me believing that there was more going on than I'd originally thought. What that was, I wasn't sure. Kelly never did say what that might be, but I could see it in his eyes, the secrets he had hidden inside.

When we arrived to the hotel, Maxwell parked out front and I said, "What are you hiding, Kelly?"

Kelly stared at me with tense muscles before opening the door and stepping out. Maxwell pulled my door open and assisted me to my feet. I hurried to catch up with Kelly and together we entered the building. "Why don't you want to talk about it?"

"Because there is nothing to talk about." His words were quick as he spoke under his breath the moment we stepped foot in the front lobby.

"What the fuck, Kelly?" My voice bounced off the marbled floor.

Kelly lifted his head and I followed his eyes to the woman working reception. He held up a hand, assuring her that there was no need to panic. Except, inside my chest, that was all I could feel—panic and uncertainty rolling through my bones.

"Can you really expect me to go along for the ride and not ask questions?"

He clamped his fingers around my arm tight enough to cause my skin to bruise. "Not here," he growled, towing me behind him as he marched toward the private elevators.

"If I'm in danger—"

Kelly spun around and was in my face quicker than my brain could keep up with. "Do you think you're in danger?"

My eyes narrowed. "Am I?"

His nostrils flared beneath bug eyes. "I don't know what Angel said, but you need to forget it."

The elevator car doors opened and Kelly yanked me inside. I liked that he was getting angry. It made him more human—more relatable. Though I wasn't stupid, either. I knew that I was walking on eggshells, pushing him to reveal more about what he knew. Our relationship was one built on sexual tension, dark desires, and money. What I was doing now, I had done my entire life. When good things came into my life, I froze. And the only way to thaw the ice was to purposely self-destruct, sabotaging all that was good and warm in my life purely out of fear of losing the identity that made me, me.

Kelly pushed me into the back corner and hovered over me with intense, unwavering eyes.

I knew that I was undeserving of his good fortune. He deserved better. Deserved to be with someone with less baggage than what I knew I was carrying. "I did forget it." My eyes darted across his strong angles. "But then she reminded me again of what it is I should be looking out for."

Kelly pushed his fingers through my hair, thrusting his hips into my soft belly. "Reminded you about what?" His voice was deep, husky.

I felt myself being turned on by him. The way he was talking to me, and the strength he had, was unbearable. Memories of the Mayor's office clouded my vision. It was impossible to forget how hard I left him after he finger-fucked me, knocking me off my axis, sacrificing his own release for me. It had to have left him suffering through intense agonizing pain of his own. "You don't want to know," I murmured.

He leaned closer to my face. "But I do, my sweet *Bella*. I want to know everything about you."

My eyelids felt heavy as I clawed at his tuxedo. "Like you said," I pecked at his thick lips, "let's just forget it."

He slammed his lips down over mine and thrust his tongue deep in my mouth. I was afraid that if I told him about the lies Angel kept spreading about him that he'd mistakenly misspeak and prove to me that what she was saying was actually true. I didn't want to know. Didn't want to take the chance and flirt with my own death. But thinking one thing and doing the exact opposite was the tendency I had when feeling cornered with no clear path out.

"Isn't this what you want instead?" I asked, reaching between his legs and cupping his hardened package. "A slut like me to fuck whenever you want?"

He pulled back, cupping his hand against my face. "That's what you think you are?"

"It's what I am, aren't I?"

A glimmer of concern darkened his eyes.

"Tell me, Counselor. How much was I worth to you?"

Kelly stepped away and turned his back. Pacing the small elevator box, I could feel his frustration building.

"Ten thousand?" I didn't move, choosing to remain with my back flush against the wall. "Fifty?"

Kelly rooted his fists into the sides of his hips and glanced over his shoulder, looking me in the eye. His pupils were tiny pinpricks of anger. I liked the danger his body expelled.

My tongue circled my lips. "One hundred?"

He stormed over to me like a tornado in the night, punching the metal wall directly next to my head. "Is that what you want? For me to treat you like a whore?"

My chest heaved through labored breaths. Instead of feeling frightened by his rage, my nipples tightened and fire spread down my belly, quivering my sex. "If you're just going to leave me once you grow tired of having me, then what does it matter?"

His eyes widened and I could feel his hot breath swirling over my face. His musky masculine scent filled my brain with memories of his touch. "Is that what she told you? That I was going to grow tired of you and find someone new?"

My voice caught in my throat. "Will you?"

"You're a submissive in training. We haven't even begun the fun part. If you think that I'm going to grow tired of this," his hand reached under my dress and plunged a finger deep inside me, "then you have me all wrong."

I grinded my hips on his hand while massaging his testicles between my fingers. "Then punish me for believing someone else's lies, Counselor."

11

Kendra

Kelly's back muscles jumped and flexed as I watched him dig through his secret closet.

My nipples were tight little razors as I stared at his firm naked butt, wondering how he was going to punish me. My pussy lips were glistening with desire and quivering in anticipation. He had me out of my dress and naked within seconds of entering his penthouse. "Will you hurry up already?"

Kelly tossed a silk scarf over one shoulder and turned to saunter over to the bed where I was leaning back, perched up on my hands with legs spread. "Tonight, we're not going to get too rough."

"But I like it rough," I mewed.

He chuckled. "You don't even know what rough is."

"I can imagine," I said, appreciating the beauty walking directly toward me.

I'd never seen Kelly's body so tight. The muscles in his arms jumped at the same time his abs flexed. A sweaty glow caught the dim lights from above and his thick thighs bounced and hardened with each heavy step he took. He was a titan, a sex god made of steel, and his cock was the thickest I'd ever seen. Without thinking about what I was doing, I touched my nipples just imagining him stretch me with that thing. "I want to get on with the kink."

He climbed onto the bed and it sank beneath his weight. Slowly, he crawled toward me, pulling my hand away from my breast. "It's a process. And you're not ready for those hard limits."

"Then what are you going to do with this?" I asked, yanking the scarf off his shoulder.

"You'll see." He stole it back and stretched it out in front of my face. He slowly brought it over my eyes, and the last thing I saw before my world went black was his long beautifully manscaped phallus hitting him in his stomach.

"I like this." My heart pounded.

"Now, it's important you do as I say." He tied the scarf behind my skull into a relaxed knot.

"Anything." I reached down, sliding my middle finger over my erect clitoris.

"If I start to do something you don't like, I want you to say," he put his lips next to my ear and whispered, "*Angel.*"

Reaching up with my hand, I pulled the scarf away my eyes and shot Kelly a look. "Really? Our fucking safe word is Angel?"

He fell back and sat on his heels. "You don't like her and if you need to say her name, you won't like what I'm doing." Then he sat upright once again and moved the scarf back over my eyes, tightening the knot this time. "It's our safe word. And if I'm doing my job and listening to your needs, you won't ever have to use it."

"Let's hope not," I muttered just as I felt a sharp pain pinch my strained nipple. "Shit!"

"Relax and remember to breath." Kelly's fingers clamped over one nipple, then the next. "I'm just warming your body up, shocking the system."

I arched my back and pushed my chest out, concentrating on each inhalation, feeling my body heat until I began sweating. With each little pain he inflicted upon my breasts, he matched it with a breath of cool air over them.

"God, you have the prettiest tits I've ever seen." His hands cupped my twins, squeezing them together while continuing to play with my nipples. "I could play with these all night."

I liked them too. If anyone asked, they were perfectly proportioned, fitting my frame with the elegance I knew men like Kelly loved in women like me. And I certainly wouldn't mind him only playing here, on my nipples, tonight.

His mouth fell to my hard pebble. Circling the dark pigment with his tongue, he sucked my nipple against the roof of his mouth. "You have me so hard."

Bright visions flashed across my eyes. The sensation of not being able to see electrified the feelings of Kelly's fingers and mouth.

"I'm stroking myself, *Bella*. Can you feel that?"

I could hear his wrist jerking back and forth. As he sped it up, the swollen tip of his cock would occasionally hit me on the inside of my thigh, causing my sex to tighten in response. "You deserve it. I should have never left you hard in the Mayor's office."

"Tell me, *Bella*, what would you have done to me if we would have stayed?" His fingers rolled my nipple and I could feel his strokes slide from root to tip.

A soft whimper escaped my lips as I began to say, "I would have set you down in his big important chair, unzipped you free, and gotten on my knees to suck you until you came."

Kelly nipped at my neck and I felt him stroke harder.

"Would I have come in your mouth," he moved to my lips and thrust his tongue against mine, "or shot it across your face?"

His lips grazed against mine and I liked the way they felt, as if he was reminding me that he was there for me, keeping me safe. "Both sound fun."

He chuckled and I flinched when he touched my pussy lips. I hadn't expected it, and with the inability to see it coming another wave of electricity shocked my system awake. "Just like your tits, I love your tight pink pussy."

I arched my spine, tossing my head back, gasping. Kelly had me panting, hot and bothered by the subtle touches of his taunting fingers. He played with my lips, spreading my desire around the smooth, bare skin. And when he gently slapped my mound with the flat of his fingers, I cried out. "I need you inside me."

"Not now." Kelly's hand retreated back to his throbbing shaft. "First, you must decide if you want to swallow my cum or have me shoot it across your tits."

"I don't care." My head rolled on my shoulders and I started smoothing one hand over my chest.

"Decide." He slapped my pussy harder. "Which will it be?"

"Across my tits," I spat, wanting to have his dirty sex coat my entire body.

"That's good." Kelly moved behind me, pulling my elbows behind my back. "It's what I would have chosen myself."

One by one, he looped another silk scarf under my elbows. Making a figure eight, he bound my arms behind my back, leaving my chest open and exposed.

"Now, I'm going to fuck your mouth." Kelly slid his muscular arm under my knees and picked me up, resting me near the edge of the bed. "Are you okay with that?"

I nodded, swallowing hard and wetting my lips, preparing for his onslaught.

Lowering my head with his hand, he dangled it over the side. I felt him leave the bed, the mattress springing up, and on my next inhale his cockhead was circling my lips.

"Stick out your tongue," he demanded.

My heart pounded fiercely against my chest as my velvety muscle left my mouth. My breath hitched when I felt his hot cockhead press against my taste buds.

"You taste that?"

I nodded, flattening my tongue to feel more of his hotness against my mouth.

"I've been hard for you all night." He spread more of his precum over my coiled tongue. "And that's all the taste you'll get tonight, so you better enjoy it."

"I am," I purred, pushing my hips up off the mattress to relieve the discomfort buzzing through my bound arms.

Kelly pushed further into my mouth, rocking back and forth. He moaned before speeding up. His satin skin grazed over my teeth, stretching my mouth beyond what I thought possible, and soon I was gagging against him. Each thrust hit the back of my throat, and I fought to breathe. Reaching down, Kelly cupped the back of my skull with both his hands and shifted the angle of his penetration, going even deeper than before. Stars flashed behind my lids and the pain I was experiencing shifted from my arms to my jaw and back again. I prayed for it to be over, but Kelly kept going.

This was what he needed. What I had asked of him. We were in this together, and I knew that if I could get through this, he would reward me with an earthshattering orgasm of my own. The pain was worth it. No matter how much it burned.

"There it is," Kelly grunted as he hooked his fingers inside my tightness. "I can feel you wanting to come."

His thick girth in my mouth kept me from nodding or responding. But, yes, I could come as easily as the push of a button.

"That's right." He pressed his thumb against my swollen nub. "Come for me." His hips rocked against my face—his balls hitting my forehead.

I flexed my core and forced myself to come, knowing Kelly

would soon follow. My arms were numb by now, and nothing about the way he decided he had to have me was comfortable. But I wasn't about to say her name—beg for relief by announcing our safe word. I was stronger than that. I wanted Kelly more than that.

Kelly ripped his fingers out of me and slammed his cock into my mouth before flinging it out and squirting hot ropes of semen across my chest. I gulped down huge breaths of air as relief swept across my body.

I laid there sweaty and sedated, covered in his hot seed, when I felt his gentle hands lift me up to a sitting position. Kelly unbound my arms before pulling the scarf off the bridge of my nose. I met his dark eyes, close to my face, and together we stared at each other, wondering what it was we were to say next.

He stroked my face and massaged my arms, getting the blood flowing back to them. Kelly Black was an enigma. How he could go from fierce predator to compassionate lover in only a matter of seconds had my head scrambling to keep up. It was these highs and lows, dips and swings, that kept me curious, always finding a reason to be turned on by him.

My hands worked over his jumping muscles, and I couldn't get close enough. I wanted to drape my body over him, melt into him, and find a way we could be one. My heart swelled for him, and when he lifted his head I knew he had something important to say.

"There is nothing I wouldn't do for you." He played with my fingers as he smoothed his free hand over my shoulder and down my arm. "And I'm not about to leave you."

My heart damn near exploded. The look in his eyes was sincere and truthful. Angel was a bitch for feeding me lies. "I'm not afraid."

12

Kendra

The truth was, I was terrified.

Holding my breath until my lungs screamed for release, I held my head under the shower stream raining down on me.

My fingers splayed against the wall and my muscles flexed.

There was so much uncertainty swinging around Kelly I didn't even know where I should begin in deciding which stone to turn over first.

My head drooped a little bit further to my chest.

Inside, my heart feared that Kelly would eventually tire of me. It was stupid, I know, considering we had barely been dating. But I didn't know his past—couldn't decide if Angel knew the man I was sleeping with better than I did or if it was all a pack of lies.

Tipping my chin back, I placed my face directly into the hot water. It streamed off my forehead and spilled down my cheeks.

Kelly's history with women was as much of an enigma as

everything else about him. Hell, that was why I liked the man. He wasn't an open book I could pick up and read without thought. There was depth and substance to him, a charming character that made me laugh and want to cry. What did it matter how many women he had been with before I came along? It didn't. And I didn't care, except for the fact that no matter what he said to try to convince me that I was his for the long-haul, I was still skeptical—all because of that bitch-faced Angel.

I rolled my neck, dipping my head from side to side, and when I opened my jaw wide, the joint popped. A shooting pain cramped the side of my face and made me wince.

But it wasn't just Kelly's history or what he was going to determine our future to be that left me most frightened. No, that was the easy part.

My chest heaved and I began hyperventilating as the mere thought of it spun around my brain.

I gasped for air, fearing that Kelly might take this whole thing too far. I knew myself well enough to know when to stop. But I also couldn't deny the reason I started working for the Madam in the first place. I wanted excitement, sought the thrill of what Kelly was now offering, and with it within my grasp I freaked and became paranoid, thinking that I would allow him to lead me down this rabbit hole of sexual experimentation to the point of danger.

I pushed off the wall, turned to allow the hot stream of water to hit my back, and hugged myself inside my arms.

It was impossible for me to know what his end goal was, or what activities he was preparing me for. Inside, my gut told me I could do the kink. He could twist me and take me in a variety of different ways, no problem. Being blindfolded and bound wasn't the issue. No. The issue was much more than that—hell, I *liked* all that.

Spinning back around, I tipped my head back and opened my mouth. A river of water poured over my teeth and when it flooded the back of my throat, my chest expanded as I gagged, choking on the hot liquid. Hurling over, I spit it out with thoughts of what it would feel like to drown—

—because that was where this was heading. And I couldn't conceive playing with death in the name of getting off.

Orgasms were cool. Death wasn't. Simple as that.

I cupped my breasts inside the palms of my hands and ran my fingers over my soft nipples and down the front of my body.

Kelly's semen was gone, washed away down the drain of his fancy shower. Half of the walls were encased in glass. The other half was black marble tiling. There were two shower heads, one on either end, with a bounty of other options of where the water could shoot out from depending on what knobs were turned or what buttons were pushed. To my left, I stared out into the empty jet Jacuzzi tub, ideally set below a stained-wooden wall of wax candles. They were unlit, but I could easily imagine the mood it set when burning.

Glancing over my shoulder, I wondered what was taking Kelly so long to join me. I was certain after what we just did that he would. I even purposely kept the door cracked open, as if thinking there wasn't any way he could pass up an opportunity like this.

This, I thought, looking around at the luxury.

No matter how awkward tonight was, I didn't want to lose this —and I certainly wasn't ready to lose him. But I couldn't continue to allow him to do whatever he wanted to do to me without first sitting his ass down and setting limits. I didn't care what paperwork I signed or how much money he paid to have me—however large that number might be. Kelly was going to walk me through his desires before I agreed to be blindfolded again.

Turning the shower knobs to off, I opened the glass shower door and stepped onto the plush bath mat. Reaching to the wall, I pulled a fresh, dry towel off the rack and wrapped it around my body.

As I headed back to Kelly, I thought about how I was going to approach this. It was best I brought it to him gently, not wanting to upset him or push him away. He was a reasonable man, and I was sure that he would recognize my concerns once he listened to the boundaries I wanted to set, convincing myself he'd understand and make a compromise.

I found him still proudly naked, standing next to his bed. I was undeniably attracted to him. He was strength and smarts packaged together in a beautiful combo and a flutter still rolled through my stomach each time I saw him—especially when I saw him like this. "Hey, so I was thinking..."

Kelly didn't move, didn't respond.

"Kelly?" I inched closer to him.

His head hung down to his chest, and when I peered to the side, changing the angle of my approach, I could see that his focus was buried in whatever he had opened on his phone.

"Hey, baby." This time I said it a little bit louder, hoping to elicit some kind of response.

A second passed before my words seemed to register. Slowly, he turned his head, glancing at me over his shoulder. One look at him and I knew that something had happened in the short time I was showering.

My brows drew together and my gaze narrowed as I studied his face.

Kelly had a wild appearance about him—feral almost. The man I was looking at now wasn't the same man I'd left only minutes ago. The lines on his face were twisted and tied, and the air seemed to have gotten sucked out of the room. His eyes bulged and he never blinked as he stared back at me with dull, dark eyes.

I reached up and touched the necklace he had given me. "Is everything all right?"

When he swallowed, it looked like it was difficult for him. "Yeah." He turned back to look at his phone as if needing to read the message one more time, somehow still not believing whatever it was he just received. "It's just a text." His voice was barely a whisper but it cut through the air like a sharp knife.

I felt the pulse in my neck tick up another notch, and instinctively I tightened the towel around my body, staring at the bright screen of his phone. It was impossible to read. I was too far away but I desperately wanted to know who it was from and what it had said. But it wasn't my place to ask. It was up to Kelly to decide if he wanted to tell me or not, yet still, I pleaded with him with my eyes to do just that.

"Do you want to tell me about it?" I asked.

Kelly looked back down to his palm one last time before closing out his phone. "Something came up."

I nodded, watching him move across the bedroom and open a dresser drawer. He dug around, pulling boxer shorts out with a pair of socks. I felt helpless, knowing that something was wrong. But without him asking for help—or knowing anything about what was unfolding in front of my very own eyes—I couldn't do anything but stand there, frozen stiff, feeling helpless.

"I've got something I have to take care of," he muttered as he skimmed past me on his way to the bathroom.

My skin prickled against the cool breeze he stirred up and my core shivered in his wake. I dropped my head inside my hand and closed my eyes. The bathroom door closed behind me and my heels flew off the wood floor.

Covering my mouth, I was visibly shaken and I had no idea what was actually going on. Truth be told, I hated how this night had turned out. In a way, I felt like this was all my fault.

As soon as I heard the shower turn on I padded lightly to the dresser in search of his phone.

Doubt crept up my spine and spread like ivy. I wanted to snoop, scroll through his list of contacts, read his messages. Except it didn't take me long to realize that his phone wasn't here —he had taken it with him.

I swore to myself that I was going to strangle Angel the next time I saw her. She was the reason I couldn't fully trust Kelly right now. Even if I was naturally a skeptical person, this had gone much further than what even I would consider healthy.

Not even a minute later the shower shut off. Kelly was out of the bathroom and digging through his closet, plucking a white button-down from its hanger and slipping his legs through a clean pair of dark slacks.

Resting my bottom on the edge of the bed I asked, "Do you want me to come with you?" The moment I heard myself say it, I knew how foolish it sounded. I wasn't even dressed.

"Stay here," he said as he stood in front of the mirror. "Get some rest and I'll be back as soon as possible."

Insecurity rolled through my limbs as I sat there staring, hating how handsome and put together he looked. He made it look so easy. Only Kelly could pull something like that off after just sticking his member down my throat. "What's going on?"

Kelly turned, finishing the last of his buttons on his cuffs, and sauntered over to me. Gently, he brushed his thumb over my cheek. I wanted to press more of my face against his hand, beg him to stay, but resisted the urge. When he stepped away, he hurried to the front of the penthouse and I followed two steps behind.

"Is it work?" My voice sounded more desperate with each question that went unanswered.

"Get some sleep." His voiced echoed down the hallway as he opened the front door. Without looking behind it closed after him, leaving me to grasp the sudden silence of his home-away-from-home.

It was much too quiet. The room began to spin and I didn't like it.

It didn't take long for loneliness to settle in. I couldn't stop wondering who he'd left me to go see. His lack of communication was killing me. And after all that had happened tonight, I couldn't help but feel that his promise of not leaving me was only another lie specifically directed at my already achy heart.

He was hiding something. And, clearly, he couldn't trust me enough to tell me what was going on. There were too many secrets and the pile was only growing taller. If he meant all the things he said, I should know these things about him. But I didn't. And that was what was killing me the most.

It was then I decided that I couldn't do this. Couldn't stay here, couldn't deal with my thoughts alone anxiously waiting for his return.

Hurrying back to the bedroom, I dropped the towel and slipped on my bra and the panties he hadn't let me wear to the Mayor's before zipping back on the dress I'd been happily wearing most of the night.

I was out of Kelly's suite and on my way to the elevator, messaging Alex.

I paced.

I sighed.

I spun in circles, waiting to hear back.

Glancing at my phone's screen for the millionth time, there was still nothing from Alex.

I entered the empty elevator car as my stomach churned. My legs were restless and it was impossible to stand still. With each passing minute, I grew anxious and impatient enough to finally hit the call button next to Alex's name.

The line rang and rang and when she still didn't answer, I dropped my phone to my side and muttered a few choice words.

As soon as the elevator doors slid open, I feared that Kelly would be in the lobby. My imagination ran wild with how he would react if he saw me. There was little doubt in my mind that it wouldn't end well. Disobeying a direct order was cause for punishment, and visions of him forcing me to retreat back into his empty penthouse, demanding I wait there until his return, filled my insecure, spinning head.

But I was leaving. Not chasing after him. He'd made the choice to go and not bring me with him. Not me.

Hugging my clutch against my chest, I searched the far corners of the hotel lobby, looking straight ahead but letting my eyes wander. There was a sea of faces, typical of this place, but not one was Kelly's.

My steps were small but my gait shortened even further when I shared a glance with the woman at reception. Her face was new to me, and that encouraged me to want to talk to her. If it had been the other front-desk employee who refused my entrance when I'd found Sylvia Neil leaving Kelly's apartment, I wasn't sure talking to her would be worth my time.

A tall man headed directly for me and smiled as he passed. I passed a few more people before I reached the front desk, thinking why in the world Kelly spent so much time here instead of the house he supposedly owned.

The woman behind the computer saw me coming and smiled. I matched her glow, and asked if she knew Kelly Black. "I do," she said with friendly eyes.

"Do you remember me?"

Her eyes searched my face. "You were with him earlier tonight."

"I was." I nodded. "Can I ask you something?"

"Of course." She angled her head to the side.

"Do you know if Kelly is normally alone or with someone when he is here?"

"Well, like we just established, he was with you tonight."

"Yes, I know." I shook my head, mildly annoyed by her response. "But what about when I'm not here?"

Her lips thinned and the warm smile she'd greeted me with was now gone. "I can't say."

I dropped my tone and leaned further over the counter. "You can't say because of policy or because you don't know?"

"I don't know." She cast her gaze to her hands. "I'm sorry."

"Thanks, anyway," I muttered, stepping away. "Have a good night."

My phone was still void of Alex's return call, and I wished she would just text me back, acknowledging me. With Nash still away, I couldn't imagine she was up to anything important. Maybe she was sleeping or working late. Either way, I was coming for her.

Pushing through the revolving doors, I stopped midstride as my eyes widened in disbelief. "Watch it!" I screamed, fearing the pedestrian crossing the street was about to get hit by the oncoming car.

The vehicle came to a screeching halt, barely missing the man, and my heart beat wildly in my chest.

I gasped, covering my mouth with a trembling hand.

The man stood mere inches from the car's hood, never getting hit, but I watched him yell against the car horn blazing. I couldn't believe the driver—the way he was acting after nearly clipping the man in the legs, like it was his fault and not the other way around. I watched them exchange words of anger, thinking that I should come to his defense having witnessed it all. But when he turned to look at me—

—my heart stopped.

With our gazes locked, the hair on the nape of my neck stood on end. I wanted to duck my head, but couldn't. My legs were heavy and I was frozen stiff, unable to move. My mind shriveled up into the helpless girl I once was. It had been so long ago, but those eyes—his eyes—were ones I would never forget. He was the man who still found his way into my dreams, haunting me at night, and now we were standing only feet apart.

My mind screamed at me to run—to pick up my legs and move. Still, I couldn't.

Slowly, his head tipped back and a knowing curve hit his mouth.

Our shared past crashed into the present as my fingers shook. I was cold. And without warning, I began backpedaling as if a higher power had come to intervene, saving me from the danger that lurked in front of me.

He held up his finger as if wanting to talk to me.

My fingers pinched my clutch so tight my knuckles went white. I could feel the blood leave my face and I was sure I was as white as a ghost.

I reasoned with myself that he might not have recognized me —only wanted to get a statement for the near-accident that had almost occurred. But I wasn't about to talk, because I sure as hell recognized him. I would never forget his face. Not after what he did to me.

A car pulled to the curb and placed itself between me and the man. I watched the driver roll down the passenger side window. "Hey."

I blinked. Then I blinked again. It was the Ugandan Uber driver I'd been seeing regularly, and without saying a word I hurried over and got into his empty backseat. He laughed, but when he saw me staring out the window he asked, "Are you okay?"

"Just drive. Please, just drive."

As soon as the wheels began to turn, the back of my head hit the seat and I sighed. Closing my eyes, I fought back the tears I felt welling behind my lids. I was convinced I was just seeing things. I just needed this night to end. When my phone started to ring, I quickly saw that it was Alex. "I just saw him," I answered the call.

"You saw who?"

"The man who raped me."

13

Kelly

My grip readjusted on the wheel as I made a left turn.

I hated that I had to rush off in a hurry, leaving Kendra behind. It was the last thing I expected to have to do tonight. But life surprised us all in ways we never expected, and my only hope would be that she would understand.

Turning my head toward the empty passenger seat, I knew that if this was anything else Kendra would be right here with me.

If I knew anything, it was that Kendra needed to be held, her body massaged. My heart felt like it was shrinking the more I thought about how tonight had played out. It started off so well—we were having fun, laughing—then after Kendra told me she needed to leave the party, everything changed. I didn't know what had gotten into me, but I knew that I had pushed her much further than I should have. What I did wasn't meant for a virgin Sub. Binding her arms behind her back and pushing my cock into her mouth expecting her to swallow a sword, was too much too soon.

My palm slammed down on the wheel. "Fuck, Kelly."

I was off my game. The way tonight transpired was my fault. It had been a while since I'd played the Dom role, and tonight it showed. Instead of establishing a foundation, I went in for the kill. Kendra talked like she knew what she was doing, and maybe that had fooled me into believing she knew more than she did. But now I knew the truth. And if I didn't work to correct the practice, it would break the entire experience I was creating for us. And the last thing I wanted was for her to be scared and ask to step away. The responsibility of a Dom was greater than anything else I knew, yet tonight I'd failed her.

Turning my head, I stared out into the pitch-dark night. It was impossible not to think of how Maria Greer had died. One wrong move on my part and Kendra could end up dead in a similar way to Maria.

But that wasn't going to happen.

That wasn't me. Wasn't my style.

My eyes grew heavy with the thought. Feeling overheated, I cracked my window.

It was better I was alone. I needed it. If only to collect my thoughts, to give myself time to decide what exactly I wanted from her. When I was leaving the apartment, I couldn't look at Kendra without feeling extremely disappointed with myself. It was too much, and my emotions would eventually get the best of me.

Kendra was the sweetest thing, and after seeing her visibly shaken by the harassment of Angelina Davis, I wanted nothing more than to protect her from whatever was being said. The more I thought about it, I couldn't help but wonder if Oscar was behind some of it. That would be his style. Friendly to people's face but looking for weakness, preparing to stab them in the soft underbelly of their gut when the opportunity presented itself. And after what I did to steal Kendra away from him, I wouldn't put it past him to do just that. Revenge inspired by resentment. Directing his assault at Kendra as a way of getting at me. It was the ugliest of truths in the world of justice, but one I was very familiar with.

Each time I closed my eyes I could see Kendra's beautiful figure. My fingers tingled with the need to touch her, make her forget the lies and rumors that seemed to be circulating about me behind my back. Maybe, mentally, she was ready to move into the submissive role, a role I wanted her to take, but clearly, I needed to put more thought into it when it came to living up to my own demands.

My phone lit up and I stole a quick glance, not wanting to take my eyes off the road for too long.

Despite my desire to please and comfort Kendra, I didn't expect to receive the text I did tonight. To say that it caught me by surprise would be a great understatement. It came completely unexpectedly, and Kaycee was the last person I thought I'd be hearing from. In the end, curiosity got the best of me. I needed to know why now, why here, and why after so many years did she decide to reach out to me tonight?

Pulling onto the interstate, I opened it up, pressing my foot further down on the accelerator, settling in for the hour drive east to San Bernardino.

As my mind slowly drifted from Kendra to Kaycee, I couldn't help but chuckle. Couldn't she have at least done me the courtesy of meeting me in the city instead of requesting to meet all the way out here?

It had been so long since the last time we'd spoken, I couldn't help but think that maybe it was her way of testing the waters to see if I'd meet her request or not. After all, it was impossible to ignore how we'd left things the last time we did see each other. We hadn't parted on a good note, and perhaps that was one of the reasons why I was so willing to drop everything—including

Kendra—in hopes of meeting some kind of reconciliation with Kaycee.

Turning the music over to alternative rock, I shifted gears and scanned the horizon for patrol cars.

If I drove well above the posted speed limit, I could get to Kaycee quicker. Knowing that I would want to speed was half the reason I chose my Audi TT versus the Thunderbird that was more for show.

A strange mix of emotions pumped through me the further I moved away from the city. One minute I was excited. The next, nervous and doubting I'd made the right decision in leaving Kendra behind so I could visit another woman.

I could see Kendra's eyes now, the look I knew she would give me if she found out, and it wasn't all that different than the way she'd looked at me when I left. Her forehead twisted with concern, those amazing doe eyes boring a hole through me. I could still feel her emotions. The paranoia and insecurity that came with it was almost unbearable. I wished that I could be more open with her. Tell her the reason that this call couldn't wait. But with her already questioning everything I was doing, I knew it would be impossible to explain without something getting lost in translation. She wouldn't understand. It was too personal, and our relationship was too new.

Up and down my emotions traveled as my mind raced. And before I knew it, I had passed through San Bernardino, winding up the mountain canyons before arriving at a gorgeous lodge at Big Bear Lake just about an hour after I stepped behind the wheel.

The air was cool and dry as I marched through the front entrance, making my way to the bar tucked in the back. Kaycee was already there, sitting with her back to me, a half-full glass of beer sitting next to her.

Slowly, I walked toward her, appreciating her strawberry blonde hair cascading down her back. She wore a black, loose fitting blouse and blue jeans. It was the same casual style I remembered she always wore, and it was impossible to not think back to the happy memories we had shared that now seemed like a lifetime ago. "Kaycee." My hand gently fell to her shoulder.

She turned her head and as soon as our gazes met, tears pooled in the corners of her eyes. "Kelly."

I pulled her to her feet, needing to wrap my arms around her. She squeezed her muscles tight around my neck as if she, too, knew that things between us could be better than the way we'd last left them.

"It's great to see you," she murmured against my neck.

"I wouldn't have missed it for the world."

Kaycee dropped her heels back to the floor, letting her eyes continue to dance with mine as she hung off my shoulders. "God, Kelly. You look incredible."

"You too." I smiled, forcing my hands to release her warm body.

Her cheeks flushed a warm, welcoming glow each time she stole a glance in my direction. I couldn't stop appreciating how familiar she was—her appearance, even the way she looked at me like I was the best thing she'd ever seen. Seeing her was like visiting home after being away for some time. Everything about her—her smell, the way her lips curled when too embarrassed to flash a full-toothed smile, the way she carried herself, relaxed, yet strong—transported me back to a younger time in my life when I thought I knew what it was I wanted to make of it.

"Can I buy you a drink?" she asked, looking toward her beer.

"No. I'm fine." I pulled out the empty stool next to her and rested my tailbone on its edge. The wooden stools were hard, butting up against a brass foot rail at a high counter with crowded booths and tables behind us. "I stopped drinking."

Her brows raised, but only slightly. "After the accident," she whispered.

I nodded. "Got sober not long after the last time I saw you."

Her mouth frowned and a small quiver shook her chin. "I'm sorry, Kelly. I should have known."

"Don't worry about it." I reached out with splayed fingers and let my hand come to rest between her shoulder blades. "It was a long time ago."

The bartender came and I ordered a sparkling water. When it arrived, Kaycee's eyes moved to my glass. "You know I'll never forget that time you, Nora, and I snuck into that party in Malibu —" her eyes sparkled as she smiled, beginning to tell her story, "—thinking that no one would notice we weren't on the guest list."

My fingers wrapped around my sweaty, cool glass as I stared into the popping fizz, nodding my head. "We nearly got away without getting caught."

"And we would have, too," her eyes crinkled with amusement as she glanced in my direction, "if you hadn't gone back for that last drink."

We both laughed.

"I'll never forget the good times we shared." Kaycee curled her lips over her glass and sucked down a gulp. "So, how have you been, Kelly?" Her shoulders drooped as sadness hit her eyes.

I knew what she was really asking. And the only response I had for her was to duck my head, nod, and say, "Good."

"The pain never goes away." Her voice was barely a whisper but it rang loud in my ears. Even through the murmurs of the crowd behind us, I heard her clear as day.

When I turned my head to meet her watery gaze, a stone formed in my throat.

A deep silence settled between us as we each thought about what could have been. I didn't know what to say or where to begin. And when I caught a whiff of her beer, in that moment, I actually wanted one even though I hadn't had a drink in some time.

The urge I felt to have a drink wasn't because I wanted to get drunk and drown out the pain from the suffering both Kaycee and I had experienced but, rather, it was a desire to go back to when my life was good, organic, and I was happy—truly happy—with where I was and who I was with.

"Sometimes I wish I could have been there to stop it." Kaycee's voice cracked.

Overnight, our worlds had changed forever. No matter how many times we replayed those days leading up to the moment it all came crashing down, it would never be enough to rewrite history.

"Me, too." I cleared my throat. "Me, too."

Kaycee tossed back the rest of her beer and slammed the empty glass down on the counter. Her frustration was clear. We both felt hopeless knowing that no matter how hard we tried, there was no turning back the hands of time.

"We've been through so much," she angled her body toward me, "shared so much of the same misery, and despite not seeing each other until all these years later, it still feels like it happened yesterday."

I watched Kaycee's hand lift to my arm. Her tender touch caused my heart to skip a beat. It was smooth and forgiving as her fingers ironed down my arm. "It's really good to see you, Kelly."

My eyes lifted and met hers. "It's really great to see you, too."

Her hand stayed on my arm. "God, it's fucking great to see you." She burst out laughing as if she couldn't believe we were here, talking again.

"Kaycee—" she turned to look me in the eye, "what's the real reason you called?"

Her hand lifted off my arm and she ducked her head, giggling with disbelief. Then she turned back to face me, shoving a hand through her thick locks. Shaking her head, she said, "Nora, she really loved coming here."

Kaycee leaned back, taking a moment to soak in the lodge's grandeur. I watched her face soften, and I knew that a part of her could feel Nora's spirit in the building. When she wasn't looking, I glanced at her ring finger. It was void of any kind of band and I couldn't help but wonder if she ever married.

"It's that time of year again," she spun her knees around so she faced me, "when I start thinking of Kelly Black." All those tears and sad faces she was making just a minute ago had now vanished with a renewed spirit.

Reaching out with palms facing the ceiling, I invited her hands to fall into mine. Kaycee didn't hesitate to allow me to hold her. I could feel her pulse against the tips of my fingers, and when I looked up at her beneath my brow I asked, "You came all this way—made me drive for an hour—just so you could tell me that you've been thinking about me?"

Kaycee's chin dropped to her chest as she snickered. "I need you, Kelly." She lifted her head to show me the sincerity twinkling in her eyes. "You have to be there for me. I can't do this alone."

I licked my lips and let out a heavy sigh.

"You know it as well as I do." She squeezed my large hands. "We are supposed to do this together."

14

Kendra

I was awake before Alex and helped myself to one of her bananas.

Angling the piece of fruit from side to side, I studied the curvature, measuring its girth by circling my fingers around it. Then I reached to pluck two bright orange tangerines out of the fruit bowl and placed them on the counter in front of me.

I looked back at the banana, then to the tangerines, then back to the banana before setting the banana directly in the middle of the two tangerines.

"Do you ever think about anything else?"

My head spun over my shoulder as I giggled. Alex had her hand fisted in her messy hair, holding it up and away from her face. "I'm debating whether or not I should eat it for breakfast," I said.

Alex's mouth parted as her forehead scrunched. "And you

thought it might sound more appetizing if you first made it look like a giant cock?"

I turned to look at my yellow and orange masterpiece. "Well, yeah."

Alex padded to the counter and pulled out a box of cereal. "There are other options, you know?"

I dropped my banana to the counter, turned so my tailbone rested on the edge of the counter, and folded my arms. "That looks all fine and dandy, but do you know how much sugar is in one serving of that?"

Alex didn't bother looking at me. Instead, she went straight for the coffee maker, loading it up with grounds and flipping the switch before pulling a bowl from the cabinet above.

"Well, let me tell you." I nodded at the box. "It's a fuck-ton. And with Kelly demanding I eat better, I think I'll stick with fruit."

Alex shrugged, opening the box of cereal and making herself a bowl.

My brows squished. "Really?"

"What?" Alex said with milk dripping out of the corners of her mouth.

"We're supposed to do this together."

"Oh, no." She swallowed her food. "That's your thing. Not mine. I can eat whatever I want."

"What about the agreement we made?"

"Huh?" Her brow arched.

"You know. The one we made at the spa?" When Alex's forehead was still twisted in confusion I continued, "The one about getting in shape with me. Working out. Eating well. Going to the gym?"

Alex spooned another large spoonful of cereal into her mouth.

"Ah, never mind," I said, waving my hand at her before peeling the banana.

We stood there in silence, watching the coffee brew. She munched away on her cereal and I chomped down the sweet banana. It didn't matter if I had to go this alone. Kelly gave me reason to think about my health, most importantly what I ate. It wasn't that my diet was bad before I met him, but I could cut out more of the processed foods that I knew weren't all that good for me.

"Hope I didn't wake you when I came in last night," Alex murmured as she finished her bowl, setting it in the sink.

"What time did you get in, anyway?"

It wasn't that Alex didn't expect me to sleep at her place again, but maybe it was a little sooner than either of us would have thought. But with the way my night had gone—with Kelly leaving and my mind struggling to comprehend what I thought I saw—there was no way I was going to sleep at my place, alone. I needed company, or at least the illusion of it, because no matter how much I refused to believe what I knew I'd seen, his face lurked in the shadows of my mind all damn night.

"After midnight," Alex said, blinking away her exhaustion.

"Nash is working you like a dog."

"It's this film. We're on a budget and a tight deadline."

"I guess you have to be careful with what you wish for." I directed my comment to Alex, but really it could be applied to me, too.

Alex floated to the coffee maker. Holding up a cup, I nodded and she proceeded to fill both of our cups to the rim. "I'll need the extra boost today," she said, handing me my cup. "I've got another long day ahead of me."

I thanked her and curled my lips over the mug. The hot liquid was robust and immediately packed a punch. "Whoa, you aren't kidding. This stuff is strong."

"How'd you sleep?" Her sleepy eyes peered over her mug as her forehead wrinkled with a hint a worry.

"Okay," I cast my gaze into the black liquid abyss, "considering."

Memories of last night immediately betrayed me. It was easy to think that none of it happened. That it was all a dream. I could go on with my day without having to confront the demons of my past or answer to a concerned friend. It wasn't that I didn't invite, or appreciate, Alex's thoughts on everything that had become my life, because I did. It was just that we didn't always see things the same way. Sometimes I hesitated in telling her too much.

"Do you want to talk about it?" Alex's lips thinned into a flat line and her face grew stern.

Determined to forget everything and move on with my life, I ducked my head and turned to my tangerines. Staring at the two orange balls, I thought more about Kelly and why he left me—whatever that reason was, I still didn't know. And even though those questions went unanswered, I still imagined him coming home to find me gone. "There's nothing more to say."

Alex watched me leave the kitchen and jump into the far corner of the couch. "I'm happy you came here," Alex moved to the window, "even if I wasn't home when you arrived." She turned to look over her shoulder. "I like finding you here."

"I'm liking this, too." I smiled. "I hope Nash never comes home."

Alex scurried over to the couch and tossed a pillow at my head. My arms deflected it and we both laughed. Taking her mind off me and reminding her what was missing in her own life was my best defense to not having to talk any more about who I might have seen or what Kelly was up to without me. Because the truth always had a way at coming out. I just didn't want it to have to be now.

Alex snuggled up against me. Pulling her knees to her chest, she hugged her legs and asked, "Does Kelly know about who you saw last night?"

My chin tipped to the ceiling until the back of my head fell to the back of the couch. "You know I can't tell him." I sighed.

"Then," Alex angled her head to look at me, "who can you tell?"

She wasn't going to let this go. Her persistence was as annoying as my own. I loved her and hated her for it. There would come a time when I felt comfortable telling her more of what my childhood was like and what happened to me, but that time wasn't now. There was too much I needed to work out with Kelly first. "I'm sure I was just seeing things."

Alex looked at me. Shaking her head, she clucked her tongue then stepped away, moving back to the kitchen where she topped off her coffee. "The way you're dealing with this isn't healthy."

I covered my face inside my hands. "But it's my way of doing things."

When I removed my hands, Alex was hovering over me. "What is it?"

"What is what?" I snapped.

"There's something you're not telling me."

I sprang to my feet and tossed my arms around Alex's neck.

"Kendra!" Alex pushed me off, wiping at the coffee I spilled on her shirt.

"I do apologize, my dear." I curtsied, getting Alex to giggle. Pulling my hair back into a ponytail, I walked away saying, "Kelly took me to the Mayor's ball last night."

"Is that where you saw him?"

My hands flung to my sides and I huffed. "Can you please just drop it?"

"Probably not. But go on." She set her mug down on the coffee table and sank into the couch with inquisitive ears. "So, your man fancied you to the Mayor's mansion?"

"That's right." My insides warmed at memories of Kelly's fingers probing me while spread on the Mayor's desk. "There's a woman I keep seeing."

"Is she nice?"

"It's not like that." I shook my head. "And no, she's not nice. She keeps telling me to be careful with Kelly."

"What? Like he might hurt you?"

"She makes me think that maybe Kelly can't be trusted."

"But you do trust him?" Her eyes peered at me from under her brow.

I tucked my hands under my armpits as I moved to the window. I felt a headache coming on. A part of me said, *of course I trust him*. But the more reserved corner of my brain reasoned that I didn't know him well enough to know what trusting him even meant.

"You do trust him, don't you, Kendra?"

"He lies for a living," I said quietly.

"Unbelievable." Alex slapped her thigh. "You can't keep having doubts about him if you want this to work."

"Do you think she could be right?" I twisted around to find Alex lift her eyes up to meet mine. "I mean, I shouldn't expect a man like Kelly to *not* have other women in his life, right?"

Alex dropped her feet to the floor and padded over to me. Smoothing her hands down my arms, she said, "It depends who you trust more. Him or her?"

I swallowed the lump down my constricted throat. "I'm afraid I'm starting to believe her."

Alex reached around my head and pulled me against her soft body. "Did Kelly kick you out?"

I pulled my head back with knitted brows. "God, no. Why would you think that?"

She shrugged. "Why else would you have stayed here and not gone to his place last night?"

I stepped back, tucking a loose strand behind my ear. "It's complicated."

"I wish you would have never done this." Alex pinched the bridge of her nose and sighed.

"And you think that you could have handled the Madam better than me?" I raised an eyebrow and huffed. "Hardly."

Alex giggled. "Have you mentioned any of this to Madam?"

"Are you kidding? With the warnings she first tossed at me, telling me to stay away from Kelly—"

"—But would she have allowed you to be with him for a month if he really was involved with another woman?"

My shoulders shrugged.

"It doesn't make sense."

Gazing out the window, I watched the white clouds spread and swirl against the blue sky. Pain hit my heart and spread across my chest. I didn't want to think of Kelly being with anybody but me.

"Madam wants to protect her interests." Alex came up from behind and hugged me. "And, in case you forgot, you're her interest."

"I know." My voice was as weak as I felt.

"What about those files you stole? Have you thoroughly searched those?"

"You think Kelly could be in there?"

"I think it's worth exploring."

"Perhaps you're right," I murmured. When I had opened them in the past, it was only to learn as much about Madam as I could. It hadn't occurred to me to see if Kelly's name was anywhere to be found as well.

"Tell me how I can help."

Skeptically I said, "I wouldn't mind if you spied on him for me."

"You know I can't do that. Kelly knows who I am, and besides, he's still after Nash for questions he has about that girl's murder."

Flipping around to face her I said, "And what if Angel is right? What if there is another woman?"

"And what if the person you saw last night really was your rapist?"

I gritted my teeth, nostrils flaring. "You asked how you can help, and now that I did, you're not willing to do it?"

Alex's chest expanded as she looked away. Her lips pursed when she blew out a heavy breath. Then she looked at me and said, "All right. I'll spy on him for you."

"Thank you," I whispered.

"But only this once."

15

Kelly

I held my breath, perked my ears up, and listened.

Walking into my apartment at such an early hour left me feeling like I had done something wrong. Kaycee got my head spinning—replaying what happened between then and now, filling me with an anxiety I couldn't suppress. It wasn't that I didn't want to be with Kaycee, but I also knew it would be wrong of me to tell her no.

Scanning the kitchen and living room, there wasn't a sound to be made.

Kicking off my shoes, I made my way inside, knowing that chances were good Kendra was still asleep. With me leaving as soon as I fucked her, I was certain that she had her doubts about my intentions. But it wasn't like that. And now that I had been gone all night—away with another woman—I was prepared to answer some pretty tough questions I could only assume were coming my way.

Draping my jacket over the back of a kitchen chair, I couldn't help but notice that Kendra's things were missing. Moving to the bedroom, my insides warmed with the hope of finding her cuddled beneath the blankets with sleepy eyes, happy to see me return. But without having to peel the covers back, I could clearly see that she was gone.

Shoving a hand through my hair, I sighed.

Kendra left me with nothing. No note or text telling me where she had gone or when I could expect to see her again. It wasn't like I could blame her for running out. This was my fault for not explaining where I was going. But it was my secret, and with that came my choice in deciding who I shared it with, fully aware of the risks involved with silence.

As I busied myself in the kitchen, making a fresh cup of coffee, I couldn't help but think that I had left last night with the expectation that Kendra would still be here when I got home. I told her to stay. Reminded her to rest up. But in the end it wasn't enough to convince her otherwise.

Curling my fingers around the coffee mug, I slumped onto the couch feeling exhausted. The longer I stared out over the city skyline, the heavier my lids became.

I couldn't stop thinking about Kaycee and what she said. She looked absolutely incredible, and I was happy that she had reached out to me. It was good to relive old memories, laugh, and also be reminded of the experiences that gave us both a little more wisdom in this life of ours.

With each swallow of coffee, my heart beat a little faster.

Lifting my hips, I reached deep into my pocket and pulled out the old photograph Kaycee had given me, insisting I take it with me. I was reluctant at first, but once I looked her in her eye, I knew that I didn't have a choice.

Staring into the faded image, I couldn't help but smile. I could see why she'd held onto this, even after all these years. The three of us looked good despite the dozens of different emotions that worked between us that day. God, we were so wrecked that day. It was anyone's guess as to what allowed us to continue standing so tall that afternoon. Because inside I knew I was crumbling. When I closed my eyes, I could still feel Kaycee hanging off one shoulder while I held Nora's trembling body on my other side.

My throat constricted and I felt a lump growing.

Raw physical pain triggered the deep emotions of that time and my heart slowed to a slumber.

I thought that together we were going to make it through the pain and come out alive on the other side. Little did I know what the future held for us all. My chest hurt just thinking of how I would have done things differently if I could go back and do it all over again. But in the end, the darkness eventually got the better of each and every one of us—eventually taking all three of us down with it.

Leaning forward, I set the image on top of the coffee table, not wanting to look at it any longer.

Kaycee said that that photograph was what helped her move on. She held on to it and treated it like a relic she could look to for advice. And when she pulled it out the other day, she knew that she had to see me.

My gut clenched when I cast my gaze to my ring finger that once housed a wedding band.

I lifted my head with wide eyes, suddenly worried that old mementos from my past life might be discovered by Kendra. I wasn't ready to tell her about my past or how I came to be working with the Madam. There was too much baggage, too much complicated history for her to understand. I wanted to keep my secrets closely guarded, at least until I thought the time was right and I was certain Kendra could handle the stories that she deserved to know.

As I searched drawers, looking for old photos of Kaycee, Nora, and I, I realized that many of those things were at my other residence. Including the wedding band I no longer wore. I was thankful for that, because I didn't want Kendra to accidently find it and get the wrong impression.

Suddenly the apartment felt stuffy and I knew that I couldn't stay here. With Kendra gone, what was the point?

Gathering my things, I thought how staying here meant tears, shame, and guilt. It was enough to weigh any man down, and the more I let my mind relive the past, the weaker my muscles became and my knees threatened to give out.

I had to leave.

And there was only one cure I knew of that would make this all go away.

The car ride to my office went by in a flash and by the time I arrived, my mind was blank. No emotion. No thought. Just in the zone, knowing that work had always been the best cure when it came to dealing with the demons of my younger self.

"Geeze, what the hell happened to you?" Giselle rose from behind her desk when she saw me coming.

"Long night," I said, picking up the newspaper she had perfectly folded and ready for me to take on the corner of her desk. "Any word from Colin?"

"He'll be in town tomorrow." She smoothed down her skirt. "Driving up from San Diego."

I quickly scanned the paper's headlines, looking for any notable news I should keep my eye on.

"I sent him the case files we have on Mario." Giselle started moving paperwork across her desk. "Minus that one file you mentioned to save for when he's here in person."

I lifted my eyes off the paper. "That's great. Thanks, Giselle."

"Kelly," she paused to wet her lips, "Colin asked to speak with you directly."

My head cocked. "Did he say about what?"

"No." She shook her head. "Just wanted me to tell you to call him."

Closing my newspaper and tucking it beneath my arm, I

moved to my office, shut the door behind me, and settled in behind the desk. A quick dial later, the line was ringing.

"Kelly Black *is* alive," Colin answered.

"How the hell are you, Cobbs?" I smiled.

Colin Cobbs and I were old law school friends and his loyalty was one that I could trust without question. It was half the reason I requested Giselle to first contact him before we started searching for alternative options. Because with the plan Wes and I had come up with, we couldn't afford to have alternative options. Colin was *the* option. With his credentials, known loyalty, and my plan to get Mario the justice he deserved while simultaneously working to bring Blake Stone down, Cobbs was the exact ingredient I needed going forward.

"Truthfully, I've seen better days." Colin sighed. "Maggie is battling breast cancer and my daughter just started driving and is running my ass up the wall." He laughed. "But I don't want to bore you with my problems. How're things with you? It's been too long."

"That it has." I leaned back, thinking back to his wedding day —the day he married Maggie. "I'm sorry to hear about Maggie."

"The prognosis is looking good." His voice was light on his feet. "But it's still a struggle."

"Is there anything I can do to help?"

"Yeah," he laughed, "you can tell me more about this murder case you're working."

Excitement pounded my heart and made its way up my body, crinkling my eyes. "We need your help."

"What for? Based off the files Giselle sent me, it seems straight forward."

"How early can you get up here?"

"Let's see," I heard his chair spin around, "I can be there first thing tomorrow morning. How does eight sound?"

"Eight's perfect. But before you make the commitment to come all this way—"

Colin laughed. "Kelly, please. A visit with you is long overdue."

"Indeed." I nodded as a pensive expression tightened my face. "But I also know you're as busy as I am and I don't want to take you away from any of your own cases."

"Really, it's not a problem. I have a great team in place who can cover for me. Besides, what I've already read about Mario is fascinating and I wouldn't pass up an opportunity to partner with the illustrious Kelly Black."

The corners of my mouth curved up into a smile. "I could certainly use your expertise."

"And I could certainly use a vacation." He chuckled. "Even if it only is for a day."

"Hopefully you'll want to stick around longer than a day after what I share with you tomorrow."

"I guess that depends on what else you have up your sleeve."

A light chuckle escaped my chest and passed my lips. "All I can say is that my involvement in this case needs to be kept secret."

"You know you can trust me," he said sincerely.

"That's why I reached out to you first." My hand smoothed down the top of my thigh. "You're the only one I can trust with this."

"What are you up to, Kelly?" There was a hint of amusement in his voice and I knew that he couldn't wait for a change in scenery.

"I can't discuss it over the phone."

"I was afraid of that."

"You don't have to commit now. Come up tomorrow. Hear me out, and then once you know everything that I'm after, you can decide if it's something you're willing to risk."

"Shit. This sounds too good to be true."

"I'm just giving you fair warning."

"See you in the morning," Colin said, ending our call.

Hanging my phone back on the receiver, I stood and moved to the door, knowing that Giselle would want to know Colin's plans. As soon as I stepped out, I knew something was wrong. Giselle had her head in her hands, gently shaking her head. "Hey," I said softly. "Colin will be here at 8AM."

She lifted her head, nodded and sighed.

"Is everything all right?"

She fluffed her hair and refused to look me in the eye. "It's nothing."

My hand reached out and I squeezed her shoulder. "Don't bullshit me."

She angled her head to show me her watery eyes. "It's John. Things are rocky at home."

My chin tipped back as my jaw ticked. "Is he home today?"

Giselle nodded. "Wanted to take me to lunch."

I took a small step forward. "And why didn't you?"

She spread her arms out to the sides and said, "Look at this mess. I have too much work and can't afford to get behind."

"Go to lunch. I'll take over. Be with John." Giselle's head spun around. Her eyes were bright and filled with surprise. "You've been working your tail off and if we're going to take on Stone's case, it's only going to get more demanding."

"Kelly, I appreciate your offer," she turned her gaze back to her busy desk, "but I can't let you do all this just because my boyfriend wants to take me out to lunch."

"It's just lunch. You'll have all afternoon to play catch up," I said, thinking of how I needed to make things right in my own relationship with Kendra.

Giselle turned to me and smiled. "Thank you, Kelly. I promise I won't let it run long."

"It's fine if you do." I grinned. "I'd hate for you to make the same mistakes I've made."

16

Kendra

K elly was possessive of me as the hostess led us to our table.

From the time he picked me up to the moment we arrived to this luxurious restaurant, his hands and lips were all over me.

His scent was now mine. His lips were imprinted on my skin like invisible tattoos across my neck and over my collarbone. When I licked my lips, I could still taste him. He left me breathless as he heated me up, turning me on.

I was happy he called. Despite my deep suspicions that I wasn't his only girl, I knew that as long as I was with him he couldn't be with anyone else.

Together we glided by a table of two and I glanced over my shoulder, unable to stop myself from staring at his incredible beauty. I had him firmly in my grasp, towing him one small step behind, fooling him into thinking that he could get away with not telling me where he went last night. He was insanely attractive in his solid black pin-striped suit. I'd give him that. It complemented his dark eyebrows, long lashes, and thick head of hair. His suit was dark as death, and if I didn't know him as well as I did, I would have thought he was Goth or on his way to a funeral. But it only added to the mystery that swirled around him like an insanely hot paradox that constantly set my insides ablaze.

Soon, I'd pounce and insist he tell me everything. But not until the moment was right.

When our eyes met, his narrowed and the corners of his lips curved upward in a devilish grin that fluttered my heart. My nipples pebbled beneath the satin of my dinner gown and threatened to reveal the exact temptation Kelly couldn't seem to take his mind off of. His free fingers seduced their way across the small of my back, constantly grazing up and down my exposed spine, flirting with the idea of having his way with me here, in front of everyone, without a care that we were in public.

I squeezed his hand and flung my hair over my shoulders as I put a little extra bounce in my step. He was guilty of something. That much I knew. I was determined to find out what exactly that was. At this point it was anyone's guess.

Eyes lifted up off their plates as they saw us coming. It was like we were a celebrity couple whose faces couldn't be placed but looked familiar nonetheless. We passed another table of two and their conversation stopped. I smiled, watching the man's eyes travel from my mouth down the center of my chest.

His date scolded him as he turned his head to watch us continue on to the back.

Kelly Black commanded attention no matter the setting. Women gazed, bit their lips, and undressed him with their eyes. The room was full of lust, and I was no exception.

I wanted him. Wanted him bad.

When we arrived to our table, the hostess seated us and Kelly was quick to order a bottle of sparkling water along with a glass of wine for me.

I settled into my side of the booth, taking a minute to look around, appreciating the darkness that sheltered us from most other patrons who were seated some distance away. Here we could talk without fear of being heard, and though I knew what it was I wanted to speak to Kelly about tonight, I also could see he had something on his mind by the heated gaze in his eyes.

"You know every man here will go to bed tonight fantasizing about you and the way you look in that dress." His voice was husky, sultry.

I cast my gaze down my front. "It's the one you picked out the other day."

His tongue darted out over his bottom lip as he nodded. "It's brilliant."

Our drinks were served and I took the liberty to raise my glass to my lips, stealing a sip. It was fruity, a bit dry, and relaxed my insides just as I'd hoped. "This place is nice," I said, looking around.

"I hope you like it." He set his drink to the side and brought his elbows to the table, leaning forward.

"Is there a reason you asked me here tonight?"

His gaze fell from my lips to my chest. Heat spread from my heart and caused my stomach to flutter. "So that I could see you wear something as sexy at that." He nodded to my bright red dress.

Pulling my wine glass away from my lips, I set it down and said, "Huh. I thought maybe it was your way of apologizing for running out on me last night."

He slowly leaned back with an amused grin filling his face. Pulling at his jacket, he said, "Do you need me to apologize?"

"Only if you're feeling guilty."

He laughed. "It's impossible to feel guilty when I've done nothing wrong."

I angled my head and narrowed my gaze as I zeroed in on him. Maybe I was only being paranoid. He looked innocent enough, but still. "So you don't care to tell me where you were or who you were with?"

"It's nothing to be concerned about."

His answer annoyed me and sent more anxiety shooting through my bones. Beneath the table, I wrung my hands over my lap between stealing small sips of my wine. I wasn't sure what to think of him deliberately keeping secrets from me. When he treated me to dinners like the one we were having tonight, I couldn't help but feel like I was his girlfriend—someone he could trust to share his life with, tell everything to, no matter what it was. It was confusing to say the least, and all I could think about was the conversation I'd had with Alex this morning and how it was all Angel's fault for making me even think that I deserved to know Kelly better than I actually did. She planted these seeds of doubt, and no matter how much I wanted to push them to the side and ignore everything she said, I couldn't.

"Can you at least tell me if it was work related?"

"*Bella,*" he chuckled, "relax."

Kelly stretched his arms across the center of the table and flipped his palms to the ceiling. I took my hands from my lap and let them fall into his. His strong fingers wrapped around mine, and the pads of his thumbs stroked over the backside of my hands.

He dropped his head to look at me beneath a sunken brow. "This is no place to talk about business."

I clucked my tongue and had to look away. No matter how much I wanted to deny it, he was right. But, at the same time, I didn't want him to think that I wasn't interested in learning what exactly he did. I wanted to know the specifics, if only to create meaningful conversation. "Then what would you like to talk about?"

"That dress."

My cheeks flamed red. I knew I looked like the bombshell I felt when wearing it. It was a V-neck cherry red sleeveless gown with a killer slit up the thigh. It was loose fitting, highly seductive, and, like Kelly had already determined, had every man drooling at the mouth. Including him.

"What do you like about?" I raised a brow.

Kelly's pupils darkened as he thought through his answer. "Besides that I picked it out?"

I nodded, thrilled with the excitement he shared for seeing me in the dress he loved so much. When he called earlier, asking me out to dinner, I knew that I had to surprise him with this gown—if only to show him that I was listening to his suggestions and that I valued his opinion. In doing so, I hoped that maybe he would trust me enough to share more of what made him frustratingly mysterious.

He leaned closer. There was fire in his eyes as he dropped his voice to a low rumble. "I could fuck you in it."

My breath hitched and I could feel my heartbeat stammering in my neck. Suddenly, the room was several degrees hotter. Kelly continued to stare, holding my hands firmly enough to make me think of being bound. He had me panting like a dog in heat. "When you blindfolded me—"

Kelly leaned closer—as if I had a magnetic pull on him—licked his lips, nodded, and wanted to hear more.

"I want more of that," I murmured in a soft voice.

The fire in his eyes grew to be an inferno. He was looking at me but I could tell he was lost inside his head. I hoped that he was thinking of me, naked, writhing beneath him. But when I watched his posture slump and retreat back to his side of the table, I couldn't help but worry that I'd said something wrong. The fiery look in his eye was gone. Replaced by something else. Something I couldn't quite put a finger on.

Was he embarrassed?

No. That couldn't be it.

The lines on his forehead deepened and a pained expression twisted his face. Kelly Black was hurt. But why?

Without thinking, compassion filled my heart with a need to comfort and take care of him. "It's okay, baby," I said, reaching for his hands.

He held my hands for a minute before saying, "Last night, I took it too far."

It was like he knew exactly what it was I wanted to hear. Without having to come out and say it myself, he was already there. Though I felt bad for the shame he was feeling, I couldn't deny how great it felt to know that he noticed it too—that we could do this, but that we needed to change up our approach.

"Kelly," the tips of my fingers stroked the inside of his hands, "it's okay. Next time, just talk me through it before you get carried away."

His head lifted and met my gaze. "I hope I didn't hurt you."

I shook my head. This wasn't worth fighting over. I knew his words were sincere, and by the way his body crumbled in on itself, I knew there was enough already eating him alive inside his own head. That was punishment enough for what he'd done to me. It wasn't worth me explaining how much I wanted to kill him last night for putting me in such a vulnerable position.

"No. You didn't hurt me. I want to go down this road with you."

The crown of his skull lifted higher, as if being pulled by a string to the ceiling.

"Next time just let me know what you're going to do. You can tie me up all you want." I smiled, but it felt forced.

Our conversation was interrupted by the waiter, stopping by to take our orders. I watched Kelly heal his broken soul in a matter of seconds. He was back to the confident man I loved to be around, taking charge, and again I was struck by how human he was. If he wasn't going to talk, then I would study his every move, diving deep into the psychology that encompassed all that he was. He ordered me a chicken breast and himself a steak, and as soon as we were alone again, Kelly asked, "Did you like any of what happened last night?"

"I did." I nodded, appreciating the way he could pick up exactly where we'd left off without missing a beat. It was that kind of attention to detail that made me believe that he wanted to see if I could be something more than an escort he could purchase for a month.

He licked his lips dry after having taken a sip of his water. "What exactly did you like most?"

I batted my lashes at him and folded my arms on the table in front of me. "The unknown. As soon as my sight was taken from me, anticipation rocked my body, sending my heart racing."

He smiled and nodded, as if he knew exactly what it was I was talking about.

"I'd never felt anything like it. My body was sensitive to every touch." I noticed how quickly I was talking, and that made me realize just how much I actually did like everything he did to me. "Like walking on pins and needles."

His smile faded and a questioning look moved over his face. He reached over and touched my jaw. I swallowed hard, knowing that it was still a little sore from his repeated cock thrusting down my throat. "It's sore," he said.

I nodded. "But I'm fine."

He took his hand away and a desire to be included in his world prickled my skin.

"That's the magic of this lifestyle." He flicked his gaze off the table and up to me.

I gave him an arched look.

"When you submit to the pain," his head gently nodded, "that's when the pleasure is most explosive."

"Don't get me wrong," I said, thinking how I had room for improvement, "I love sucking your cock."

Kelly chuckled. "Is that right?"

"You have no idea." I nodded.

He looked to the center of the restaurant. It was filled with people engaged in conversation and happily enjoying their meals. Then the next thing I knew, Kelly began opening up his pants.

"Kelly?" My eyes couldn't leave his lap. "What are you doing?"

He smirked. "Exactly what you think I'm doing."

"What?!" I whispered with the same intensity as if I'd yelled it. "Here? You're fucking loco."

"Crawl under the table."

I leaned back, pressing my thighs together in a failed attempt to suppress the heat now damping my uncovered sex.

"I'm your Dom." He reached his hand inside his pants. "And you're my Sub. You must do as I say. It's our agreement." His eyes darkened. "Don't you remember?"

I refused to look at him. Instead, my eyes darted across the room as fear of someone seeing us paralyzed my body. My muscles were tense, but I couldn't deny the thrill of doing what he was asking. I *wanted* to do it. But the more rational part of my brain kept me from taking action.

"There is nothing to fear. We're safe here." Kelly's voice was hypnotizing. "Now get on the floor and crawl over to me."

My head snapped over to him and I barred my teeth as I said, "If you need to feel like you're in total control, I can give it to you, but within reason."

"I'm dying over here. Feel me. I'm so fucking hard." His hand started moving and I knew he was stroking himself. "C'mere. Let me feel how wet you are."

I hated how right he was. There was a pool gathering between my thighs and it threatened to soak through my dress. I was without underwear, knowing that something like this might happen tonight. It was Kelly's way, and no matter the fight I was putting up, I knew that eventually I would submit to his demands and suck him off—even if it was here, right before dinner.

"You want me to crawl on my hands and knees and suck you off?"

Kelly sucked his bottom lip into his mouth. "It's not a want. It's a demand."

Turning my head away, I huffed a quick laugh. When I turned back, Kelly's eyes were locked on mine. "Tell me I'm your only girl."

Kelly's shoeless foot lifted to my calf and slid up my leg, traveling between my thighs where his large, sock-covered toe sliced between my folds. "You're my only girl."

I hated how my body betrayed the lie I was hoping to tell. But he had me. Called my bluff. And now I was about to go all in. Kelly continued to stroke me with his toe, and the thin fabric of his sock was enough to get me to squirm. He had me panting, biting back the whimper that threatened to escape past my lips.

Kelly pulled his leg away and came to sit next to me on my side of the booth. Reaching under the table, his hand traveled beneath my dress and he pushed his fingers inside me. I gasped and clung to him. "My cock is waiting."

I couldn't take it any longer. Without thinking, I reached my hand inside his pants and pulled his length out. Wrapping my fingers around his base, I stroked him before lowering my head and taking him into my mouth.

His hot, satin-skinned cock twitched against the roof of my mouth and I swirled my tongue around his pulsing tip.

I knew there was a chance someone would see us. And I was slightly embarrassed at the thought of getting caught. But once I started I couldn't stop. I needed him as much as I hoped he needed me. If anything, when I was with Kelly, he made me feel alive.

"God damn, your mouth feels amazing," he grunted, holding my hair off my face.

I took him a little bit deeper.

"Tell me not to come."

Lifting my head away from his member, I said, "Don't come."

He pushed my head back down and my cheeks hollowed as I bobbed my head up and down. "Oh, shit. I'm going to come."

"Don't you fucking do it," I growled between slurps.

Writhing against the booth, Kelly's hand reached around my back and cupped my left tit. His moans grew louder and I knew we were just asking to have the cops called on us for sex in public or indecent exposure.

But I didn't stop. He insisted I keep going, his hand guiding my head over him.

"Shit, woman." His teeth grinded. "I can't hold it any longer. Give me permission to come."

"Not yet," I said, pumping him harder, loving this game.

It was tormenting us both. He wanted the release and I was having fun denying it. With each thrust the intensity between us grew, and suddenly I realized why Kelly insisted I deny him his orgasm. I could feel his need, feel the way my own need for orgasm grew inside of me. The harder I worked, the more light-headed I became. Bright flashes of light sparkled behind my lids and my mouth was dry from the lack of breath.

His finger dug deep into my firm breast and I could feel him about to explode. "Come. Now, Kelly. Come." As soon as my lips circled back over his cockhead, I felt his entire body clench just before his dick twitched and spurt his hot seed to the back of my throat. Thick ropes of semen coated the inside of my mouth and there seemed to be no end in sight. When he was finished, he fisted my hair and pulled me by the roots, guiding me to his mouth. My mouth crashed over his as I whimpered against his lips.

And just like that, I was shuddering through my own release.

"You naughty girl." Kelly chuckled against my lips, tucking himself away.

It was a small orgasm, but an orgasm nonetheless. Never had I experienced something like that without being provoked. But I was so hot and bothered by everything that just happened, my body had no choice but to go along for the ride.

Shaking inside Kelly's arms, I said, "Now, if you'll excuse me, your girl would like to freshen up."

Kelly slapped my ass as I stood to walk away. Nervously, I glanced around with a lowered head, hoping that no one had noticed me blowing my man right before dinner as if we didn't have anything better to do.

Hurrying to the women's room, I took a quick sit on the toilet before staring at my own reflection in the mirror, washing my hands. "What has he done to you?" I said to myself, swishing around mouthwash between my cheeks.

A woman covered in expensive jewels and wearing a designer dress walked in, smiled, and joined me at the sinks. She played with her hair and touched up her makeup before saying, "What do you think? Do I look fat in this dress?"

Taking my eyes off my sex-flushed face and disheveled hair, I looked at her and said, "You look great."

She turned to the side and sucked in her gut. "You're just saying that."

"Honestly, that dress looks amazing on you." It was the honest truth. She was amazing.

"God, are you kidding?" She turned to face me. "You're gorgeous. What I would do to be your size."

I shifted my eyes to her in the mirror. "Don't tell me that a man is making you second guess yourself."

She nodded, taking her gaze off of me and turning it back on herself. "First date. I'm doing the whole online thing. You know how it goes." She worked her lips. "What about you, here with a boyfriend or husband?"

I saw her glance at the ring Kelly had given me. "Boyfriend."

She pulled back and tucked her things away inside her clutch. "He's lucky. You're gorgeous, sweetie. Don't make him forget it," she said, gliding her hand across my shoulders.

"And do me a favor?" I said just as she was about to leave.

She paused and turned back to me.

"If he thinks you don't look like a million bucks, leave his ass."

Her head tossed back as she laughed. "You got it, sweetie."

I watched her leave and wondered if Kelly thought he was lucky to have me or if I was just a temporary solution to a problem in his life. When I stepped back into the restaurant I caught sight of the woman I'd just met and watched her make her way back to her table. There was a man there waiting, and when he stood to pull out her seat for her, my hand flew over my mouth as I gasped.

Refusing to believe it was him, I quickly looked away.

For her sake, I hoped that it wasn't him—because I doubted she knew that he'd once raped young girls.

Ducking my head out of fear of being seen by him, I hurried back to Kelly, convincing myself that I was only seeing things. It couldn't have been my rapist. Not here. And certainly not with the woman who was beyond friendly in the restroom.

But as I approached Kelly, I also couldn't deny that maybe Kelly *was* the cause of my hallucinations. After all, this wouldn't be the first time he'd set off a trigger that made me want to run away forever.

17

Kelly

I caught sight of Kendra stepping out of the bathroom.

God, she was gorgeous. It was no wonder half the men here tonight couldn't stop staring in her direction. Look at them now. The way they easily forgot the women they were with, lost in fantasies of what it would be like to experience Kendra's natural beauty and spontaneity.

A chuckle filled my chest knowing that she was mine—all mine—and I wasn't about to let her go.

That dazzling cherry red gown was like a beacon of hope in a sea of mediocrity. It caught my eye the first time I laid eyes on it, and without seeing how it would look on Kendra, I'd known that she and that gown would be an incredible match. And what a way to surprise me with purchasing it, just for me, as if this world-class meal wasn't enough.

The smell of grilled meats and sweetly scented dressings

made me smile. My stomach grumbled and I gave the young man serving me a knowing look.

"Enjoy your dinner, Mr. Black." He smiled.

I eyed him, checking if he could smell the sex I'd just had here in the booth. There wasn't anything in his face that told me he could, and I liked that we were able to get away with a quick release before we moved into what I hoped would be a thoroughly enjoyable dinner.

"Before you go," I held up my finger, "more drinks. The same."

He nodded. "Of course."

Seeing as Kendra's first glass of wine was nearly finished, I wasn't about to let her talk me out of not having another simply because I wasn't drinking alcohol with her. It didn't matter. I knew she would want another, and I wanted her to enjoy herself. Tonight was meant to be relaxing, an escape from the stresses of my job and a way to better get to know one another.

As I marveled at the presentation of both our meals, my hands tingled and I felt weightless. Not wanting our dinner to grow cold, I turned my attention back to Kendra. She hadn't moved from where she was standing and I wondered what—or who—had stolen her attention.

She *was* the most beautiful woman here tonight. That much I knew for certain. Her skin radiated against that dress, and the way she had her hair done in a French twist was enough to get me hard all over again.

The young man was back with our drinks and I thanked him before sending him on his way, reminding him, "We're good. I'll call if there is anything else we need." I didn't want to chance him returning if for some reason Kendra and I decided on a repeat of our appetizer.

When I turned my attention back to Kendra, I watched her make her way to me. She floated on her feet and I appreciated how gracefully she moved between the tables. Grinning from ear to ear like a school boy in love, I was eager to see how many men stopped mid-conversation to watch with a dropped jaw as she passed. But when she approached, the smile that filled my face slowly drooped into a concerned frown.

Something was wrong.

Without hesitating, I went to my feet, grabbing Kendra's shriveled body in my hands before she fell over. "*Bella,* what is it?"

Her chin hung low as she shook her head. I slowly guided her into the booth, seeing just how pale her face really was. Her unblinking eyes were dull and she didn't answer, just stared quietly down at the table.

"Are you feeling okay?"

It was like she wasn't even there. Then, after a minute of my mind racing to understand what had happened to my fun date, she snapped out of it.

Turning to look at me, I knew immediately that dinner was no longer on tonight's menu. She was cold to the touch and without asking I said, "Grab your things. We're going home."

She blinked. "What about the meal?"

I pulled her to her feet and threaded my fingers through hers. I didn't give a shit about the meal. It was her that had me worried. And whatever it was that happened in that short time she was gone, I knew that the only chance I had at taking her mind off of it was to leave now.

We weaved through the maze of tables as we briskly walked to the exit. This time I didn't care who was looking or watching. We passed a table of two and the woman looked up with a face like she knew who Kendra was. Glancing over my shoulder, I noticed Kendra duck her head as a tremble worked its way down her arm.

I didn't think too much of it, instead concentrating on leaving the building as fast as we could. Once outside, Maxwell pulled to the curb and I assisted Kendra into the backseat with me quick to follow. We rode in silence, the partition up, not bothering to buckle up.

My arm draped over her shoulder and I pulled her against my chest. She quickly snuggled deep into my side without saying anything. I could feel her heart beating like a drum into the night, and with each minute that passed, her fingers clenched more of my shirt.

"Do you ever see things that you think are real," her voice was barely a whisper, "but really aren't?"

Angling my head down to hers, my hand lifted as I petted her hair. Quietly, I wondered what it was she was talking about. And when I had nothing, I asked, "Did you see something at the restaurant?"

Her head lifted off my chest and she clawed up my body with heavy lids. Without answering my question, she pressed her fluttery lips against mine.

Her skin was still frozen to the touch as I held her in my arms. Lightly pressing my tongue against hers, I tried my best to warm her. With each panting breath, I attempted to smooth out the prickles covering her body. They refused to go down no matter what I did or how I touched her.

A full body tremor rocked her core and had my eyes go wide. Kendra was like a broken child needing protection and an agonizing pain twisted my insides knowing that no matter what I did nothing seemed to ease the pain she was feeling deep inside.

When I felt the motion of the vehicle stop, I turned my head to see that we had arrived back to my penthouse hotel. "C'mon. Let's get you inside."

Kendra peeled herself away from me and pulled her dress down her legs. Taking her by her hand, I snaked my other arm around her waist and held her on her feet as we marched through the lobby without stopping.

With each step we shared, I felt Kendra grow stronger.

We shared a glance and I smiled, appreciating the way she

gathered the broken pieces of her soul and collected them into the woman who was holding her head high. She radiated a sense of strength that I hadn't seen on her until now. And I liked what I saw.

Once at the elevator, I dug inside my back pocket and pulled out my keycard. Flashing it in front of the reader, a car was on its way and I turned my attention back to the woman who made me believe that anything could be possible.

"You feeling better?" I took her shoulders into my hands and squeezed.

She nodded. "Thanks for recognizing my need to leave."

Leaning forward, I pressed my lips against hers. She kissed me back, adding more heat than what she'd offered on the drive here. I knew she was strong. Knew that she could handle adversity. But this was different. This was divine.

When the car doors slid open behind me, I released Kendra and guided her inside first. Together, we watched the doors close and as soon as we started our ascent to my penthouse level, Kendra turned to me and pushed me back against the wall.

Smashing her lips against mine, I parted my mouth and she instantly recognized the opportunity to dart her tongue against mine.

We clawed at each other until we became breathless.

Her fingers worked to untuck my shirt and freed me from the confines of my suit.

Lowering myself, I reached between her legs as she dove her hand inside my pants. I cupped her hot mound, thrusting my finger between her slick folds as she squeezed my shaft. She was as needy as I, and a deep, desperate passion grew with each thrust of a tongue and pump of a wrist.

The moment Kendra's tongue left my mouth, I pushed off the wall in an attempt to flip her around. Surprising me, Kendra held her ground, and with one hand firmly planted in my chest, she shoved me back, refusing me to leave the wall.

I chuckled and only got harder.

Whispering close to my ear, she said, "Tell me how much you like my tight little cunt."

My finger was soaked as I move it around inside her. "I love your tight little cunt."

She squeezed my length hard enough to make me wince. I watched her face fill with satisfaction. "Now push my face into the wall and tell me not to make a sound."

Digging my nails deep into the soft flesh of her arm, I muscled her away from me and spun her around until I found myself caging her against the wall with all my weight. Once again, I reached under her dress, quickly finding her hot pussy waiting for my pursuit. Thrusting her with two fingers, I growled next to her ear, "Now don't make a sound."

Her face twisted with agony as I pressed the flat part of my palm against the side of her head, pinning her face against the cold metal wall. I could tell she liked it as her hips writhed on my hand. Her walls tightened around my fingers and I knew she was close to coming.

"Tell me you can have me whenever you want," she snarled as the elevator slowed to a stop.

Licking her ear, I repeated her words. "I can have your tight pussy whenever I want."

She screamed into the wall and let out a monstrous moan.

As soon as the doors opened, I pulled my hand away and pushed her out of the car and down the hall toward the door to my apartment. Kendra hung off my shoulder as I worked to unlock the door. Whatever had gotten into her wasn't about to end. I could see it in her eyes. The way she searched my face, looking for answers that to puzzles that had to be solved. I was so painfully hard, I couldn't wait to kick this door open and continue my assault on her.

"Fuck me from behind, Kelly," she barked as soon as I kicked the door open. "Pull down your pants and fuck me from behind."

Fire burned in my belly and my nostrils flared as the primal need to claim her zipped down my spine. Without hesitating, I tossed her face-first over the couch with enough force to knock the wind from her lungs. Dropping my pants to my knees, I thrust myself deep inside her.

Kendra grunted into the pillow with each powerful lunge I inflicted upon her fragile body and my muscles tightened as I held her head down.

"You want it rough?" she cried.

My arm and leg muscles flexed as I bucked my hips harder.

"That's it."

I slammed into her quick and fast with selfish need. "This little cunt is mine," I said, pushing her face harder into the pillow. "Don't you fucking say a word," I growled through gritted teeth, feeling the heat spin fast at the base of my spine.

Stars flashed across my eyes and the room spun when my cock thickened in agony. Moving inside her faster, soon I was shooting my seed deep against her cervix, curling over her and hugging her tight around her sweaty waist.

I stayed there, allowing my lungs to fill with air, and didn't move until I went limp. Kendra was silent and lifeless. Her eyes were wide and I wondered where she'd gone—yet again.

Then a tear streamed down her face.

Stepping back, my heart broke thinking that I had something to do with her crying. "*Bella,* no. What did I do to hurt you?"

Another tear fell from her eye and she sniffed. "It's not you."

Moving around the couch, I dropped to my knees so that I could be there next to her. "Tell me." I gently stroked her face. "I hate to see you crying. What did I do?"

She blinked and several more tears scurried down her cheek. "I can't, Kelly. I just can't."

My head lifted and I slowly backed away from her face. Inside I felt hollow and helpless. I didn't understand what she meant. Was it me she couldn't do? Or just the sex? "Talk to me, *Bella.*"

Kendra finally pushed herself up, backing away from the couch she was draped over and said, "Me, talk?"

I looked at her with big round eyes filled with fear.

"What about you?" She wiped her cheeks dry.

"I can't help you if I don't know what's wrong." I swallowed the stone forming in the back of my throat.

"Touché," she said, curling into a tiny ball on the chair opposite the couch.

Not wanting to argue with her, knowing full well that something much larger was going on inside her head, I made my way to the master bath and started filling the tub.

It hurt me to see her like this. Broke my heart to think that I'd done something to make her crumble inside. As I watched the steam fill the air, I replayed the events of last night and today, trying to figure out what was happening to the woman I thought I knew.

Once the tub was filled, I found Kendra still in the chair, hugging her knees to her chest, staring out into nothing in particular. Without asking, I bent down and picked her up. She hung on to me as I padded my way back to the tub. Once inside the bathroom, I helped her undress before slipping her into the water. A second later I joined her. Wrapping my arms around her I held her, thinking we were going to have to put our game of submission on hold until I knew exactly what was eating her up inside.

Because, if we didn't, it might just be enough to destroy us.

18

Kendra

"Your tight little cunt feels so good."

I squeezed my eyes shut, not liking the smell of his hot alcoholic breath on my face.

"God, girl." He dug the tips of his fingers deep into my hip bone. "I'm here to take care of you."

Lifting my hips, I reached my hand above my head and took the bedsheets between my fingers. Gripping with all my might, I tried to claw my way to freedom. He pulled me back beneath him and worked to undo his belt. A second later my back arched up off the blankets as he slammed into me hard.

"Stop! You're hurting me," I cried as he tore my insides apart.

I kicked and flailed, wincing between the sharp pangs of excruciating pain. It felt like he had set a fire between my legs. It burned and there was nothing I could do to get away. He was so big, too strong, and no matter how much I cried for him to stop, he didn't.

"Shut up!" His fingers tightened around my skull and smashed my cheek further into the mattress. "Don't make a sound."

My pleas for help were drowned out, suffocated by the comforter of my bed. A hot liquid dripped from my insides and he kept going.

Soon I'd get used to the pain—grow numb to it.

This wasn't the first time he visited me at night. He said Dad told him to come. It would make us sleep better, he said. But I never did ask Dad after the first time, too embarrassed by the bleeding the day after. It hurt to sit, and concentrating in school was impossible. All I could think about was him and how he'd hurt me and how much I wished that I wouldn't see him again.

He grunted over my body, his heavy belly coating my back in his sweat. My jaw clenched and I kept my eyes closed. If I tried hard enough, I could fly away and be somewhere else. My imagination was that good. But I had to try really hard, and he wasn't making it easy for me to think about anything other than the shooting pain zipping up my spine.

He told me that he loved me. That he would do anything for family. But I didn't believe him. He was a monster at night, and monsters lied and hurt innocent girls.

I couldn't breathe. He was too heavy. So heavy he crushed me. And when it all got to be too much, the pain resided as the warm metallic taste of my own blood filled my mouth.

Gasping for air, I flung my hands around my neck. Springing up in bed, I coughed the blood into the palm of my hand. Feeling my tongue swell against my molars, I knew that I had bitten it, clenched down on the soft muscle just like the hundreds of times before.

Hanging my head, I sighed.

Wiping the sweat off my brow, I stuck my finger in my mouth and touched the injury to see if it was as deep as some of the other times. Each time I bit my tongue—even if it was only an accident during a meal—it transported me back to those dark and ominous nights as a child I wished I could escape.

Reaching for Kelly, I frantically searched the bed before coming up empty.

He was gone.

I didn't know where he was, just that he wasn't here now. My mind struggled to recall the events leading up to when we decided to finally come to bed. I knew what happened at the restaurant. What I thought I saw and how Kelly ordered we leave without first eating. I could remember the way I acted in the elevator and how Kelly held me tenderly without saying a word while soaking late into the night as our bodies floated in the tub.

My eyes widened as I began to hyperventilate.

Inhale.

Exhale.

Again and again, I worked to calm the anxiety threatening to erupt inside me. After I managed to settle the panic attack working its way through my body, loneliness took over.

Looking around with a longing gaze, I was too afraid to breathe. My limbs were frozen in place and I feared Kelly had abandoned me. But could I really blame him if he had? I was broken. An emotional wreck. And if I kept having these hallucinations of seeing my rapist and sweating through nightmares that came along with it, it would only be a matter of time before he decided I wasn't worth it anymore.

My head turned and my ears perked.

The room was too quiet and I didn't like it.

My insides jumped at the crackling of a heater or the quiet hum of the refrigerator. Even from the back bedroom, I could hear the sounds in the kitchen. Finally, I found the courage to flop back onto my pillow and close my eyes.

A minute later, my heart settled and found its normal rhythm.

I continued to breathe as I stretched my hands far above my head.

The longer I laid there, the more I convinced myself that my brain was playing tricks on me. This was all just a bad dream. It wasn't Kelly's fault any more than it was my own. He was my happy place, the reason to get out of bed every morning. It was important that I didn't associate him with any of my nightmares or triggers to bring my horrible past back into the present. *He* was my present. A gift to be treasured, not taken for granted.

Rolling onto my side, I raked my fingers over Kelly's pillow. It still had an indentation of where his head had been resting. And though his spot was cold, I wondered how long ago he'd left. "You should have kissed me goodbye," I whispered into the darkness, making myself giggle.

I laid there in bed, wrestling with my racing mind. I thought about everything from Kelly, to my rapist, to my family before drifting back to Alex and Nash. Soon night turned to dawn, and I knew that finding any kind of rest again tonight wasn't going to happen. I kicked off the covers and headed for the master bath. It was there I found a note from Kelly, along with a new outfit.

Bella, sorry I couldn't stay. Work robbed me of sleep and I headed into the office. Stay as long as you need. Here is a fresh outfit for you to wear. Food is in the fridge. Yours truly, K.

My lips curled at the corners as I set the note off to the side. Turning my attention to the black backless slip dress, I held it out in front of me and lifted my eyes to the mirror.

Angling my body from side to side, I knew that I would look good in it. Kelly constantly surprised me with his inherent sense of style. He knew what he liked and, even better, he knew what I would look good in. And because he'd chosen the color black once again, I couldn't help but laugh. But before I put it on and got ready to take on the day, I padded my way to the kitchen.

Opening the fridge, I found nothing but health foods waiting. There was oatmeal, fruits, and vegetables. Whole grain breads, humus, kale juice, and eggs.

I shook my head and clucked my tongue.

It wasn't that none of that sounded good. In fact, I appreciated his desire to eat well and keep in shape. But despite him gifting me another gorgeous outfit—one which I truly loved—I wasn't starting today off great. I was still feeling low, reeling with the last bits of my nightmare, and if I knew anything about myself, it was that when I felt like this all I craved was junk food.

And junk wasn't anywhere to be found.

Closing the fridge, I looked around for alternative options. Nothing sparked my interest so when my phone dinged with a message, I naturally went straight for it.

Morning doll. Meet me at my office in an hour. Don't be late. It's important. ~Madam

Setting my phone down, my shoulders curled over. Suddenly, I wasn't as hungry as I thought I was when I'd first rolled out of bed. Making my way back to the master bath, I dragged my feet over the hardwood floors as I thought of excuses on how to get out of having to go see the Madam.

I knew what this was about and I wasn't interested. I told her that, too. But she never listened. And if it wasn't for my debt to Alex, and for me finding Kelly through Madam's indirect introduction, I would be breaking my contract today and telling her to go stuff it.

But I owed it to more people than just myself to keep going. So, I took a quick shower, slipped on my dress, and was out the door on my way to meeting my Uber pick-up a couple blocks from Kelly's.

"Seriously?" I said, opening the door and seeing who it was. "How do you keep making this happen?"

"Now that is a question I should be asking you." His fantastic white smile filled his face.

It was the same driver from Uganda as I'd had two nights ago and so many times previously. Closing the door and buckling in, I said, "I feel like if we keep having this happen, then I should at least know your name."

"Lucky." His eyes found me in the rearview mirror.

"C'mon? Really?" I cocked my head. "Your name is Lucky?"

He nodded.

"If that's true, then I would love to know what your last name is."

"Charm," he said without missing a beat.

I shook my head and huffed a disbelieving laugh. "Lucky Charm."

When we stopped at a light, he pulled his driver's license from his wallet, and showed it to me. "See. It even says it here."

I pinched the card in the corner and read his name. *Lucky Charm.* Just like he said. Unbelievable. "And your parents gave that name to you?"

"Who else?"

"Okay." I showed him my palms. "Well, nice to meet you, Lucky. I'm Kendra."

"Kendra. I like that name."

"It's okay." I turned to look out the window, realizing we had just pulled into Madam's neighborhood. "Certainly not as cool as your name."

"I guess I was just lucky." He laughed and it was the kind of laugh that made you naturally want to join in on the fun.

When he pulled the car in front of Madam's building, I set my hand on the back of his chair and leaned forward. "Ever been here before?"

He leaned across the middle and took his time taking in the red bricks that seemed to be glowing today. Slowly his head shook as he frowned. "No. I don't recall ever being here."

"No worries." I opened the door. "I was just curious."

"Sorry."

"Would you mind waiting for me? I shouldn't be long."

"For you? Of course." He smiled.

Slipping my arm through the shoulder strap of my handbag, I thanked Lucky before scurrying up the stairs. Janine lifted her head and greeted me as I passed her desk. I mumbled a quick hello back and continued on. When I rounded the corner, naturally Kelly filled my head with thoughts of the first time I met him. Without allowing myself to overthink things, I found Jerome standing with a wide stance and his hands folded in front.

"Hello, *dah-ling*," I teased him with my impersonation of the Madam. Flipping my hair over my shoulder in a dramatic fashion, I said, "A bit early for us to be working, don't ya think?"

Jerome cocked a brow and flicked his wrist. Glancing at his gold watch he shook his head. "Nope."

"Well, you're no fun," I said, stepping past his bulk and heading directly into Madam's office.

She lifted her head with bright eyes and smiled. Her red lipstick made it hard to focus on any other part of her face as I took the liberty to plop my butt down in a chair directly across from her. "Kendra, baby. It's good to see you."

Curling my fingers toward my face, I glanced at my nails. "What can I do for you on this fine morning?"

"You could start by telling me where you got that dress." She folded her hands on top of her desk and straightened her spine.

I cast my gaze down the front of me. The hem had ridden up my thigh and I liked how I felt like I wasn't wearing much at all. "Do you like it?"

"I do." She angled her head and gave me a thin-lipped smile. "It has Kelly's name written all over it."

"Funny you mention him." My gaze rolled up to meet hers. "He's the one who gave it to me."

Relaxing her otherwise stiff posture, Madam's attitude was nonchalant. "How is he doing?"

"Good. Great. Busy." I barked off everything that came to mind.

"Are you enjoying your time with him?"

Her line of questioning was making me nervous. Suddenly my nerves were raw as I flashed her a questioning look. "I am." My words were slow to roll off my tongue.

"That's wonderful, dear." Her smile seemed forced, and that alone had me anxiously waiting to see where she was taking this.

We stared at each other without saying anything. I could hear the clock ticking on the wall and if it weren't for that, I would have thought time had stopped all together. Then, finally, I said, "Did you think I wouldn't?"

"No. I didn't." Her eyes flickered like a candle. "The question-naires I had you both complete didn't align."

"Oh?" I cast my gaze to my lap and picked at an imaginary piece of lint on my thigh.

"Based on your answers, your interests conflict."

"Well," my brows raised when I looked up at her, "I guess you'll have to update your questionnaire."

She cocked a brow.

"It seems to be flawed."

Madam turned her head and cackled. "You think so?"

I shrugged. "Well, yeah, I mean—"

"I meant what I originally said about Kelly Black." Madam's voice grew stern. "You don't know him the way I do and I ask," she looked down long enough to center herself, "because I don't want either of you to walk away from this month together feeling disappointed."

"What is it I should know that you're not telling me?" My lips pursed. "Does he have other women in his life I should know about?"

Madam's face was stone as she stared back at me. Her lips were sealed and I wasn't surprised by her lack of desire to share what she knew about Kelly. "It's not my place to tell you those things."

My chin tipped back slowly as my eyes narrowed into tiny slits. "But you took the liberty of telling me that Sylvia was receiving death threats?"

"You trusted me to look out for you, and that's what I did when I learned of what was happening with Sylvia."

"Shit!" I slapped my thigh. "Then what makes Kelly different?"

"Kelly can tell you that," she wet her lips, "but only if he wants."

I turned my head away, growing frustrated with how the Madam picked and chose which news was important enough to share with me and which wasn't. I heard something heavy fall to her desk and when I turned to see what it was, my jaw dangled on its hinges. "Oh, fuck no," I said, staring at the envelope I knew was full of cash.

"Oh, fuck yes." Her eyes glimmered like she knew I didn't have a choice. "As long as I have you under my wing, you'll do whatever it is I ask."

My mouth snapped shut and my jaw twitched as we stared each other down.

"Don't think I won't tell Kelly about your past."

Reaching to the table, I snatched the envelope inside my hand with nostrils flaring. Standing, I turned to the door without saying another word.

Inside, I debated which was worse: Me telling Kelly about how I was raped, or him finding out from Madam that my pussy was far from being pure. And no matter how much I tried to convince myself that I didn't care, I did. But I also knew that I wasn't ready for Kelly to know my secret, either.

With one foot out the Madam's office, she said, "Oh, and Kendra darling?"

I stopped, tipped my head back, and sighed before turning around.

"I've spoken with Emmanuel." She stood, balancing herself with five fingers firmly pressed onto the top of her desk. "Let me know if he misbehaves. I'd hate for him to get the wrong idea about you."

19

Kelly

I set my cell back on the empty table after reading the text from the Madam.

Stroking the sweat dripping from my cold glass of sparkling water, my mind went back to thinking of Kendra. Mojito wasn't open to the public but since I had Wes coming to meet Colin Cobbs, I was let in early by the bartender preparing the place to open for lunch.

My lips pursed as I blew out a weighty sigh, unsure what to do about Kendra.

Like last night wasn't already heavy enough, now she had to go to the Madam with questions she had about me? Our relationship was unraveling quicker than I'd imagined it could. It was balanced on a thin wire.

Adrenaline pumped through my veins, paranoid she could discover something she might not want to know. It wasn't like I had tons to hide. But what I was keeping from her was for her own good.

Lifting my glass to my lips, I sipped a healthy gulp back and slammed the glass down much harder than I intended.

I still couldn't make sense of what happened last night. Why Kendra started crying or what got into her head with wanting me to say those things to her. It was fucked up and twisted but, hell, I wasn't going to tell her no. God, she was doing so well meeting my demands but now, with her digging into my past, she was asking for a fight.

Glancing to the door, I wondered when they were going to arrive.

My knee bounced beneath the table and I continued to work on my drink.

The truth was, I didn't know what the best approach with Kendra was. When things were good I wanted to fuck her, tie her up and continue easing her into the submissive lifestyle. But now I had my doubts that she was cut out for it.

I rubbed my face inside my hands and grumbled with uncertainty.

Leaving her last night was the best choice for both of us. This meeting that was about to happen was huge and, not that I wanted to discredit the way she was feeling, but I knew that I couldn't let her be a distraction when mentally preparing for today.

Rolling my neck, I could only hope that that was the best decision—knowing that would be what I would have wanted if it were me. Inside, I hoped she would recognize it, too. Except, instead of being alone—like I wanted her to be—she went running to Madam.

"Fuck." My muscles twitched.

None of this had gone as I'd hoped. Kendra was too delicate and if we were to continue moving forward in our relationship, it was important that I didn't move too fast. We were barely into our month together, and the last thing I wanted was for it to end now. At least until I understood what was actually going on in that head of hers.

"He the man you're waiting on?" The bartender pointed toward the door.

I glanced up and saw Colin pressing his face against the glass. "Yeah, that's the one." I stood, moving to let him in.

"Kelly Black." Colin threw one arm around me. "Good to see you, man."

I pulled back, smiling, and patted him on the shoulder. "How was the drive?"

"Excellent."

I waved for him to follow, and together we strolled lazily back to the table. "Did you find this place all right?"

"On Rodeo Drive, are you kidding me?" His enthusiasm crinkled his eyes. "But I would have liked to see your office."

We slid into our chairs and settled in. It didn't take me long to realize that Cobbs had aged considerably since the last time I'd seen him. The wrinkles around his eyes and across his forehead were deep and defined, complementing his once-brownish, now-greying hair. Though I could still see that youthful spirit shining in his eyes when he looked back with a satisfied grin.

"I would have loved to show you the lab, but," my hands folded on the table in front of me, "with the secrecy behind this plan I'm going to further explain to you today, I just couldn't risk you being seen there."

"I'll admit, all this talk about the big plans you have," he laughed, "is half the reason I agreed to come."

"And here I thought it was because you wanted to see your old college buddy." We shared a laugh before I continued. "There's someone else I wanted you to meet."

His brow arched.

"Speak of the devil," I said, catching Wes walk through the front doors over Cobbs's shoulder. "Here he comes, now."

Cobbs turned to look over his shoulder, and together we watched Wes walk in wearing a bright white three-piece designer suit, holding Kami on his arm. She was in an ocean blue loose fitting dress that fell all the way to the floor. They looked incredible.

"C'mon." I pushed back from the table. "Let me introduce you."

Cobbs followed me to the front and watched me first greet Kami with a soft kiss to the cheek before turning to hug Wes. "Wes, this is my old friend, Colin Cobbs."

Cobbs extended his hand, offering it to Wes. Wes shook it and said, "So you're the one Kelly has been talking about."

Cobbs glanced at me. "I guess so."

When Wes released Cobbs's hand, Wes turned his attention back to me. "Have you been here long?"

"Long enough to enjoy my first drink." I winked.

He glanced toward the bar and nodded at his employee. "And what about food? Who's hungry?" He clapped his hands together and circled the group with his eyes.

"Wes owns the joint." I turned to Cobbs. "Mojito has some of the best food in town."

"Not to mention drinks." Wes nodded. "Make yourselves at home and I'll go put in an order."

Cobbs and I watched Wes and Kami stride toward the bar holding hands. I could tell Cobbs was working through something inside his head as he stood there stroking his chin. When I glanced at him with an arched look he said, "I've seen them both in the papers."

"Wes's empire stretches across industries and beyond LA." I nodded. "He's Hollywood royalty."

Then he turned to me and whispered, "You doing all right?"

With hands stuffed into my pockets, I turned to face him with a quizzical look.

"The accident." He frowned. "I don't think I've seen you since."

I reached out and laid my hand on his shoulder.

"I should have asked you when we spoke yesterday, but with everything going on in my own life—"

"I get it." I nodded, squeezing his shoulder. "I'm doing just fine. Don't you worry about me."

It wasn't worth reliving the accident or what happened afterward. That was a long time ago, and with Cobbs having to worry about his own wife's health—while managing to keep his firm running—it was best we focused on the matter at hand rather than shit that in the past.

"Kelly," Wes called over from the bar. "Let's move to the back. More private there once we open."

I nodded and turned to the table I had taken up residence at and began quickly gathering my things. Cobbs walked by my side to the table Wes now occupied.

Our drinks were served, Wes and Cobbs with a bloody Mary and me with my iced sparkling water. Cobbs never did mention me not drinking alcohol, and I liked that I didn't have to explain myself. We settled in and made more small talk before we jumped into discussing the reason I'd called everyone here today.

"So, before we begin, I would just like to remind everyone that whatever is discussed today stays between us." My eyes darted between the two men.

They both nodded, understanding the implications if someone were to leak information. But when I saw Wes keeping one eye firmly on Colin, my eyebrows drew together.

Wes's bartender served us our food and as soon as he left, Colin asked with a thumb pointing over his shoulder, "Should we worry about him?"

Wes's hand fisted on the table next to Colin's plate. "I serve you food, provide the drinks, and welcome you into my restaurant only to have you question the loyalty of my employees?"

Colin leaned away from the table, retreating. "I didn't mean to offend you, but Kelly is making this meeting sound top-secret."

"And I don't know you." Wes's voice was deep and firm.

"Wes," I said, "Colin is only covering his own bases."

The two men stared each other down.

"We can all trust each other here," I reminded them, my voice strong but soft. "Wes has his employee's full loyalty. We're all on the same side, let's not forget that."

"Well then," Colin humbly said, averting his gaze to his food. "The food smells delicious."

Seeing that the tension was already buzzing between the two men, I dug in my bag and pulled out a manila folder, sliding it to Colin. "This is the reason I have you here."

He eyed me for a second before opening the folder to a thick file on my next client. "Blake Stone?"

I nodded, taking the utensils in my hands and slicing up my breakfast burrito. "That's right."

Wes held up his hand. "And before we go any further, I'm going to need your personal information."

Colin rolled his eyes over to me with a look of disbelief filling his face.

Wes pulled out a pen and paper and set them down in front of Colin. "Your home address." He tapped the paper. "Along with the name of your wife, all your children—their ages and where they attend school."

"Is he fucking serious?" Cobbs asked, looking me straight in the eye.

Slowly, my head nodded. "We need to establish a form of insurance."

"Unbelievable," Cobbs huffed, leaning back and tossing his napkin to the table. "Kelly, you already have that information."

"But Wes doesn't."

Cobbs glared at Wes. Wes stared back without a hint of emotion giving away what it was he was thinking. "Can't you at least tell me more about what it is you want me to do before I give this asshole my information?"

"I wish I could, but this case is too big to take any chances," I said, plopping a fork full of burrito into my mouth.

Cobbs cursed under his breath and quickly scribbled down the information Wes demanded of him. "There, you happy, asshole?" he sneered, sliding the paper over to Wes.

Wes took the paper between his fingers and read it. "And when you can," Wes glanced back to Cobbs, "I'll also need photos of these people."

Cobbs pushed his plate away and fell back into his seat, curling his shoulders. "Kelly, if you want me to do anything illegal, tell me now and I'll leave."

"It's nothing illegal."

"Good. Because what I've already read on Mario has me convinced he's innocent."

My face lifted, pleased Cobbs recognized what I saw in Mario's case, too. "He is. And I'm glad you saw that, too."

"So, what do you need and how is this asshole," he pointed his thumb to Wes, "involved?"

Wes chuckled into his drink.

"He's the one who came up with the plan." I went on to tell Cobbs about our plan to convict Stone. "You'll be representing Mario and feeding me what you learn about what your new client knows about Stone. And I'll take that information and use it against him, ensuring he gets convicted."

"Let me get this straight." Cobbs clasped his hands in front of him. "You need me to represent Mario and use the information I learn from him to set him free, in order for you to get the client you're representing convicted?"

"That's right," Wes interjected.

Cobbs blinked and shook his head. "Did I miss something here?" His eyes darted between me and Wes. "Kelly, you're a criminal *defense* lawyer, right?"

I nodded, smiling. "LA can't afford my client to be set free. It's my job to ensure that it doesn't happen."

The crease between his brows deepened as he read more of the paperwork I had on Stone. "Why not just let a judge decide the case? It seems like an open and shut trial."

"The consequences are too grave." I nodded between bites.

Wes told Cobbs about what Stone had done to the movie industry, how he was destroying many people's lives through the drugs he was trafficking, and how he opened up a market that didn't seem to want to go away. We shared our theory of how if we didn't make him an example, that someone would quickly fill that gap left behind in the market—without mentioning Madam by name.

And, all the while, I allowed my mind to drift back to Kendra, deciding how best to approach her the next time I saw her.

"Wow." Colin rubbed his face with his gaze cast down. "This is fucked up and twisted. I knew Stone was a bad motherfucker, but," he turned to look at me, "is he really worth ruining your winning reputation?"

I set my fork down and lifted my water to my lips. "I wouldn't have called you here if I didn't think you'd see what was at stake."

"It's big."

"Together, we can make this work." I nodded. "Everyone will win. Mario. You. Even me and my reputation. As well as the citizens of Los Angeles County. We're in the business of bringing justice to our people, even if that means bending the rules to achieve that." My cell began ringing inside my pocket. Reaching inside, I took it out and saw that it couldn't wait. "Excuse me," I said, leaving the table, taking the call.

"Kelly, I couldn't do it." Kaycee's voice was frail and immediately caused my stomach to clench. "I thought I could do it. But I couldn't go through with it."

I shoved a hand through my hair and blew out a sigh, realizing that I might have opened up something I shouldn't have the other night when I drove to San Bernardino to see her. "What happened?"

"I turned around. I can't leave without first visiting. The other night was great, and I would like more of that—more of us. I need you with me."

"I'm in the middle of something right now." My eyes closed.

"Please, Kelly. Come with me. Be by my side."

I turned back to the table, seeing Cobbs talking with Wes. My hope was that they could learn to trust each other after the shit Wes pulled about requesting Cobbs's family information. It might have been too much but, then again, we couldn't risk getting this case tossed, either.

"You know it wouldn't be right without you there," Kaycee pleaded.

My heavy lids closed, knowing that she was right. No matter how hard I tried to ignore it, I needed to be there next to Kaycee. It was up to me to make things right, to be there for her, even if it was only one more time.

"Where are you?" I asked.

"I'm in LA. I don't know how much longer I can stay."

The muscles in my face sagged. "I can't see you today."

"I don't have much time. Are you sure you can't meet today? I'm not sure I can come back again."

"Tomorrow, Kaycee."

"Kelly, I'm a wreck," she cried.

"Tomorrow." I tipped my head back and stroked my chin. "Tell me you will wait until tomorrow to see me."

Silence hung on the line as anticipation built. "I'll wait. You know I'll always wait for you."

"Keep your phone on. I'll call you in the morning." I ended our conversation with problems mounting. When I got back to the table, I found Cobbs more on board than ever.

"Wes told me about what happened to Adrianna." Colin's face

flared with anger. "The more I learn, the more I want to kill this asshole myself."

Wes nodded when I caught his gaze.

"You have no idea how boring my life has been. Finally, thanks to you guys, I'll be working on something exciting." Cobbs laughed. "You know, Kelly, I'd do anything to make things right."

The corners of my lips curled upward.

"Besides, it wouldn't be the first corrupt trial I've worked." He chuckled. "It would be my honor to help you bring Stone's ass down."

20

Kendra

My fingers drummed nervously on top of my thigh.

Visiting Emmanuel was the last thing I wanted to do. And what did Madam mean by not wanting Emmanuel to get the wrong idea about me? I tried to wrap my head around that for far longer than I should have but as soon as I glanced down at what I was wearing, I suddenly regretted not stopping back home first to change.

A new song changed over on the radio and Lucky's head bounced to the reggae music. He had such a lively spirit I couldn't stop myself from smiling. As soon as I'd taken my seat in the back, opposite of where he sat behind the wheel, he asked if he could listen to his favorite music—reggae. I happily agreed, knowing that it would leave me plenty of time to scramble through the thoughts swirling through my head.

My eyes were open but I couldn't tell what was going on in the world outside. Lucky weaved his vehicle in and out of traffic until we left the heart of the city, exchanging it for the industrial area where I was instructed to make this next drop for Madam.

A hand fluttered to my neck. I played with the black diamond white gold necklace Kelly gave me as I stared at the cube shaped package sitting on top of my handbag.

Without having been told, I knew what it was—money. How much exactly, that was the question I wrestled with. But by the weight and size, I would have guessed it was easily mid-five figures.

The moment Lucky turned into the entrance he hit the brakes. "Are you sure this is it?"

"I'm sure," I said, seeing his eyes flicker with concern when passing over the barbed-wired fence entrance with security cameras perched up on the roof.

With a great deal of hesitation, Lucky's foot let up off the brake and the wheels began to roll once again. A shiver prickled my scalp and I hugged myself warm. The place was a mess, much more so than the last time, as litter blew across the pavement finally getting caught on a rust-pitted dumpster leaking something disgusting from the bottom corner.

Lucky kept glancing back at me in the mirror as if he could feel my unease growing.

A strange mixture of rotting garbage and motor oil filled the air and I couldn't decide if the feeling hardening in the pit of my stomach was from the sight unfolding before my eyes, or if it was simply because I knew exactly what—and who—I was going to have to deal with today.

My last visit with Emmanuel didn't exactly inspire me to want to ever come back. His appearance was only half the reason I thought of him as disgusting. He tried to flirt with me but it wasn't flattering. He wasn't my type and if I had to be honest, I was way out of his league.

When I turned my head forward, I caught Lucky's eyes staring at the side of my head. I forced a smile, if only as a weak attempt to hide the bile rolling my insides over. "Watch it!" I screamed.

Lucky slammed on the brakes making the tires squeal. My entire body lurched forward as the sudden stop sent my heart racing. In a split second, we'd gone from nearly clipping the backside of a feral dog running in front of Lucky's hood, to skidding to a complete stop.

We both stared at the dog as it scurried off into the shadows.

"Are you okay, Ms. Kendra?" Lucky turned to look at me with big round eyes.

The pulse in my neck ticked hard and fast as I held up a hand. "Yes, I'm fine."

Lucky turned his focus back to where we saw the dog trot off. "I don't know where he came from."

"The dumpster," I said, dropping my forehead into my hand. "He was licking something at the dumpster."

"Oh, my. I'm sorry about that." He shook his head, clearly disappointed in himself for not seeing the dog before I did.

"Its fine," I said, pointing through the windscreen. "Park there. That's where I need to go."

Rubbing my temples, I worked to collect my thoughts before going into my meeting with Emmanuel. He wasn't one I wanted to show weakness to. Madam was right, I didn't want him to get the wrong idea about me. I was here on business. We weren't friends and I didn't have to stay and chat, pretending like we were.

Lucky kept both hands on the wheel as he drove slowly to the parking space I'd pointed to. I quickly recognized the same unmarked delivery truck backed into the loading dock as during my last visit. And the front metal door was propped open. A man stood staring back at Lucky and me, sucking on a cigarette.

"He doesn't look friendly," Lucky muttered in a low voice as he stared at the man smoking. "Are you sure this is where you wanted me to take you?"

"I'll be fine." I unbuckled myself and set my hand over Lucky's right shoulder.

He blinked, barely recognizing my touch, and by the look on his face I knew that he too was having the same feelings as I was. Something didn't feel right.

"You recognize that man?"

Lucky's eyes narrowed, continuing to study the man. "I can't remember."

"Perhaps from the nightclub you take the girls to?"

"Yes. Maybe." He turned his head to look over his shoulder at me. "But I can't say for certain."

Then the man flicked his cigarette butt, turned, and walked inside.

"Well, I guess that's my cue." Digging in my bag, I made sure that the envelope was securely tucked away before stepping outside.

Lucky turned to show me his pained face and without him actually saying anything, I knew that he was worried for me. But he didn't have to be. I could take care of myself.

Opening my door, I firmly placed one heel on the ground, catching scent of the last remnants of the man's tobacco smoke burning down to the filter. "Wish me luck."

Lucky's voice was drowned out in all the noise going on inside my own head. I was sure he wished me luck or said that he was there if I needed him. But I heard nothing.

Looking around, I pushed all the fear I felt boiling inside me to the side and blamed Kelly for my frayed confidence. He was the one to have left me when I needed a body to snuggle with. He was also the one to have first triggered my flashback to the time I was raped. If it hadn't been for any of that, I wouldn't be feeling as weak as I was now.

I was strong—not a fragile little girl who couldn't fight off my assailant.

As soon I stepped inside the building, I pulled my sunglasses off my face, taking a moment to look around. My brows raised, surprised to see the entire layout had changed from the first time I had visited, barely a week ago. Men swarmed between boxes, cars, and motorcycles. When one of them whistled after seeing me I turned my head and smirked.

"Hey, gorgeous. I told you to wait for me at home," a man said, getting the others around him to laugh.

Despite my heart pounding against my chest I remained calm, choosing to ignore it all. Holding my chin high, I found myself floating through the harassment in hopes of finding Emmanuel quickly so that I could get on with my day.

"As soon as I heard the men erupt, I had a suspicion it was because of you." Emmanuel smiled with arms spread wide as he seemed to emerge out of nowhere.

I dodged his attempt at a kiss and I ducked my head to the chaos swirling around us. Whatever was happening here today, they were preparing for something big. Boxes, crates, and the general hustle of preparation buzzed in the air. "What happened to the beauty products?" I asked above the noise.

Emmanuel laughed, reaching his hand around to my lower back, nudging me forward as if he didn't want to talk with me here. "All sold out." He grinned.

With Emmanuel at my side, I tried to stay inconspicuous with my unrelenting observation but it proved impossible. Curiosity always got the best of me. Even when I knew it wasn't any of my business. I was just dying to know what was going on. So when we passed a vehicle being torn apart, I turned to Emmanuel and said, "That's too bad."

Emmanuel flashed me a questioning look.

"I was hoping to get my hands on more of that perfume I had last time."

His eyes drifted down to my chest as he smiled.

"Let's talk in my office." He winked. "Perhaps I have a bottle of what you're looking for in there."

Stepping out of the way of an oncoming forklift, Emmanuel opened the door to his office and was the first to step inside. I quickly followed and as I passed him, my vision tunneled.

Suddenly the room spun and I felt dizzy.

The smell.

His smell.

It was something I recognized. A smell that went straight to my head. I knew what it was—knew it so well that I wished I didn't. It was a sweet woody smell that flooded my head with memories of him—my rapist. And just like that, I was once again thrust into the ring, running for my life.

I blinked.

Then I stumbled.

And when I turned to see Emmanuel, he had beady reptilian eyes.

I watched his tongue slither over his bottom lip as I fell back into the empty chair behind me. My palms heated and began to sweat. I knew that look he was giving me—the face of a predator searching for weakness in his prey. I shook my head and tightened my abs, preparing for a fight. Staring into his eyes was like staring into those of a lion.

Emmanuel shut the door and I jumped.

He chuckled.

My hand flew over my mouth as I gasped. Closing my eyes, I let out a heavy sigh telling myself, *Get it together*.

"Relax, Kendra." Emmanuel's hand smoothed down my bare upper arm as he passed, taking a seat behind his desk. "We're friends here."

I watched him thread his fingers together, resting his hands over his stomach. My mind was on overdrive and I knew that I'd overreacted to the smell of his cologne. But it sparked terror inside me and instinct took over. I hated that this terror I'd been feeling inside seemed to be following me wherever I went. I didn't know what I could do to forget about what happened to me as a child and move on with my life.

But one thing was certain: If I kept experiencing triggers that reminded me of my traumatic experience, Alex's idea of seeking professional help seemed more like something I *had* to do.

"Look, I don't have much time, but," I reached inside my handbag and pulled out the envelope, "here's the gift from Madam."

Emmanuel extended his arm across the desk and took the envelope from my hand. He squeezed it and lifted it to his nose, sniffing it. I thought it was a weird gesture but, then again, that was the adjective that defined him—*weirdo.*

"What's the money for, anyway?"

He remained silent, keeping his eyes closed as if thinking of all the things he was going to do with whatever amount of money I knew was stuffed inside. Then, one by one, his lids opened and glared at me. "Madam said you might misbehave."

My jaw dangled on its hinges. "Excuse me?"

"That's right. I was warned about you."

My thoughts recoiled back to Madam's warning about Emmanuel. I didn't know what kind of game she was playing but, clearly, she was telling two different stories depending on who she was talking to. "That's funny," I mused with an arched look.

He quirked a brow and tilted his head.

"She had the same warning about you."

Emmanuel dropped his chin and shook his head as he chuckled. "Deliver a message to Madam," he said, lifting his gaze back to mine. "Tell her that if we sit on the eggs any longer, they'll hatch."

My eyes narrowed. "What the fuck does that mean?"

He lifted his index finger and wagged it at me. "Language. It's not attractive on a beautiful lady."

My brows pinched, wanting to rip off his paternal finger wagging its ugly head at me.

"Just tell her." He stood. "Now, if you'll excuse me, there are things I must be attending to."

I showed him my palms, stood, and was eager to leave his shitty ass warehouse before I really did break down and begin hyperventilating. I hated it here and was beginning to hate Emmanuel even more.

Sit any longer and the eggs will hatch? What the fuck did that mean? Psychopath.

"What about the perfume?" I asked.

"Next time." He nudged me back into the chaos.

Dodging more cat calls from his men, I flipped them the bird over my shoulder as Emmanuel escorted me to the exit. Without saying anything else I left, wondering if Madam purposely was trying to create mistrust between her associates or if it was just the feeling I had.

Lucky was standing with his arms folded across his chest, leaning against the hood of his car when I stepped outside. When he saw me coming, I nodded and he slid back behind the wheel, starting the engine. "I was starting to get worried," he said as soon as I opened the back door.

"About me?"

He turned and smiled, watching me settle into the backseat. "Who else?"

"You're such a sweetheart but I can take care of myself."

Lucky tipped his head back and laughed. "I never doubted it."

The ride back to my apartment went by in a flash. Once again I was oblivious to my surroundings, choosing instead to focus on the thoughts skidding between my ears. I thought about Madam and what exactly the money was for and if it was money earned from girls like me. Despite the dangers that came with knowing too much, I wanted more.

I began to think about the files I'd stolen on her and how maybe I had missed something inside them when I first went digging. Promising myself I'd check as soon as I got home, Lucky tried to make conversation but I mostly just nodded. Once he pulled over, letting me out on the same corner I always instructed him to, he wished me a good day and I did the same, leaving him free to find his next customer.

As I walked to my building, my senses were on overdrive. That same sweet woody scent intoxicated my brain. Faces I passed on the street shared similar features with the man in my nightmares. His smell, his face, and even the way he touched me haunted me like an old ghost who refused to go away.

Mr. Anderson lifted his head as soon as he saw me push through the front entrance to my building.

"Hey, Mr. Anderson, are you staying out of trouble?" I smiled as I passed him.

"I should ask you the same, though I probably wouldn't want to hear your answer." He laughed.

The elevator doors opened as soon as I arrived and I took the short lift up, anxiously waiting to research all that I had about Madam. Adrenaline pumped viciously through my veins all the way to my door. Taking my keys out, I unlocked the door, stepped inside, closed the door, and quickly turned the deadbolt back over. Leaning my back against the door, I inhaled a deep calming breath, then rushed to close the curtains.

It was silly to think someone was watching, as if knowing what it was I was going to do. But I didn't want to take any chances. Pulling my hair back into a ponytail, I pulled out the files I had hidden away and began my search.

Over the next hour, I read, filed, and made notes on everything I thought might get me one step closer to solving who exactly the Madam was and what it was she was involving me in.

There was paperwork on the business entity, tax classifications, forms that legitimized a corporation in the eyes of the state and federal governments, among many other necessary but boring paperwork to make a business legit. Thinking that I had nothing new to go on, I flipped over one more file and that's when I discovered it.

Peeling it away, I couldn't believe I had missed it before.

One measly piece of paper was stuck to the back of another. Possibility surged through me as I hung on to hope, thinking that this could be it—my golden ticket to knowing exactly what it was I was doing.

Once free, I quickly scanned the document. It was an IRS audit with personal notes jotted down on the side. Through the chicken scratch I could read, *Shell company for illegal escorting service?*

Lifting my head, my mind raced.

I knew the Madam's business probably wasn't exactly legal, but if she set it up properly—with professional expertise—she could get away with having women like me date men like Kelly for her own profit.

My eyes dropped back to the form and I read more of the lawyer's notes stating how the Madam's business was a dating agency and set up as such, *NOT* an illegal escorting operation.

Okay, I nodded.

I went on reading, scanning to the very bottom, and my heart stopped when I saw the signed name—*Kelly B.*

Dropping the paper in my lap I leaned back, wondering what more the Madam was having Kelly do to make her operation look legit. And more importantly, what was in it for Kelly? My eyes closed as exhaustion took over and all I could hear was Kelly telling me, "It's not what happens that matters. It's how the story is told."

21

Kelly

As I approached my office building, I searched for Giselle's car on the curb.

When I found it parked in front of a large silver pickup truck, I couldn't decide if I was happy she beat me to the office or sad that she didn't take an extra half-hour to mend her relationship teetering on the edge of collapse. Though, in the end, it wasn't my call to make and her dedication to my firm was admirable.

Springing up the steps, I reached for the door handle just as a car honked behind me. I turned to see who it was and immediately recognized Madam's limo slowing to a stop.

I frowned, wondering what it was she was doing here. It wasn't like her to visit unannounced. I figured it must be important.

A second later, Jerome stepped out wearing a royal blue three-piece suit with a bright fire-truck red tie. "Kelly, the Madam would like to have a word with you."

Looking up and down the street, I knew that I had no choice but to see what it was she wanted. Our business relationship wasn't top-secret or anything like that but, still, I didn't like risking being seen with her, especially at my office.

"Madam dress you?" I said, tugging on Jerome's suit as I passed him before stepping inside the limo.

Jerome didn't comment and when I ducked my head inside, I found Madam sitting in the corner bench with her white-gloved hands folded in her lap. "What's wrong with the way Jerome is dressed?" Her eyes sparkled with curiosity.

I took the empty space across from Madam, leaned back, spread my knees wide, and watched Jerome struggle his way back inside. He shut the door and I felt the vehicle begin to move. "Nothing." I snickered, suddenly realizing they matched better than I'd originally thought. Madam's interview dress was the same red color as Jerome's tie, and her blue jacket was identical to the color of Jerome's suit. "You two look cute."

They glanced at each other as if noticing for the first time that they matched. Then Madam turned her attention back to me and cocked her head. "Was Kendra with you last night?"

My brows pinched. "No, why?"

Jerome smoothed his flat palms over his thick thighs.

"Is she okay?"

Madam glanced at Jerome who continued staring at me. "Relax, Kelly." A smug smile filled her face. "I'm sure she's just fine."

I knew I should have called Kendra last night—checked in to make sure she was okay. I'd debated it and then tossed and turned throughout the night, regretting my decision not to.

But I also didn't want to push her into having to think that she needed to see me again so soon after her complete meltdown. I wanted to give her time to heal, to be alone, to get her thoughts straight before I took her out again. When it was just us we were fine. But if I was to continue bringing her to important dinners where people of influence attended, I couldn't continue to risk my career because she refused to let me in on whatever the hell was going on with her. "Then why are you here?"

"You're right." Madam dropped her gaze to her hands, but only for a second. "I'm wasting your valuable time."

I moved my eyes over to Jerome. He remained silent with a stoic look stamped across his face.

"Kendra stopped by my office yesterday," Madam said with a sigh.

"Yes, I remember the text you sent me." I rolled my eyes back to the Madam. "What did she want?"

"Kelly," her tongue darted out of her mouth and wet her lip, "Kendra isn't like the other women I employ."

I arched a brow, thinking that I already knew that. Kendra was better than those women. *Way better.*

"She's..." Madam shared a quick glance in Jerome's direction before turning back to me, "How do I put this without it coming out wrong?"

My lips pursed as I waited for her to continue with a fluttery, empty stomach.

"Kendra, well..." her eyes looked up and to the left, "...she's broken."

Madam locked gazes with me as I replayed how the events from the other night unfolded inside my mind. It was something I was still reeling with myself, and could only hope that it was an anomaly to how she generally was. Because it broke my heart to see her crying, feeling her frozen stiff inside my arms as I hugged her tight against my chest in the steaming hot bathtub. "Broken." I swallowed. "I don't see it."

Madam's eyes darted over my face before she said, "She was asking lots of questions about you."

A pang of worry twisted my gut as I couldn't help but wonder if Kendra's visit with the Madam was because she was having regrets about being with me. I wasn't a fool. I recognized the pattern, saw that I may very well be the cause of Kendra's anguish she was fighting through. Though, worst case scenario, I hoped she was only testing the waters to see how difficult it would be for her to break free from the agreement she'd made with the Madam—which I knew wasn't ever going to happen until Madam squeezed her to the last drop.

"Have you told her anything that might get her curious?" Madam's lids hooded over and she pressed her lips flat.

"Curious about what?" I twisted my watch on my wrist, pulling up my sleeve to check the time.

"Your past."

I shook my head.

"Why it is we work together?"

Again, I shook my head, feeling my heart slow to a pitter-patter.

"Or the cases you're currently working on now?"

I rubbed my mouth inside my hand, thinking she was now digging for clues. "I don't see how any of this is relevant."

Madam's cackle was as light as the feather dangling from her ears. "You know how I don't appreciate someone trying to dig up dirt on stuff they don't know anything about."

I waved my hand through the air. "You're overthinking it. Kendra is doing just fine."

Madam gave me a skeptical look.

"You don't believe me?"

She dropped her chin and looked up at me from under her brow. "Let's face it, we may be looking at the same woman, but trust me when I say that we are not seeing the same thing."

"So, what would you like me to do about it?" My shoulders shrugged.

"Well," she sighed, "she is yours for a month."

The right side of my face smiled.

"Since she's your problem—"

"—No problem," I interrupted her. "Kendra is just fine."

"See it as you will, but," Madam lifted her face, "I would like to see you break her into complete submission."

I turned my head to the front, seeing that we were rounding back to my office. "What do you think I'm working on?"

Madam laughed. "Then what is taking you so long? Are you rusty?"

I turned my head and glared at her.

"After all, it's been a while since you've played the Dom role."

The limo pulled to the side and slowed to a stop.

"Make it happen soon, Kelly."

Madam's focus drifted to something behind me, and when I turned to see what it was, I caught sight of Kaycee making her way down the sidewalk on her way to my office. I cleared my throat and frowned, pissed at her for showing up like this without first waiting to hear back from me. Cracking my knuckles, I thought how Kaycee was seriously testing my patience and I had to make sure she knew it wasn't cool for her to just show up like this.

"I'd hate for Kendra to discover something that would make her question our arrangement."

I turned back to find Madam's disapproving eyes traveling across my face. The stuffy air inside the limo was sucked out the moment Jerome reached across my lap for the door handle. Opening it, I heard Kaycee's footsteps stutter to a stop. "Kelly?"

I turned and smiled. "I'll be right in."

She nodded, seeing that I was busy with the Madam.

"Naughty boy, Kelly." Madam cackled. "Perhaps I understand Kendra's concern about you not being loyal to only her." She glanced at Kaycee walking up the stairs. "Though I must say, you have a particular taste in women."

"Thank you," I mumbled as I stepped one foot out onto the pavement.

"They all look the same." Madam reached over and touched Jerome's thigh.

Jerome snickered.

"I'll be in touch about the Stone case," I said, leaving her limo.

"Yes, honey. I know you will." She laughed. "And Kelly," I dipped my head back inside, "if it's Kendra who is not fulfilling your own desire," she leaned forward as if to emphasize her point, "you can always give her back to me."

"Thanks, but no thanks." I grinned.

"Then don't let her find out about her." Madam nodded to Kaycee as I shut the door, not in the mood to hear anymore of her concerns. Turning back to face Kaycee, I knew that I had enough problems on my plate already.

22

Kendra

Stretching my hands above my head, I yawned.

After spending my night digging through the files I had on the Madam, exhaustion finally took over and blessed me with the best sleep I'd had since one of the first times Kelly sexed me up real good.

Rolling on my side and tucking an arm under my head, I glanced at the clock and couldn't believe it was almost noon already. That was something to smile about. Reaching to the nightstand, I turned my phone on and after a minute of it booting up, my doorman app dinged me with a message. A package was waiting for me in the lobby.

Placing the phone back on the stand, I rolled onto my back thinking it had to be from Kelly.

I stared at the ceiling for another minute before tossing my covers and rubbing my face. My feet hit the floor and I quickly stepped into a pair of shorts lying next to the bed before finding a tee and pulling it over my head.

I had my hair tied up into a messy bun on top of my head and one glance in the mirror was enough to tell me that I looked good enough to retrieve the package but not hot enough to go any further than that. After all, it was only Mr. Anderson I was going to have to actually converse with so what I was wearing was perfectly fine.

Snatching my keys off the kitchen counter, I locked the front door behind me, paranoid that if I kept it unlocked something bad would happen. I didn't have to wait long for an elevator and once inside, I tried not to think too much into Madam's deliveries to Emmanuel. The less I knew the better. However, that still didn't ease my mind with what I already assumed was going on. The money I was making with each delivery was outstanding, and that was on top of the weekly checks being deposited into my bank account for escorting for Madam. Yet, still, my stomach remained unsettled.

Lowering my head, I pinched the bridge of my nose thinking there had to be a way to convince Madam I wasn't her best option.

It wasn't rocket science and another girl could easily pick up where I left off. Because my heart told me that I needed to find a way out. If there was even a possibility of doing that, I needed to find it fast.

Lifting my head, I folded my arms over my chest and leaned back against the wall.

But like most things in life, discussing the theory behind something was the easy part. Presenting it to her, and making a convincing case to leave, was something entirely different. I didn't know how best to go about it. After all, it was my decision to take on Alex's contract and fulfill the obligation she'd promised Madam, not the other way around.

I tilted my head and nodded, thinking that maybe Kelly could help.

He would be much easier to convince. I knew what he thought about me, how much he wanted me. All I would need was for him to see that I was worth the fight and then he could take his court-room skills straight to Madam and convince her that my contract was only a silly piece of paper we could all learn to ignore.

My entire face pursed.

Except after finding what I assumed to be his signature on the files related to Madam's business ventures, I wasn't even sure he would want me to step away from Madam's operation. And *maybe* it was his idea to have Madam use me as her delivery girl in the first place.

Tipping my head back, I closed my eyes and sighed.

I didn't know what, or who, to believe. But one thing I was certain of: I was probably letting paranoia control more of my thoughts than the more rational side of my brain. Besides, I only saw the name *Kelly B.* It didn't mean that it was *my* Kelly Black. In fact, there were millions of last names that began with the letter 'B' and probably another million Kellys in this world, too.

Looking up to the ceiling, I tapped my chin.

Who was I fooling? This wasn't just coincidence. Of course that signature was my Kelly. I swore I needed to stop reading fiction and stop listening to the news. Too many conspiracy theories clouding my judgement. As soon as the elevator slowed to a stop on the lobby floor, I stepped forward only to be met by a sea of people waiting to get inside.

"Pardon me," I said, stepping between the crowd.

Somehow I managed to brush shoulders with only one or two people before emerging on the other side. My feet danced across the floor, and when I rounded the corner I saw Mr. Anderson busy with paperwork. Smirking, I flung my body across his desk. "Sorry I'm late. Had a late night."

He arched a brow.

"Doing work." I wiped my forehead with the backside of my hand. "You know, keeping myself busy."

"Uh-huh." He nudged his forearm against my shoulder and swept me off his paper.

"Anyway," I slid back to the floor, "I have a delivery?"

"Ah, right." He held up his finger, working to finish his paperwork before retrieving my delivery from the backroom.

My foot tapped anxiously on the floor as I couldn't wait to see what it was, though I was certain it was from Kelly. I mean, who else would it be from? Before he'd come around, I hardly got anything more than junk mail.

Spinning around, I rested my tail against the edge of the desk and smiled at the neighbors who came and went. We all recognized each other but our relationships never matured past a friendly nod here and there. And I was fine with that. I didn't need to get involved in building gossip. Mainly because I had a feeling *I* was *their* gossip.

"Here you are," Mr. Anderson said behind me.

I spun around so fast my hair flung over my shoulder. My hand flew over my mouth as I gasped. "Mr. Anderson," I teased. "For me?"

He laughed.

"You're such a sweetheart."

He rolled his eyes, one to quickly recognize my sarcasm and roll with the punches. "Seems you are making quite the impression."

Flinging my arms forward, I clamped both my hands around the bouquet and brought the dazzling array of colors to my nose. Closing my eyes, I got lost in their amazingly warm scent. As the swirls of smells made their way into my brain, my imagination reminded me of rainbows and butterflies and fields of happy hippies hula-hooping. All things that made me smile and keep me hopeful that this world was going to be all right after all.

"I assume they are from Mr. Black." Mr. Anderson's eyes sparkled.

Rocking back and forth on the backs of my heels I pulled the flowers into my chest, smiling. "He really likes me."

"What's there not to like?"

My lids popped open and I frowned. "I haven't been completely honest with him lately."

Mr. Anderson's face twisted and I knew there was something he wanted to tell me.

"You don't have to bite your tongue when you're with me." My brows pinched as I firmly nodded. "Go ahead, blanket me with your wisdom."

He cast his gaze down to the floor. But only for a second. "I'm not here to tell you how to live your life—"

"—Then don't." I shrugged.

"But if you like him," his bushy brows rose, crinkling his forehead, "then keep your relationship honest."

I stood there with wide doe eyes staring back at my wonderful and honest doorman. "Thank you. I will keep that in mind." I nodded as I knocked my knuckles against his desk. "Now, if you'll excuse me, I have breakfast to go make."

He glanced at the clock.

"I know." I lifted my hand and waved my fingers over my shoulder as I turned to the elevators, walking away. "It's already afternoon. But you know what they say—breakfast is the most important meal of the day!"

I could hear him laughing all the way to the elevator. Feeling appreciative, I couldn't stop smiling. The flowers were gorgeous and I couldn't wait to read the note stuffed inside.

What was it Kelly had to say today? I silently wondered.

Would he apologize for doing something he wasn't at fault for? Or was he going to ask me out and forget everything that happened the other night? I felt like such a fool for acting the way I had but my imagination was quickly running away from me.

I followed one other person into the elevator and wedged myself in the back corner so that I could open and read the note in private as I got whisked up to my floor.

My pulse increased and I raised my brows, looking around the small elevator car nervously as I slowly opened it. Acting like I was reading something I shouldn't be allowed to have, I bit my cheek and dropped my eyes to the paper.

I can't stop thinking about you.

My hand moved over my heart.

Sorry I didn't call.

My lips curled upward as I looked around.

I need to see you again. Call me when you get this. ~ Kelly

I stepped off the elevator feeling as beautiful as the flowers. Truthfully, I was glad he didn't call yesterday. I needed the time alone to figure some things out. But that didn't mean that I was going to tell him that. As far as he was concerned, he was right. He should be feeling guilty for not calling to check up on me.

Fucking asshole, I giggled.

Skipping down the hall, I plowed through my front door and marched straight for my cell phone still sitting on top of the nightstand. Scrolling to call Kelly, the screen lit up and it started ringing.

My eyes popped wide open and my heart skipped a beat as I waited to see who it was, hoping that it was Kelly. Then I let out a monstrous growl when I saw that it wasn't him, but instead Alex.

"Did you think I was dead?" I answered with narrowed, teasing eyes.

"What? No."

"Oh." My shoulders curled as I moved back to the living room and collapsed onto the couch. "I thought maybe you would have since I didn't stay at your place last night."

"Where are you?"

"Home." I lifted my feet up from the floor and hugged my knees to my chest. "Why, what's up?"

"I've been thinking."

"That's a first." I snickered.

"Kendra, I can't stop thinking about your boyfriend's questioning into Nash's involvement around that dead girl and the missing money."

Letting out a heavy sigh, I said, "And I couldn't stop thinking about what we talked about the other day."

"Did you look?"

"I did," I said, glancing to the stacks of files still left out from last night.

"And?"

"Kelly's definitely Madam's lawyer."

"No surprise there."

"Except I think he might be more involved in her escort business then he initially led on."

"He told you he was part of it?"

"Well, not really. Only a suspicion I had."

"So you don't have enough information on him to prove your theory one way or another?"

"No. Not yet." I dropped my head into my hand, feeling a headache coming on.

The line went silent and then I heard a car engine turn over.

"Where are you?" I asked.

"Outside his office."

My feet dropped to the floor and I leaned forward, resting my elbows on my knees. "Kelly's office?"

"I can't believe it either."

"No, that's great." My voice floated softly through the air as I tried to imagine what she was seeing.

"You sound surprised."

"Because I am." I wet my lips. "I didn't think you would actually spy on him for me."

"Me neither, and I don't know why I am. There's nothing going on here."

A slow smile spread across my face.

"Oh, shit."

"What?" My brows furrowed. "Do you see something?"

"Kelly just came out."

"Did he see you?"

"No."

"Then what is it?"

"You're not going to like this, but he's with another woman."

My stomach hardened. Staring down at his promise ring and still smelling the flowers sitting only feet away from me, I knew I shouldn't be feeling the jealousy that flowed through my veins. "What does she look like?"

"She's gorgeous."

"Not helpful." The crease between my brows deepened.

"Long blonde hair. Curvy, even behind the loose-fitting yellow dress. And he just said something to her to make her laugh."

My hand balled into a tight fist as I punched the soft couch cushion.

"She just hooked her arm through the crook of his and..."

"And what?" My hands trembled.

"They're getting into a car."

"Alex! Follow them." I stood and began pacing across the floor of my living room. "Whatever you do, don't lose them. I need to know where they go."

"Okay, I'm on it." I heard her switch over to speaker. "Can you still hear me?"

"Talk louder." She tested the line again. "Much better."

"Who do you think she is?" Alex asked once she'd started driving.

"I don't know, his sister?" Sarcasm laced my words. Her guess was as good as mine.

"With our luck, it would be his daughter."

Alex snickered, thinking back to the time we spied on Nash, catching his daughter kissing him on his cheek. We'd overreacted then and I could only pray that we were doing the same now.

Alex announced the cross streets of every turn she made. Her descriptions created a good visual for me to follow inside my own head but, still, I wanted to see it with my own eyes.

"You must have seen this coming," Alex murmured. "Otherwise you wouldn't have asked me to spy."

"Where are you?"

"Slowing down. They just turned into—"

"Turned into where?" The line went silent. "Alex!"

"What the heck?" The line crackled.

"Alex, where did they turn into?"

"A cemetery?" Her voice sounded skeptical, like she couldn't believe what she was seeing.

My mind raced to understand why he was at a cemetery and why he would bring a woman Alex described as gorgeous there. Then my head snapped up to my own front door when I heard a knock coming from outside.

"Kelly has his arm over her shoulder. Her head is down." Alex continued the play-by-play. "It looks like she might be crying."

There was another knock on my door. This time a little bit louder. Hurrying to see who was at my door while still listening for what Alex had to say next, I turned the doorknob without thinking and answered it.

"Hey, Kendra." He smiled but it never hit his eyes.

Slowly, I lowered the phone away from my ear. I could hear Alex screaming my name, asking if I was still there, but I couldn't move. I was frozen with big unblinking bug eyes staring directly into the face of my uncle.

"Can I come inside?"

23

Kelly

Pushing through the front glass doors, I stormed into Kendra's building with my blood boiling hot.

"Mr. Black." The doorman approached me.

"Where is she?" I hurried to meet him with furious eyes darting across his face.

"I don't think now is a good time," he said with a slight head shake.

I narrowed my eyes and rubbed my face. "What do you mean? She's home, isn't she?"

Clenching my hands into tiny fists, I watched Mr. Anderson's gaze travel the length of my arm. "I can't let you go upstairs when you're like this."

My nostrils flared as I bore my gaze deeper into his unwavering eyes. He was older and shorter but a hidden strength kept him standing firm. It was admirable but it wasn't going to be enough to stop me from getting what I wanted. "I need to see Kendra."

He held up his hands, showing me his palms. "Like I said, now is not a good time."

I took one step closer, peering down over the man dressed in his silly black suit. "Don't make me regret this."

He nodded, still holding his palms an inch away from my chest. "She has a visitor."

My eyes widened as fury zipped to my extremities. Without hearing anything more, I stepped to the side. Mr. Anderson grabbed me by the arm but I broke free and hurried to the elevator with him threatening to call security. I didn't have to ask who Kendra was with because I already knew. His tone gave it away.

Kendra was with another man.

Stepping in front of the elevator, I repeatedly jabbed the button like it would speed things up. My breath was steaming through my nostrils as I clenched my teeth. Looking down, my hands were still balled in fists and my heart beat fast enough to cause a heart attack.

I didn't know who she was with but just the thought of her being with another man was enough to make my head pop. "C'mon!" I screamed while sending my fist into the metal door a second before they opened.

I pushed the woman stepping out of the car to the side, only to turn and see Mr. Anderson on the phone staring in my direction. He wasn't the kind of man to bluff so I knew my time was limited before security would track me down and kick my ass out.

The journey up to Kendra's floor couldn't have taken longer. Time slowed and there was nothing I could do to make it speed up. I tapped my toes anxiously on the floor, wondering if security would be waiting for me before I had a chance to see who Kendra was with.

I paced.

Rolled my neck.

Cracked my knuckles.

By the time the car slowed to a stop, I flexed my muscles, puffed out my chest, and held my breath, waiting to see what I would be met with once the doors opened.

Peeking my head around the corner, the hall was empty. I sighed.

Marching at a quick clip, I pounded my fist against her door, demanding she open it. "Kendra!" I continued knocking, the force of each blow growing more intense with each second that passed. "Kendra. Open up!"

The door creaked open. "Kelly?"

Her eyes were bright with surprise.

Glancing over her shoulder I could smell the scent of another man.

"I was just about to call you." She opened the door all the way, and without waiting for an invitation I pushed my way inside.

I looked toward the couch. Nothing. Then I hurried to the bathroom. Still nothing. I searched her bedroom and her closet. The man was nowhere to be found.

"What's going on?" She followed me around like a lost puppy. "Is something wrong?"

Making my way back to the front, I saw the flowers I'd sent her and thought back to what I had written in the note.

"They're beautiful." She clasped her hands down in front of her and flashed a weak but appreciative smile. "Thank you."

"Last night," I took a deep breath in, "where did you sleep?"

She furrowed her brows and gave me a questioning look. "Here."

I cocked my head to the side and gave her a look.

"I swear. Kelly," she hugged herself inside her arms, "what's going on?"

"I don't like not hearing from you." I watched her eyes glance over to the note folded on the table next to the bouquet of flowers. She was right, they were beautiful. "Contrary to what I said in that note—" I pointed to the flowers, "—you need to let me know where you're at—at all times."

Silence hung in the air between us and I watched Kendra plant one hand into her hip while the other lifted to rub her forehead. "I see." Then she turned to face me. "How did you get up here, anyway?"

The muscles in my neck tensed.

"Fucking shit, Kelly," Kendra cursed. "If this is the way you're going to treat me, you can't just come up here and expect me not to consider this visit an invasion of my privacy."

My brows raised. "You're supposed to do as you're told."

She jumped, bringing her heels together and standing tall while saluting me. "Yes, sir!"

"It's our arrangement."

"Why didn't you call if you missed me so much?"

I stroked my chin, staring at her out of the corner of my eye. "Huh?"

My head gently shook as I couldn't stop looking at her thick moist lips and the way her tongue slid over them.

"And since you brought it up, maybe I should ask where you were early this afternoon." Her brows raised as she took one step toward me. "Huh? Who were *you* with?"

I pinched my runny nose between my fingers as thoughts of this morning's anguish filled my head. I didn't ask how Kendra knew because I didn't care. My visit to Nora's grave with Kaycee was our affair. Not Kendra's. Those were our memories, our emotions, and if I started talking about it now, I knew that it would cause more unnecessary distress than even I was prepared to handle in this moment.

Turning my back, I rooted my hands into my hips and tipped my chin to the ceiling.

"I should have known," Kendra murmured.

What I couldn't say was how I silently wished for her to have called me this morning so that I could take my mind off the past and concentrate on what made me hopeful for a better tomorrow. "Who was the man you had here?"

When I turned around, Kendra shifted her weight to her opposite leg. Her cheeks blushed with guilt and she looked so damn cute I couldn't stand it.

"Was it your way to get back at me because you're jealous of something you know nothing about?" I asked.

"It's not like that."

"It's not?" I slowly strode toward her, closing the gap between us.

She shook her head. "No," she whispered.

"You're mine." Hooking my finger beneath her jaw, I forced her to look me in the eye. "Say it."

Her beautiful greens danced with mine as her beating pulse ticked in her neck. "I'm yours."

My eyes crinkled from the happiness filling my heart. Her voice was light, soft, and sexy all at the same time. "And I won't allow you to invite other men into your apartment without my knowledge."

Slowly, her hand lifted to my arm. She smoothed it over my bicep before letting her fingers come into contact with my face. Her other hand grazed over each ripple of my abs as she looked up at me beneath her brow. "You can't have it both ways."

I arched a brow.

"If you expect me to be loyal, then I expect the same from you." There was a glimmer of strength in her eyes that got me hard. "There are no double standards here, Counselor."

"The Madam said you're afraid I might have another woman on the side."

Her lips parted.

"Madam tells me everything." I smiled.

Kendra dropped her gaze and flattened her hand on my chest, pushing herself away.

My stomach clenched as I asked, "What was it you were doing with the Madam?"

She moved to the window and stared outside without saying anything for a long minute. Then at last she said, "Madam called me in to see how things were going with me. Checking in with her," she made quotation marks with her fingers, "*investment.*"

My mind swirled with deciding who to believe and who was only telling me half of the story. Kendra was hiding something, I could feel it, but I didn't know what it was. But what I did know was how manipulative the Madam could be when it came to using people. And I refused to allow that to happen to my sweet *Bella*.

Kendra turned around and started cleaning up magazines lying aimlessly around her living room. "Her investment is doing just fine." She flicked her eyes up to me as she plopped the stack directly on top of a pile of manila folders. "In case you're wondering."

"The clothes in your bedroom," I paused to look in that direction, "it looks like you're packing your things."

"I'm leaving here." She moved to the side of the couch and leaned against it with arms folded across her chest. "My cover is blown."

She turned her head away and I watched her eyes scurry over the place she called home with a look on her face that said she wasn't planning to come back. I didn't ask what she meant by her cover being blown but I did care to know where she was planning to go. "Where are you going?"

"Anywhere but here." She lifted her head and met my gaze, adopting a sullen look somewhere along the way.

My brows drew together. "What's wrong?"

Her arms unfolded and she covered her face inside her shaking head.

"Kendra?"

"Stop, Kelly." Her voice was muffled but clear as day. "I'm leaving."

"I don't know what's going on with you, but this shit needs to stop," I barked.

Even from behind her hands, I saw her face twist with pain and she began to cry. As soon as the words were out of my mouth, I regretted it. Whatever was going on wasn't just something that she could wash away.

Closing the gap between us, I wrapped my arms around her trembling body and held her tight—wanting her to know that I was here for her, would always be here for her. And as she cried into my chest, all I could think of was how Madam warned me of Kendra being broken. I'd seen it. But I'd refused to believe she was right.

Until now.

"C'mon. Let's finish packing your things. You're coming with me."

24

Kendra

Sitting in Kelly's passenger seat and staring out the window, it didn't take me long to know where he was taking me. His penthouse was his go-to place when it came to us, and I was perfectly fine with that.

Rolling my head, I glanced at him out of the corner of my eye.

He had one hand on the wheel, his other up by his face, deep in thought.

A tiny smirk lifted my frown, thinking how amazing a man he was. Even though I was beginning to trust Kelly more with each passing day we were together, I was still too afraid to open up to him completely. My story, my past, the reason I felt shattered inside was a story that would make me entirely too vulnerable— even with someone as intelligent and forgiving as Kelly made me believe he was.

Turning my attention back to the world outside, I let my

thoughts continue to roll through the ups and downs of the emotions traveling through me.

The person I'd been this last week wasn't me. I was stronger, happier, and not nearly as fragile as I knew Kelly thought I was. When I thought about how I must look to him, I hated myself for appearing so ugly, despised the way I seemed to constantly be breaking down and crying in front of him like an immature, entitled girl.

Reaching my hand over, I let it come down on his thigh.

Kelly didn't react. He kept his eyes forward, his hand firmly gripping the wheel. He was cold to my touch and that only caused more of the ache I was feeling to twist my gut into a tight knot that kept my body feeling crippled.

Choosing to keep my hand there for as long as he allowed, I thought back to my brief but intense visit with my uncle. He'd snuck past Mr. Anderson, and so had Kelly. Determined to let Mr. Anderson know I wasn't happy about it, I let up on my determined pursuit of justice when Kelly and I finally made it to the lobby and saw security waiting. They didn't have to escort Kelly out, I was already doing it for them. But how did Kelly and my uncle not cross paths?

Squeezing my eyes shut, I shook my head.

It wasn't cool of my uncle to show up uninvited. Up until just an hour ago, my apartment was my place of refuge. I worked so hard to keep it mine, carefully ensuring I kept it a secret from the outside world. And now it was compromised. I wanted to thank Kelly for stealing me away, but I also wanted him to be the first to break the cloud of silence that hovered over us.

I glanced in his direction.

Kelly's face was filled with tension, making his jaw muscle dance.

I loved the flowers he'd sent, appreciated the note he'd written even more. He showed me his cards, let me know that he was jealous of the fact that I had another man visiting. As desperate as it was, I liked that I had that effect on him. It told me that I meant something to him even if I knew he was seeing another woman on the side. "I know you were with a beautiful blonde this morning."

He dropped his free hand and readjusted his grip on the wheel, casting a quick gaze to my knees.

I'd had enough of the silence and needed to get my own jealousy off my chest. His eyes lingered on my knees for a second longer—acting like he was afraid to look me directly in the eye—before lifting them back to the road.

"Did she also know the person in the cemetery you were visiting?" It was a wild speculation on my part—only guessing that Kelly knew the person laid to rest—but by the way his nostrils flared, I was convinced I was on the right track.

Kelly slowed the vehicle and made a sharp right turn.

"You want to know more about me." My body naturally gravitated closer to him. "I can't trust you with my secrets if you can't trust me with yours."

His fingers loosened as he readjusted his grip, curling them back over the wheel, squeezing hard enough to get his knuckles to turn white. The engine revved and he began driving faster.

"That man you were looking for?"

Kelly turned to look me in the eye. His gaze was dark and dangerous and hot enough to send a flutter through my aching heart.

"He was my uncle."

A slight moan escaped his lips as he turned his head to face forward.

Silently, I watched his chest rise and fall through heavy breaths for a couple minutes before I said, "How did you know where to come look for me?"

He tipped his head back as if annoyed by my questioning and licked his lips. "It doesn't matter. What's done is done."

With shaky limbs and a soft pleading voice I asked, "Are we done?"

Tears welled behind my eyes when Kelly didn't respond. His hands didn't move, his eyes unblinking. And if it wasn't for the way he maneuvered his vehicle in smooth, confident swerves around other cars who were driving much slower than us, I would have checked his pulse, making sure he was alive.

"Kelly," I said again, this time reaching over to cup his manhood. "Are we done?"

He clamped his fingers tightly around my wrist and flung my hand away. Angling his head to me, he glared. Determined not to lose the only thing that seemed to be going right in my life, I went for him again. This time he didn't push me away. Slowly, I unzipped him and reached my hand inside his pants, wrapping my fingers around his thick girth. "You can tell me the truth."

His cock hardened more with each stroke of my hand. I pumped him until he groaned.

"You saved me today." My wrist worked up and down his pulsing shaft. "I was coming for you and you came for me."

Kelly slowed the vehicle and pulled into his parking garage, quickly killing the engine once parked in his assigned spot. He unbuckled his belt, leaned over, and threaded his fingers through my hair. Staring into my eyes he said, "I'd do anything for you, *Bella*."

I swallowed hard and blinked away the threat of tears while I continued to stroke his erection. I knew he was angry with me. And rightfully so. I hadn't been as fun a date as I knew I could be —as I knew I should be. He had every reason to want to be done with me. "Kelly, I'm ready."

He looked at me with hard, searching eyes, and it didn't take him long to know what it was I was saying. A glimmer of recognition flashed across his eyes as they hooded over with heavy lids.

His satin flesh was hot and I knew that I had him close.

Stroking him harder I said, "Take me to your playroom. I know you're angry with me. Take your anger out on me."

He fingers curled in my hair. Pulling me close, he panted against my lips, tugging at my roots. My tongue darted out and I closed my eyes, working him harder, faster, finally getting him to come.

Thick ropes of hot semen oozed over my knuckles and I liked the feeling of control I had over him in this moment of weakness. His body convulsed and I milked him for all he had until he softened in my hand.

Asking Kelly to have his way with me—have him take his anger out on me—was my gift to him, but also my way of forgetting that my uncle was here in LA and with him, the family drama that I tried my entire life to escape.

"Tell me what you want," I mewed.

Kelly thrust his tongue into my mouth.

"You can do anything to me." I swirled my tongue over his. "I'm ready. Ready to obey your every demand."

25

Kelly

G lancing over my shoulder, I saw Kendra strapped face-down to the bed and panting into the silk sheets.

My cock twitched at the gorgeous sight. Reaching my hand down, I squeezed my cock stiff, ballooning my head a deep shade of purple. I lingered on her body for another quiet minute, appreciating each soft curve that I adored more than anything, before turning my attention back to the closet.

I tapped my toe on the wood floor, considering which option of punishment she was going to receive. It was important I didn't forget how well she obeyed my every command once we were safely closed inside my penthouse apartment.

She listened when I told her to undress as I watched.

She listened as I told her to tie the scarf over her eyes.

And she nodded when I told her that she should be careful what she asked me to do when I bound her to the four corners of my California king.

Here, my options seemed endless. I could do anything I wanted. All these toys were new, recently purchased, knowing that the time would come when I would be able to use them on my sweet Kendra.

Because a time would come—though maybe not today—a time would come.

I couldn't ignore the severity of what implications might come from the looming decision I was about to make. The stakes were high and I knew that the fate of our relationship rested solely in the palms of my hands.

Stroking my shaft, I shifted my weight to my opposite leg.

Kendra kicked her feet and jerked the chain, causing it to rattle. Turning my head, I could see her pussy wet with desire, yearning for me to relieve the aching pulse working her insides over.

My chest tightened and my core burned.

One wrong move on my part and she would break, go back to that fragile girl that seemed to still be living somewhere deep inside of her. And that was what had me most curious. I wanted to know who that girl was and what her reasons for crying were. There was a reason for it. There always was. And if she couldn't tell me what those reasons were, then maybe I could use sex to get her to talk.

Reaching inside the drawer I pulled out anal beads, knowing that this would get her to open her mouth and tell me what it was that was bothering her.

Hearing the chains rattle behind me, it was like Kendra could hear my thoughts playing out inside my head. Her patience was waning. But learning to wait—biting back the intense desire I knew was burning inside her, too—was a practiced art and I was determined to teach her the skill today.

Stroking the beads between my fingers, I could only imagine the intense, searing burn Kendra would feel as I worked each ball past her very tight muscle.

The chains rattled once again and I knew Kendra's mind was racing to know what exactly I was doing, what I was preparing to bring back to the bed with me. It was all part of my strategy to get her to open up and confess. I'd make her wait before driving her to the edge only to retreat again and again until she was begging me to give her the release her body craved.

Setting the beads back where I found them, I exchanged them for a pair of nipple clamps.

Smirking, I thought how I could attach these to a cock ring and with each thrust they would tug on her nipples and make her sing into submission.

But, then again, I didn't want to push her too far like the last time I caused her to break. No, I had to be careful in my pursuit of complete dominance.

Dropping my chin to my chest I closed my eyes.

Kendra's fragile mind was what was making my decision so damn hard. It didn't matter what she thought I wanted from her. Submission wasn't about breaking a person down. It was about using pain to find intense pleasure, allowing them to discover their own escape. And even though those were the exact things I needed after my morning with Kaycee I knew that when it was over, none of that would satisfy my own needs—at least not until I was certain Kendra could survive the punishment without first completely shattering.

Glancing over my shoulder, my pulse raced out of control.

Pumping my shaft, I turned my head back around and that was when I saw it. It was perfect. There it was, shining in the light as if calling me to tell me this was what Kendra needed—what we both needed.

Extending my arm, I took the dildo into my hands and turned back to Kendra. Two steps later I was raking my splayed fingers over her hot, quivering body. First up her legs, between her soft thighs, up and over her gorgeous firm ass, before reaching around to wedge my hand beneath her stomach.

Kendra sucked in a breath and I grinned at her fluttering belly.

She was angelic. Her pussy lips glistening pink and soft, it took every muscle in my body to control my darkest urges to plunder her goods without remorse. I wanted to be inside her playing, spreading, licking.

God, she was flawless.

Stepping to the head of the bed, I bent down and pressed my lips to her apple-red cheek.

Her lips curled into a smile and I couldn't peel my eyes away from her. She was stunningly beautiful with a youthful inno-cent glow. I felt guilty for being part of the reason it would someday spoil. But her look was also deceiving in who she really was.

The bed crumbled under my weight as I climbed over her and positioned myself between her spread legs. Taking my cock at the base, I placed the head at her slick entrance and squeezed it inside her.

All four chains pulled tight as Kendra adjusted to my thick girth.

Slowly, I began to thrust shallow strokes in and out of her tight cunt that kept me hard and filled with agony. She had so much spunk for a woman who appeared to be innocent.

She arched her back and changed the angle of my penetra-tion despite her limbs being bound to the bed. Only a girl with sexual experience could have made a move like that.

My hips rocked back and forth, circling my hardness against her velvety walls.

No, Kendra wasn't as innocent as she looked.

My hand took a fist full of her fleshy ass and I held on tight as I jabbed into her quickly.

She moaned and mewed, reminding me that I had to leave her before the intensity building inside me grew any hotter. "Remember, don't speak unless asked," I said, pulling out of her.

Her body writhed against the mattress in protest of the sudden loss.

Settling my face against her pussy, I lapped between her folds, knowing that I couldn't go any further without first stealing a quick taste. The sweet nectar of her juices was an immediate reminder of what it was I was fighting for—what kind of lover I was training her to be. She wasn't innocent. Far from it. Innocent souls didn't break down and drift off into space the way she did. Only broken ones did.

When her breath labored, I climbed back up on all fours and lunged myself back inside her. Again, my thrusts were slow to begin, then grew with intensity as I got drunk on the incredible way she felt. There was nothing better than this, than her.

Her pussy squeezed my cock and I lunged hard and deep, holding her hips down firmly to the bed with my weight. And just when I felt myself about to come, I pulled out and climbed off, leaving her body begging me to come back.

Even with her face hiding behind the black blindfold, I knew she wasn't happy to have me quit. But coming inside her wasn't the goal. The mission was to get her to open up and tell me everything—no more secrets, no more deception, only truth.

I set both of her wrists free. First her left, then moving around the bed to do the other. Then I moved to her ankles, flipping her around before spreading her legs and clipping them back to the corner, locking her in place, preventing her from moving. "Remove the blindfold," I said in a deep, husky voice.

She slowly reached up to her face and pulled the scarf back over her head, revealing her eyes. Her gorgeous green gaze traveled the entire length of my naked body. My cock was pulsing, clenching my stomach and painfully hard. I ached to be inside her—losing myself in the pleasure she offered—but there was something else I had in mind.

Reaching to the bed stand behind her, I picked up the vibrating dildo I had taken from the closet and set it down next to her thigh. Without saying a word I backed away, letting my feet fall flat to the floor.

Kendra glanced down at the curved, balled, dildo. "Kelly—"

"Don't talk," I said firmly, taking my cock into my hand.

She nodded, wetting her lips.

"Only listen."

She nodded again and I watched her pulse tick fast in her neck.

"There is something going on with you. I don't know what that is and I refused at first to believe it was true. But now I know." My hand tightened around my shaft. "Maybe I was too blinded by my own desire to be the first to recognize it myself, but until you can let me help you this is how we're going to continue to fulfill our contractual agreement."

"Kelly," her eyes pleaded with me, "I wish I could explain—"

"Don't talk." I held up my hand. "Now's not the time to explain."

Her chest rose and I let my gaze fall to her beaded nipples. I could taste them from memory, knew how much I loved them in my mouth, clamped between my teeth. I wanted to touch her—smooth my hands across every inch of her body—but I knew that the consequences of going any further than I already had were too grave. There was the potential of another fallout, and that was a risk I wasn't willing to take.

She watched me stroke my cock, licking her lips as if she wanted them wrapped around it. "You want to get fucked?" I asked, taking a step closer to her.

She nodded.

My dick twitched at the way she was looking at me—eyes burning with sexual desire. "Then take that dildo and slide it into your wet pussy and show me how much you wish it was me playing in there."

She swallowed hard before glancing at the dildo.

"Take it." I lowered my gaze. "You know you want it." Widening my stance, I started to work myself harder.

As if she didn't want to feel left out, Kendra picked up the dildo and brought the tip of it to her moist entrance, still pulsing from when I was stretching her only moments ago. She wet the tip, then plunged it fully inside her. Her head tipped back as she cried out.

My stomach flexed at the sight. She was so incredibly hot. I knew that I could find my own release at the mere sight of her. Though I'd much prefer her lips wrapped around my cock than my own hand, watching her drive herself higher and higher was doing things to me that I never expected. Slowly guiding my wrist back and forth I asked, "What's our safe word?"

Kendra's head lifted forward, and through heavily seduced lids she spat, "Angel."

"Yes, you are." I began stroking myself again after Kendra flashed me an angry look.

She wouldn't be needing to use it tonight. Not a chance. I just wanted to hear her say it, to make her angry with the thought of the woman she hated interfering with our sex life, coming between us right before I was about to make her climax.

Her lids fluttered closed as she continued to grind herself down over the dildo.

"Tell me, what does it feel like?"

"Not as good as if you were fucking me," she moaned.

Tonight was all for me. I needed to see how she reacted after she got herself off. If she would become the person she was the last couple times we fucked. It was important I knew how she reacted after I attempted to touch her, and how I refused to allow her to touch me. She couldn't break down. I couldn't allow it to happen and I wouldn't give her the orgasm she craved, instead I'd make sure she drove herself to the edge to make certain I wasn't the cause of her torment.

"You're so beautiful. You see how hard you have me?"

Her eyes flickered open. She took a minute to stare at my manhood before she nodded.

"You do this to me. You make me this fucking hard." I squeezed and stroked harder, grinding through gritted teeth. "There is no other woman in my life. You *are* my woman." I groaned and squeezed my eyes tightly shut. "Fuck yourself as hard as I am."

I could hear Kendra working herself harder, pushing herself closer to the edge of no return. Soon, her cries filled the air, and when I knew she was close I shouted, "Now pull it out."

She stopped, and so did I. Our gazes locked, and together we stared into each other's eyes as we both fought to catch our breath. I was teaching her what it meant to be a submissive—my submissive—and she would do as I said.

"Now turn on the vibrator."

She flipped the switch and the quiet buzz of the device filled the room.

"Stick it in your pussy," I paused to lick my lips, "and make yourself come."

She did exactly as I said without protest. This was good. She was good. Because it was important that we established our roles in the relationship we shared sooner rather than later. I didn't only need her to obey when in the bedroom. The rules transferred over to daily life, too. It was important that she understood that.

"Grab your tit and play with it."

Her fingers dug into her soft globe, massaging it through mewling pants. The dildo was slick with her juices and I was incredibly jealous that it wasn't my dick covered in her arousal. Kendra rolled her head and when her abs flexed, I knew she was extremely close.

Working myself harder, not wanting to be left out—she was a reflection of me as much as I was of her—and together we would come.

Her head fell back between her shoulders as she cried.

"Now stop."

Kendra's hand stopped moving between her legs and she flashed me an annoyed look. Understandably so. But it had to be like this.

"Ask me who I was with earlier."

Her brow arched and her lips parted.

"Now fuck yourself." My gaze dropped to her sex.

Kendra took the device inside her once again. "Who was she?"

"Harder!"

She touched the vibrator to her clit and her mouth rounded.

"Harder!"

"Oh, fuck!" she screamed. "Who was the woman you were with?!"

"Now come!"

Kendra's face twisted as she shuddered through her climax. Feeling my own release working its way up I stepped closer to her, and as she was still shaking through her own orgasm I shot my hot semen over her chest and belly, coating her with my mark.

"Who was she, Kelly?"

Shaking my dick over her body, I growled until the last drop. Then I turned around and walked away. "You'll be staying here with me until I say otherwise."

26

Kendra

I heard the shower turn off in the bathroom.

Glancing over my shoulder, my ribs squeezed.

After Kelly refused to tell me who the woman was he was with yesterday morning, I didn't bother asking again. It wasn't worth the fight and since he said that I would be staying with him until further notice, it was enough reassurance to convince me that I was in fact the only woman in his life who truly mattered.

Plopping down on the edge of the bed, I couldn't stop myself from staring at the many photographs of Alex's family. They both haunted me and created a sense of envy, wishing sometimes my family life could have been like hers.

My bottom lip curled and pouted.

I was here to collect my things, pack them up and move them to Kelly's. Not that I had a whole lot here to begin with but enough to want to clean up the mess I'd created since I moved in and occupied the guestroom in Alex's apartment. Besides, Nash was soon to be home and I didn't want to be staying here once he got back. I could only imagine the shenanigans he and Alex were going to get into upon his return.

Dropping my head into my hands, I couldn't stop thinking about my uncle and how I wished I'd never agreed to meet with him later today. But it was the only thing I could say to convince him to leave yesterday. I didn't want him at my apartment, and it already freaked the fuck out of me that he knew *exactly* where I lived.

A dullness spread across my chest.

Light footsteps padded across the hall and when I lifted my head, Alex was leaning her shoulder against the doorframe. She was beautifully wrapped in a bright yellow towel, her hair wet and smelling of fruits and flowers. I watched her eyes travel over my clothes laying in the center of the bed before giving me an arched look.

"Sorry, I should have called. But it was too early and I didn't want to risk waking you."

She smiled and floated across the room before filling the empty spot directly next to me. We leaned into each other, letting our heads come to rest against the other's. "I have another busy day." Alex sighed.

"You don't regret the position, do you?"

She shook her head. "Absolutely not."

We both laughed.

"Nash requested lots of iterations to the current project and I still have a lot more editing that needs to be done."

"He's such a dictator." I smirked.

Alex snickered. "But he's *my* dictator."

"And when does this tyrant come back to rule your castle?"

"Two days." She frowned.

Reaching around the back of her shoulder, I wrapped her up in the best hug I had to give. Closing my eyes, I nodded. "I'm really going to miss this."

Slowly, Alex pulled away and flashed me a questioning look. Then she glanced over her shoulder to my pile of clothes. Reeling in my arms, I ducked my head and stood, turning to face the bed. I couldn't even look her in the eye without the threat of me gushing tears. It wasn't like I wasn't ever going to see her again but that was what it felt like.

"Just leave them," Alex pleaded.

"It's useless," I said, beginning to rip the sheets off the bed. "Once Nash is back in town I won't be staying here anyway."

"It's not like he's coming back tomorrow." Alex scooped my clothes off the bed and tossed them into the suitcase I'd brought with me.

"You and I both know that I'm not going to want to be here when he does return."

Alex glanced up at me and pursed her lips. "Are you all right?"

Diverting my gaze, I knew by the twisted concerned look on her face that she knew I wasn't feeling completely myself. "Yeah, I'm fine." It was a lie but I didn't have it in me to tell her about what was really dragging me down.

"Hey." Alex moved closer and smoothed her hand down my upper arm. "Sit."

I nodded and we sat once again on the edge of the bed. My head hung to my chest the moment I closed my eyes. "You're waddling around, you know that?"

My hands moved to my stomach and I held it as if something inside me was preparing for the sharp pain I felt looming, waiting to strike down upon me any minute. I knew I had to tell her that I was with Kelly last night. It was important she knew. "I stayed at Kelly's last night."

Alex's eyes widened as she turned her head forward. A minute passed where neither one of us said a word. I could only imagine the disappointment she was feeling knowing that she didn't think I should have gone back to Kelly so soon after seeing him with another woman.

"You're mad at me, aren't you?"

She shook her head slowly. "I'm not mad." Her voice was soft, forgiving. "I just thought that maybe you would give it more time until we figured out what was going on is all."

"He gave me flowers." I smiled.

Her brows lifted on her forehead and she nodded once. "Is that right?"

"They were beautiful."

She cast her gaze to the pile of clothes she'd dumped into my suitcase. I knew what it was she was thinking—that Kelly had bought me those, too. And she was right.

"Did you ever figure out what he was doing at the cemetery or the name of the woman he was with?" I asked.

Alex turned her gaze to me and shook her head.

"What about whose grave they were visiting?"

"I don't know," Alex whispered. "Kendra, that's your job. I thought you would have at least asked him."

"I did."

"And?" Alex's voice raised, along with her spine.

"He says I'm his only woman."

"And you believe him?"

Our eyes danced but my words hesitated. "I do."

"Then what is it?" Her brows pinched.

"I didn't get a name because I couldn't find the strength to push him."

"Honey," Alex's forehead wrinkled, "This man is killing your spirit."

"Kelly's not dampening my spirit."

Alex's mouth slackened.

"My uncle showed up." My eyes rounded above my flat-lined lips. "To my apartment."

Her brows drew together and by the look on her face, I knew

that this was news to her. Alex didn't know I had an uncle, let alone an open and active relationship with any member of any part of my family. As far as she was concerned, I was an orphan because that was the family dynamic I self-imposed upon myself in an effort to flee the drama that consumed much of my childhood.

"I didn't realize you had an uncle in LA."

Tipping my head back, I stared at her wall of family photographs. "I don't."

"Judging by your reaction I assume he wasn't invited."

And just like that, I managed to steer her concerns of Kelly away and present her with a much greater personal dilemma. "Just showed up out of the blue," I said, thinking that I saw this coming. Knew it was lurking in the shadows waiting for the opportunity to present itself. When I turned to look her in the eye, I said, "Baby, my family is fucked up."

She bit the inside of her cheek as concern flashed across her eyes.

Standing, I went back to gathering my things, packing them up in preparation for taking them to Kelly's. "I'm meeting with him today. My uncle. I don't know why he's here, now, after all these years, but I can't imagine he'll be sharing any good news with me."

Alex tugged on her towel and glanced at the clock near the bed stand. "I have time for a quick breakfast. Do you want to talk about this over bagels?"

Shaking my head, I said, "I'll take a raincheck. When Kelly learned my uncle was in town he insisted I stay with him until he stated otherwise."

"Shit, Kendra." Alex stood and cocked her head. "I know you're totally gaga over this man, but don't you think that you need to know more about who he is before moving in with him?"

"It's only temporary."

"And so is my offer." Her hands rooted into her hips. "Stay here. Stay with me."

"Look," I took her by the shoulders and smiled, "I'll be fine. I'm supposed to be having lunch with my uncle and have a million other things I need to finish before then."

Alex gave me a hard look. "Promise to call me after your lunch?"

I smiled and nodded. "Pinky-swear."

We hugged.

"Oh, and before I forget," I spun around and started digging through my purse. "Let me give you this back."

Alex stared at the key to her apartment.

I wanted to give it back so I didn't have an easy out if things got tough with Kelly. I wanted my relationship with him to work and with my apartment compromised and knowing Alex's place wasn't an option, I knew deep down that I would try harder to make things work with Kelly.

Shaking her head, she lowered my hand and clasped my fingers over the thin piece of jagged metal. "Keep it. As long as we're friends, you'll always have a place to stay in my house."

27

Kelly

L eaning back in my office chair I blew out a heavy, controlled breath, feeling deflated.

Despite the stresses of the job staring me down from my desk, I couldn't stop thinking about Kendra. I wondered if she'd slept at all or if she just laid awake the entire night staring up at the ceiling. She tossed and turned and was rolling out of bed way before first light. I couldn't let her leave without making sure she understood that I meant what I'd said.

Closing my eyes I could still see her tense face, reluctant to agree to my latest demand.

Kendra would stay with me, living at my penthouse apartment, until further notice.

This wasn't a game. She didn't have a choice.

And she knew it.

There wasn't a reason to fight me on this because in the end she would lose. I left no room for discussion. It was just something that I needed her to do until we worked through whatever the hell was tearing her apart inside.

Spinning my desk chair around my eyes opened and I stared out the window, watching the palm leaves blow with the breeze.

It pained me to know that she was hurting and that she didn't ask me to help. I wanted to help. Even if I might be the cause of the anguish she was fighting, it had to be me to help her recover. That was what I'd agreed to—the commitment I'd made the moment she signed my contract.

Dropping my head into my hand I pinched the bridge of my nose, thinking back to how I demanded she make herself come.

I feared she would lose control of her emotions afterward once the sweat dried and the labored breathing calmed. But she never did. Though choosing to remain quiet, she never curled back inside herself like the times before that kept me on edge, waiting to see another relapse. And that was something to smile about. Because if I was the cause of her trigger, I didn't know how we could go on and make this thing we had work.

But it wasn't me. It was something else.

Lifting my gaze back outside, I wondered how things were going. The searing kiss I left her with early this morning still tingled on the tip of my tongue and left my lips feeling numb. There wasn't any way she was leaving without me first making sure she wouldn't forget who cared about her most. I was carving my place in her life, and it was important she knew that I was serious about her.

But that didn't come without first setting up a couple necessary precautions. That was why I had Maxwell be her driver, be the one to look after her. Kendra was my prized possession. And past all the filth of my job, I had only her to fall back on.

I let my desk phone ring twice before spinning around to pick it up. "Kelly Black."

"Kelly, its Mike, from the gym."

Mike Ricci was my personal trainer and the man I'd first called when arriving at the office early this morning. "Thanks for returning my call."

"Of course. What's up?"

"I have a friend who I'd like you to start working with."

"Great. What can you tell me?"

"She's a woman I just started dating—"

"You want me to tone her up? I can do that." He laughed.

"Yes. But more importantly, she is dealing with lots of stress and I know you can put her through a program to help her relax a bit."

"I know just the plan," he confirmed without hesitation. "My schedule is flexible for you, Kelly. You know that. Just send her over or have her call me and I'll get to work on her."

"Thanks, Mike."

"Anything for you."

"She's important to me so, please, treat her with care."

"Goes without saying."

Hanging up the phone my lips tugged at the corners, knowing the kind of magic Mike was sure to create. Between his workout regimen and me continuing to ease Kendra into a more submissive role, it was only a matter of time before she'd relax and realize that as long as she was with me there wasn't anything to worry about.

Glancing at the clock I saw that it was almost eight. Giselle would be arriving any minute.

Maria Greer's case file laid open and I started to think more about her; what she was like, how she'd spent her final days, and how Colin should be meeting with Mario now. But beyond Maria and Stone and all my other work, I had to be sure to get this right with Kendra. I couldn't live through another ordeal like the one Kaycee and I just relived.

Reaching out to the far corner of my desk, I took the framed photo of Nora into my hand and brushed the tip of my finger over her happy face.

She had been gone five years and it never got easier. Time continued to pass, but the raw ache of her absence carried on. The memories Kaycee and I shared were there—reliving tales of how the three of us once lived a more carefree life before shit got real. I would never forget, even if somedays I wished I could. Her photo was a simple reminder to not take the good in my life for granted because, without warning, one day it might disappear.

Setting the image of Nora down on the desk in front of me, I wondered how Kendra knew I was with Kaycee. I could only assume that the Madam told her as a way to control our relationship from the sidelines.

I heard the front doors open, and soon after Giselle was dropping her things behind her desk. "Morning, Giselle," I called.

She peeked her head into my office. "Hey, Kelly."

"How are things at home?"

She cast her gaze to the floor and frowned. "Not good."

The way her shoulders drooped reminded me of Kendra. "If there's anything I can do to help you'd let me know, wouldn't you?"

Her eyes flicked up to me as she nodded. "Yes."

It seemed like we were both battling our own relationship troubles. Though neither of us would admit how much it truly bothered us—for fear of it interfering with our work—the fact remained. We both had an important decision to make and, with it, we were deciding between having a career or being with the one we loved.

"You miss her, don't you?" Giselle's eyes were locked on the photo of Nora.

"More than anything." I stared at the image and swallowed down the stone that had formed. "Love isn't easy," I glanced up at Giselle, "nor is it easy to find."

"No," she folded her arms over her chest and leaned her shoulder against the doorframe, "it's not."

I kept my eyes on Nora when I shared a story from my past. "She didn't like all the hours I put in, and, truth be told," I lifted my gaze up to Giselle, "even after what she did to me, I deeply regret not stepping away while we still had a chance."

Giselle's eyes rounded and watered.

"Don't lose John. If he's worth fighting for, do whatever it takes to make him stay."

She blinked and a tear fell from the corner of her eye when she nodded. "I love what I do, Kelly."

"I know you do," I said solemnly.

"You can't do it alone. I won't let you." She laughed, wiping her cheek dry.

I chuckled, appreciating her loyalty to the practice, but her response made me question if she hadn't already given up on him.

"I better get that," she said when her desk phone started ringing.

I clasped my hands together and rested my elbows on my desk. Keeping one ear on her conversation, I thought about what she said and I wondered if we'd both die alone. This business was demanding, brutal, and unforgiving in its constant demands. It would put a strain on anybody's personal life and had ruined many marriages along the way. I could only hope that Giselle wouldn't follow in my own footsteps—having to live with regrets every day.

I angled my head when I heard the urgency grow in Giselle's voice. Something had happened. "I'll transfer you to, Kelly," she said.

Giselle peeked her head in my office just as I was placing the receiver over my ear. "This is Kelly."

"Kelly, it's Colin. I'm afraid I have some bad news."

I swallowed with pinched brows.

"Mario refused my counsel."

My eyelids closed as I hung my head, wondering what we were going to do now.

"He wants to go this alone."

28

Kendra

It was awkward sitting at the same table as him.

He kept one eye on me and I couldn't look at him without wanting to duck my head.

I'd dragged me feet when coming here. Hundreds of possible excuses played out inside my head on my journey downtown. But like everything else, it wouldn't go away without first confronting it.

"They're supposed to have the best burgers in town." My uncle's voice was much softer than I remembered from my childhood.

I glared at him out of the corner of my eye before lifting my iced tea and curling my lips over the rim. The cool drink moved over my tongue but did nothing to settle my uncomfortably dry throat. Setting my glass down, I picked up the menu to decide what I wanted to eat. After a quick browse, nothing sounded good. "The Tower Tavern has the best burgers." I folded the menu and set it off to the side. "Not this place."

"Then I guess I should have done my homework." He lifted his gaze up off the menu he was reading and snickered. But I didn't find it amusing.

When I knew he wasn't looking, I took a minute to study the clothes he was wearing. He was dressed in a maroon button-down with an open collar. It wasn't tucked into his blue jeans, and his leather shoes could use a quick polish. But other than those minor infractions, he presented himself better than I would have thought.

"Not funny?" His smiled touched the corners of his eyes.

Rolling my eyes, I refused to play into his hand.

My uncle was a large man and in his prime, had muscles to prove it. Though he wasn't the same youthful man I remembered. His muscles that once stretched his shirts were now replaced by soft fat. He still had a shaved head, though I imagined that his jet-black hair—the same color as my own—would be salt and pepper now if he ever let it grow out.

"It's in Beverly Hills. You probably didn't even think to look past the city." I rolled my eyes and turned my head away, annoyed by my having to be here. "Look," I turned back to find his amber brown eyes waiting, "I know you've been in town for a while."

Setting down his own menu, he lowered his gaze and nodded.

This time it was my turn to stare into his face without the fear of him looking back. His facial features reminded me of my grandfather, his lips and ears the same as his sister—my mother. "If you knew I lived here, why didn't you come to me sooner?"

Glancing up at me from under his brow, I knew he was taking his time, choosing his words slowly. Resting one hand on top of the other, he sighed. "It's been so long. I just wanted to make sure that the woman I was seeing," he turned his head away, breaking eye contact, "was actually you."

I leaned back into my booth, casting my gaze down at my fumbling fingers. "And now that you found me?"

He grinned hard enough to deepen his dimples. "It's you."

"No shit," I mumbled under my breath.

The waitress came to take our orders. My uncle insisted that I order first. Not sure I was even hungry anymore, I ordered a regular cheeseburger with a side of fries. And as my uncle ordered his bacon cheeseburger, I felt sick to my stomach as I watched him be so kind to the woman—like he was free from the guilt I knew he should be feeling.

As soon as it was just us, he turned his attention back to me. "Your mom has been asking about you."

Scratching my forearm with my nails, I let my gaze travel from table to table, looking for my way out. "Is that your reason for being here?" I turned to meet his wide gaze.

"They miss you, Kendra." He leaned forward and lowered his voice. "You have no idea the kind of anguish you have put them through."

My eyelids hooded as I fought back the urge to scream in his face. It was difficult for me to believe the bullshit he was feeding me. If my parents really missed me they would have come themselves. "Did they send you to come find me?"

His forehead twisted as his eyes pleaded with me to calm down. My blood boiled and my heart pumped the anger I was feeling through my entire body, spreading the fire threatening to explode on him. After what my parents did to me, they were the last people I wanted to see.

He turned his eyes to the same tables I was just looking at. Then he rolled his neck back to me and said, "I live here now."

My eyes widened as I openly stared at him. He was serious. He lived here. In LA. The city I called home. How long? And why was I was just learning this? So many questions raced through my brain, it only scrambled the confusion I was already experiencing. This couldn't be; was he serious?

He nodded as if seeing my own disbelief spread over my face.

My chin tucked back into my neck and I shook my head, feeling my last breath of air catch in my throat. Recoiling back inside myself, my brows pinched and my heart beat erratically as I thought that not only did he know where I lived but, now we both lived in the same city. LA wasn't big enough for the two of us —let alone just me.

"Kendra." He reached out and went for my hand, balled on top of the table in a tight fist.

Pulling it back before he could touch me, I held both my hands against my pounding heart. The diamond ring Kelly gave me caught the light and sent rainbow prisms scattering across the nearest wall. It was strangely beautiful despite the betrayal I was feeling inside.

I watched my uncle stare at the kaleidoscope of colors dancing over the wall before turning back to settle his eyes on the ring. "Someone special give that to you?"

I dropped my hands, hiding them beneath the table. I didn't want to discuss Kelly, or anything about my personal life for that matter. He didn't deserve to know—at least not until I understood what it was he was truly after.

Then his gaze moved to my neck.

This time it was the black diamond white gold necklace his eyes were after.

Feeling exposed, I lifted my hand to touch the necklace. But it was a mistake. I failed to remember that I was also wearing a family heirloom bracelet on that wrist. One given to me by my grandmother—his mother—and something I knew he would most certainly recognize.

"Well, regardless of who gave that to you," he leaned back but kept his forearms on top of the table, "it looks like you're doing well."

Glancing down my front, I regretted not dressing more

conservatively. Though I was wearing clothes that I would have worn any day of the week, my open shoulder collared shirt wasn't enough to keep him from making me feel uncomfortable.

"What do you do for work?" His eyes were warmer now that they had traveled over every inch of my body.

Looking around, I knew that I was safe. We were in public and there were too many other people around for him to do anything. Yet I still closed the top button of my shirt, wondering if he even knew I'd gone to law school. "If it's money you're after you can go look somewhere else."

His lips were wrapped around his straw when I said it, but as soon as he swallowed down his drink he began laughing. "That's not why I'm here." He wagged his finger at me. "Though, with our family history, I could see why you would think that."

My body tensed as my mouth curled with distaste.

He continued to laugh, each one getting louder than the last.

Pulling my cell phone free from my clutch, I checked the time and said, "You know what, I'm busy, and can't stop my life when you just show up out of the blue like this."

He leaned back with a rosy face and wide grin.

Gathering my things, I scooted out from behind the table and said, "Don't worry about lunch. I'll pay for it on my way out."

His cold hand clamped around my elbow, catching me before I got too far way.

The room spun as I stared into his beady eyes.

A glass fell from a table behind me and shattered when it hit the floor.

My feet jumped off the floor as my heart lurched up my throat.

Time all but stopped.

My heart pounded.

I tried to jerk my arm free but his grip only tightened. "Let me go," I said through a clenched jaw. Black spots began filling my eyes. I felt claustrophobic, like I couldn't breathe. Panic started to settle in and just as I was about to scream for help, he let go of my arm.

"It's your parents," he said sharply. "That's the reason why I'm here. Kendra," his brow wrinkled, "they're in trouble."

29

Kelly

"Fuck!" I tossed the stack of papers I was reading on Stone against the far wall.

Giselle came hurrying inside. We both shared a look of concern.

"I'm all right." I held up a hand. "I can't think straight."

Giselle followed my gaze to the papers scattered over the floor. "Let me help, Kelly."

Rubbing the back of my neck, I was left with scrambling to find a solution. Mario's decision to refuse Colin's counsel threw me for a loop. I hadn't seen that one coming. I needed to get Mario to listen, to recognize that Colin was the lawyer who would get him off.

Giselle knelt on the floor and picked up a paper on Stone, beginning to read it.

"I have the rough draft already written."

Giselle gathered the rest of the papers and stacked them into a neat pile before standing. She didn't look at me, only stepped to my desk, setting the stack she had gathered on the corner. "Let me handle this," she said, plucking my request to represent Stone off the top.

"I can't represent them both." I blew out a heavy breath of frustration. "This was our plan, the plan we all needed," I murmured.

Giselle finished reading what I had written and when she looked up, she fixed her eyes on me. "We'll work through this."

I held her gaze. "What is Mario thinking?"

Her eyes widened as she sucked in a deep breath. "He's confused. Probably feels betrayed by us." The power in her voice lost steam. "What we did," she flicked her gaze back to mine, "walking out on him after earning his trust, it wasn't cool, Kelly."

I wished it hadn't happened like that either. "Did I make a mistake?"

She shook her head. "There is only one way to go, and that's forward."

I inched my way to the edge of my desk and plopped enough of my bottom down to sit comfortably on its edge. "It was the only way if we're going to represent Stone."

"I know," she said solemnly, just as my desk phone started ringing. "I'll finish writing this up," she held up my request to represent Stone, "and after reading it, Stone will be begging for you to represent him." She winked.

I mouthed a quick *thank you* and answered my phone. "This is Kelly Black."

"Today was the day your friend was meeting with Mario, wasn't it?" Wes asked.

"It was." I closed my eyes, not looking forward to explaining this one to Wes.

"Have you heard anything?"

Convinced I could fix this, I said, "Still waiting to hear."

I knew Wes was afraid Colin wasn't the right person to handle the job. I couldn't tell him what I knew without talking to Mario first.

"Hit me on my cell," Wes said without any kind of emotion attached to his words. "I'll be waiting to receive a confirmation."

The moment I hung up the phone I pressed my hands flat on the desk, closed my eyes and hung my head. If Mario wasn't testing us, then I had a solution to scare him into accepting Colin's services. It was our last shot and I had to give it everything I had.

Shoving a hand through my hair I gathered my things, tossing my jacket over my shoulder, and passed Giselle's desk saying, "Get that request written up and deliver it when you're finished."

"Where are you going?" Giselle asked as she stood.

"To visit Mario." I stopped in my tracks and turned to face Giselle head-on. "He and I need to have a talk."

30

Kelly

Pacing the visiting room, I wondered what was taking so long. I knew my visit was unannounced but it shouldn't have taken them this long to fulfill my request.

"Hey, have you forgotten about me?" I asked the guard.

Slowly, he turned his head and flashed me an annoyed look. "They're working on it."

"Fuck." I flicked my wrist to check the time. The minutes were ticking away and I was stuck with having to wait. Not wanting to waste another second, I moved to the seat behind the table and began working through a possible Plan B.

My toes tapped.

My fingers drummed.

And I was still convinced that Mario was innocent. Together, Colin and I could win this case for him. I knew it. Mario would be a free man and washed clean of the guilt that was hanging over the head of Maria's true killer.

Turning my head, my mind soon drifted back to Blake Stone. After writing up the proposal to request him as a client, my only hope was that he would accept my counsel. After that, it would be all hands on deck. But, first, I needed to know what Mario knew about Stone and if it was as big as I needed it to be.

My knee bounced and I couldn't sit still.

The longer this went on, the less I liked the plan we were pursuing. The weight on my shoulders only grew heavier with each new agenda that got placed on the table. I wanted Stone put away as much as anybody, but I was having doubts that Madam's plan to get him convicted was worth sacrificing my own reputation for. Though with what she had on me, I also knew that she wouldn't let me walk away without a fight.

Hanging my head, I rubbed my brow, working to release the tension mounting as best I could. The door finally squeaked open and my head snapped up to find Oscar Buchanan standing there with a smug smirk crossing his face.

"Why is it that whenever you're in the building, it just feels colder?" He flashed me a questioning look.

Ignoring him completely, I glanced at my watch again.

Oscar's shoes clacked against the floor as he circled around me. "Why does it seem like you haven't got anything better to do than annoy the fuck out of me?" He peered down at me with hands stuffed into his pockets and laughed. "How is she?"

"Ahh." I nodded. "Still bitter about me stealing Kendra away from you?"

His eyes narrowed as he grinned. "I've moved on."

"Then why'd you ask?"

"Curtesy between colleagues."

"Then I guess I should ask you how Angel is."

He bit his bottom lip and grinned.

"Divorce is treating you well." I gathered the paperwork I had been working on and closed my notepad.

"Can't say I didn't know it would." He tucked the folders he was carrying under his arm and moved to the window.

"I know she's not Madam's girl." I stared at the back of his skull but he didn't move. "Should I ask where she came from, or would you prefer I guess?"

Slowly, he angled his body to face me.

Locking eyes, I said, "No. I didn't know you had it in you but you do, you sick son of a bitch." I laughed.

His brow arched.

"Paying for sex." I dropped my voice and covered my mouth.

He tipped his head back and I watched his face redden.

"I'd hate for the media to get a hold of that story."

He dropped his head and chuckled as he strode back to the table. "Careful, Kelly." He looked up at me from under his brow. "Don't think that I don't know how you've helped arrange Madam's business to skirt the law."

The muscles in my legs tensed at hearing his threat. "Then you shouldn't forget that we have records of you doing business with Madam." Pushing back, I stood to meet him at eye-level. "And despite how it sometimes may seem, we both want what's best for our city. Isn't that right?"

His eyes danced with mine for a minute. The air between us hung in suspense before he finally backed down. "I hope you're right," Oscar pulled the folder out from under his arm and tossed it down in front of me, "because I don't think that Timothy Parker would say the same."

Flashbacks of the night I kicked Timothy's ass in a jealous rage came rushing back as I opened the folder and began fingering through the images Oscar just tossed my way.

"Is the stress of Mario's case getting to you?"

Without taking my eyes off the images, I asked, "Where did you get these?"

He snorted. "I'm the fucking district attorney."

My mind raced to understand why he was bothering to show me, and worse, what he planned to do with them.

"I can only imagine what will happen next if Stone *actually* allows you to represent him."

Pinching the corner of one particular image, I lifted it and brought it in for a closer look. Timothy was pointing at me, yelling something as I lead Kendra away. The look on her face said it all—she wanted me to fight for her and prove that I had it bad for her. Which I did.

"It seems as if Kendra is a free-spirit that can't be tamed." Oscar's voice was filled with arrogance as he moved to the exit. After opening the door, he paused and glanced at me over his shoulder. "Anyway, the real reason I'm here is to tell you that Mario has refused to meet with you."

My head snapped up.

"Give up, Kelly." He smiled. "Accept that you've lost and move on. You're wasting your time."

31

Kelly

A s soon as I collected my items from security, my cell phone
started to ring.

"Sorry to bother you, sir." Maxwell's even tone filled my ear.

"Not a bother, Maxwell," I said, stepping outside, heading in
the direction of my car. "I'm just leaving County now.
What's up?"

"I'm afraid the reason I'm calling is because I don't have
good news."

My heels dug in, my legs coming to a sudden stop. "What
is it?"

"It's Kendra, sir."

I lifted my head and looked around with pinched brows.
"What happened?"

"Well, there's no good way to say this..."

"Just say it," I barked.

"She ditched me, sir."

I clutched my phone into a white-knuckle grip and gritted my teeth.

How could he let this happen? And what kind of games was she playing? Maxwell was there to get her around the city safely. That was it. My assigned protector in a city that seemed to be tormenting her.

"Where are you now?" Hurrying to my vehicle, I unlocked the door and slid behind the wheel.

My mind raced, wondering if Kendra was purposely adding to my already high level of stress, or if this was a cry for help—a way to get my attention. She could be so infuriating at times, and chasing her down was the last thing I needed to do with my already full plate. But it had to be done. I needed to know why she ditched Maxwell, and for what.

"I managed to follow her across town," Maxwell interjected.

"Where, Maxwell?" I cranked the engine over and put it in gear. "Tell me where you are, dammit!"

"I think you were right, sir," he mumbled.

Confusion pounded in my temples.

"I brought her to visit her friend, Alex. Then, as I was parked outside waiting for her return, I saw her leave the building and get into another car." He sighed. "It all happened so fast. There was nothing I could do."

"Maxwell," I inhaled a deep, calming breath, "tell me where you are."

Maxwell told me the cross-streets and the name of the burger joint Kendra was now at before stealing my attention by saying, "Kelly, she's with a man."

My heart paused for a beat as I looked up and peered over my steering wheel. "A man?"

"Yes."

My mind swirled to try to figure out who the man might be and what it was she was trying to hide from me. "What's he look like?"

"Big. Casually dressed. Bald."

I got the point. "Are you inside?"

"No, sir."

Pulling the rearview mirror down, I needed to get a good look at myself, wondering if I looked as bad as I felt. My head pounded and I could see the dark circles forming beneath my eyes. After what Oscar just pulled in the visitor room with images of Timothy Parker getting his ass handed to him, I worried that maybe this was Kendra's way to get back at me after she learned that I had been secretly spending my time with Kaycee.

"Do you still have eyes on her?" I asked after a couple minutes had passed.

"They ordered meals not long ago. Nothing has happened. Just talking."

Taking my foot off the brake, I began heading in the general direction of where Maxwell said he was. "I'm coming for you."

"I'm in the parking lot adjacent to the restaurant."

Pressing my foot down on the gas, I switched over to my Bluetooth connection and kept Maxwell on the line. We didn't say much as I drove but I could still hear shuffling on his end every few seconds.

My conversation with the DA didn't sit well. We had both threatened each other and whenever that happened, I knew the stakes to win were high. Oscar was like me. We would do whatever it took to win. And with that drive came paranoia—silently wondering who I could trust and who was deceiving me into thinking they were my friend.

"I'm two minutes out," I said.

"They're still here."

Slowing around the corner, I dropped a gear and sped up.

"On second thought..."

I glanced at my phone's screen, holding my breath.

"She's getting up to leave."

My foot pressed harder on the gas. I couldn't let her leave without me getting to her first.

"Oh, shit."

The crease between my brow deepened and I knew something big just happened. Maxwell rarely cursed. "Maxwell, talk to me." I jerked the wheel and passed the vehicle in front of me. "Tell me what's happening."

"He just grabbed her arm."

My heart slammed against my chest, the vein in my neck ticking.

Whoever Kendra was with I promised to strangle myself. No one laid a hand on her but me. She was my woman and I'd do anything to protect her.

Turning on to the street restaurant's street, I knew I couldn't be too far. I craned my neck, searching for an address. Back and forth my head went, looking for the name of the restaurant but it wasn't anywhere to be found.

"Kelly, she's leaving. Where are you?"

"I'm close." My head whipped back and forth, my eyes searching.

"No way." I heard Maxwell's engine start. "Not again."

"What is it?"

"She just got into a car."

Frantically, I weaved through traffic, knowing that if I didn't get there soon I might not see who the hell she was meeting with. "What color is the car?"

"You're too late." Maxwell's voice deflated.

"Follow her!" I slammed my hand down on the wheel. "And don't you fucking lose her this time."

32

Kendra

I reached for my phone with shaking hands.

Putting it to my ear, I listened to it ring several times on the other end before going to voicemail. "Alex, baby. You're probably working but I just met with my uncle. Call me back, ASAP. We need to talk."

Ending the call, I turned my focus outside. Peering out the window, deep inside I knew that it wasn't good to have my uncle come back into my life. Nothing good could come of it. And I doubted that my parents were in any kind of *real* trouble, rather it was just a way for him to get my attention—which he did. Mission accomplished.

Sinking further back into my seat, I dropped my head and pinched my brow, fighting back the tears I felt swelling behind my lids.

I hadn't spoken with Mom and Dad in what felt like forever. Once I was awarded my grandparents' inheritance, we all kind of went our own ways. It was for the best. Though despite their resentment for my unwillingness to share any of the money with them, I was certain that was the reason my uncle was also here. He wanted a piece of the pie—a slice he felt he obviously deserved.

Hugging myself, I rubbed my arms in an attempt to smooth down the goosebumps covering my skin. I still couldn't believe my uncle grabbed my arm the way he did. The feeling of his hand on my arm left my hairs standing on end. My entire body shivered knowing that he now lived in LA. I didn't know for how long he'd been here and that made me nauseous, unsure of how much of my life—and in what detail—he knew about.

Lifting my head, I found the driver with both his hands on the wheel staring ahead.

"Hey, do you know Lucky?" I asked.

He glanced at me, and with the rearview mirror framing his eyes he shook his head. "Sorry. Does he also drive for Uber?"

"Yeah," I breathed out.

Wishing it was Lucky driving me, I turned to look out the window, knowing that he would have found a clever way to lighten my mood. I guess I couldn't have it all. I should be thankful that I managed to hide my request for a lift from my uncle without him seeing. I hadn't planned it and hadn't thought I'd have to leave so suddenly, but once I saw his eyes go from worry about how our reunion would play out to sparkling with an all too familiar dangerous confidence, I knew that I shouldn't have ever agreed to meet with him.

I sighed and glanced at my phone.

Praying for Alex to return my call, I didn't know where I was going or where I would end up. All I knew was that I didn't want to be alone. And because of that, I was left with very few options. I couldn't go to Alex's or back to my apartment. Both places I would be by myself but, more importantly, my place would be the first destination my uncle would seek if he had the urge to come after me. He wasn't going to like me leaving without learning what kind of trouble he said my parents were in. It was only a matter of time before we met again.

My cell vibrated and I glanced down at my lap to see who the incoming call was from. The corners of my lips curled upward and my insides danced when I saw that it was the one person I had hoped to be hearing from. "Hey, baby."

"Hey."

Just hearing Alex's voice dropped my shoulders. Relief washed over me, knowing that as long as I could speak with her I was safe.

"How did lunch with your uncle go?"

I exhaled heavily before answering. "Not great."

"I'm sorry."

I knew by her tone that Alex was frowning. "He lives in LA."

"Are you kidding?" Her voice screeched in surprise.

"I wish I was. But, you know what? I'm not that surprised. I knew he did, I just refused to believe it."

"What are you talking about?" Alex spat. "You knew he was in LA?"

"Yeah." My lids fell as I sighed.

"For how long? And why is he just reaching out to you now?"

Flicking my lids open, I glanced outside but was blind to what was actually in front of me. "He said my parents were asking about me," I paused to wet my lips, "and that they're in trouble."

I could hear Alex's fingers tapping away on her keyboard as we talked. "Trouble, like how?"

Touching my arm with my free hand I could feel the bruise forming from where my uncle's fingers had dug into me. "I don't know."

"He didn't say?"

"I didn't stick around to hear him out." The line went silent and I knew that Alex had put her work on pause to consider my decision not to hear my uncle out. "He's not here for my parents."

"I wish I could understand," she said in a soothing tone.

"Trust me, you don't. These people aren't the family you have." I felt the muscles in my face tighten as my body heated with anger. "My uncle was here for himself. Just like everyone else in my family, he's looking for the easy route—"

"Easy route to what?"

Looking at the bracelet my grandmother had given me, I said, "To next month's paycheck."

"Really? I mean, I don't know much about that money you received in the inheritance other than you have a lot of it, but I thought that was settled a long time ago."

Leaning forward, I tapped the driver on the shoulder motioned for him to pull over at the next corner. He nodded as I fell back into my corner. "It's never finished with my family when it comes to money," I said in a harsh tone filled with resentment.

The vehicle slowed before pulling over. Once it was stopped, I stepped out and glanced over my shoulder. An underlying fear knotted my belly into thinking that my uncle had followed me and would want to pick up the conversation where we'd left off. Because that was my family—never seeming to let go of things.

"Kendra, baby, I know you don't want to, but have you considered that maybe he's actually telling you the truth?"

My eyes rolled. I knew Alex was only trying to talk some sense into me, but she wouldn't understand. Even with her parents dead, her family troubles were so much different than my own. Even the family members she had left—and was still in contact with—were solid individuals. Mine, not so much.

"My parents deserve to burn in hell," I murmured as I gave a hard glance over my shoulder. "Along with my uncle for what they all did to me." I swallowed hard, still unable to wrap my head around how none of them did a damn thing to stop any of it from happening. I knew they knew. What they did to me was unthinkable. And no little girl should have had to experience the nightmares that I had to go through.

"Well, that's a bit harsh, don't you think?"

"You don't know them the way I do," I said, pushing open the front doors of a small boutique and stepping inside.

The lady standing by the front counter smiled. I acknowledged her and began browsing the many racks of clothes. My skin was still sensitive to the touch and my conversation with Alex was having the opposite effect as I had hoped. Instead of making me feel better, it only made me feel worse. And with it, all my suppressed emotions threatened to surface with just one wrong word.

"I better let you get back to work," I mumbled.

Alex was reluctant to end our call but I knew she had a desk full of work that needed attending to. "Talk to you later," she said, ending our conversation just as I was pulling a cute blouse off the rack.

I couldn't stop myself from thinking that the woman I was today was because of me leaving the family bullshit behind. I didn't know why my grandparents chose me for the inheritance over the others. I didn't ask for it and they didn't tell me it was coming before they were both gone. Maybe they saw something in me that wasn't seen in anybody else. It wasn't like I was the only one they could have singled out. My family was large, yet for some reason I was the chosen one.

Checking the price tag, the blouse was more than I wanted to spend.

Who knew where I would have ended up without my grandparents' money. The inheritance paid for my schooling, allowed me to get out with a degree debt free, and opened up opportunities I wouldn't have otherwise had. I wasn't entirely convinced that any member of my family knew any of that about me but, if they did, I could see how they could be jealous of what I'd worked so hard to achieve.

Slowly, my feet scooted across the floor as I continued browsing the clothes I wished I had but didn't.

I could only imagine how quickly the money would have disappeared—spending it on worthless shit—if my uncle would have gotten his hands on it.

I trailed my fingers over the assorted colors of cotton and thought how his assumption that any of the money was even left over was a rather bold one to make. Maybe he was just hopeful there was. And as far as my parents were concerned, I wasn't going to completely disregard the fact that they very well might be in trouble. Anything was possible. I just didn't want to hear it from him.

I stepped forward and was quickly jerked back when I felt several strong fingers wrap around my elbow.

The hold slowly tightened as my heart raced with fear.

Terror widened my eyes as I snapped around, ready to fight him off.

But as soon as the flat of my hand came into contact with a solid, muscular chest, I blinked and was wrapped into familiar arms. "Jesus, Kelly, what are you doing sneaking up on me like that?"

His hand smoothed over the back of my skull as he kissed the top of my head.

My arms snaked around his waist and I held him tight, closing my eyes, taking a minute to soak it all in. When I finally pulled away, I found myself smiling at his tussled hair. His dark eyes matched his stealth black suit and danced with mine for a silent moment before he said, "You had Maxwell worried."

His dark gaze raked over me and caused my nipples to harden. "I'm a big girl. I can take care of myself."

"Courtesy goes a long way, you know."

His husky deep voice was reassuring as it warmed my insides from the cold fear of having my family know exactly where I was and what I was doing. I could listen to Kelly all day long.

Taking his hand inside of mine I asked, "How did you know where to find me?"

Threading his fingers through mine, he turned me around and led me swiftly through the racks of clothes until we found ourselves standing outside. "Despite you leaving him, he never left you." Kelly pointed at Maxwell sitting behind the wheel of his tinted windowed black SUV.

I wasn't sure I liked the thought of Maxwell following me throughout the day. From Alex's to my lunch with my uncle, all the way here. Maxwell was there, always one step behind. Fighting down a parched swallow, I was afraid that Kelly would discover my secret before I had a chance to tell him myself. I didn't want that to happen. He had to hear it from me first. "You had him spy on me?"

"You did that to yourself," he said, spinning me around and pushing me into his car.

He opened the door for me and I didn't put up any kind of protest to get inside. As long as I was with Kelly I was untouchable. And even though I wasn't about to admit it, the fact that Maxwell stayed within reach today somehow made me feel better about the dangers that may have been swirling around me.

Kelly glanced at me out of the corner of his eye as soon as he settled in behind the wheel. His head slowly shook and I knew he was disappointed in me. How could he not be? I'd ditched his driver, the one man who would ensure my safety, and tried to sneak off to have a private meeting with someone I didn't want either of them to know more about than what they already did.

"I didn't ditch Maxwell," I said, buckling myself in.

He flashed me an arched look.

Pulling down the mirror, I smoothed out my eyebrows and checked my makeup. "I just didn't want to bother him with having to wait for me."

"That's what I pay him to do." His voice floated through his lips, firm yet sexy.

"Then you must also know that I had lunch with a man." My brows raised.

Kelly didn't respond, only looked on with unwavering eyes and a thin-lipped expression that told me nothing about what he was thinking. He did this often and, still, I didn't know him well enough to be able to read it any better than before.

"Okay, I'll take your silence as a yes. And it's true." I looked away but only for a second. "I had lunch with another man."

His chest expanded and there was a mild nostril flare. But other than that he hid his thoughts well.

"You're pissed. I get it." Reaching over, I settled my hand over his. "But what are you most pissed about?"

He turned his head forward and was clearly thinking how best to respond.

"Me having lunch with another man or me ditching your spying driver?"

Kelly's jaw ticked and I knew I was pressing his buttons. But I wanted him to explode, tell me that I couldn't do what I did today, that I was putting myself in danger and that I shouldn't do anything to jeopardize our relationship. I needed him to say something. I wanted him to tell me all those things but before he had the chance my cell started ringing.

Kelly glanced at my purse but I let it go to voicemail.

Then, when it started ringing again, Kelly demanded I answer it.

"No," I said as strong as I could.

His eyes flickered across my face.

"Not until you tell me what you're most angry about."

The phone continued to ring and we both knew that it would soon go to voicemail if I didn't answer it. I didn't care but he seemed to want me to answer it. "Both," he barked. "I'm angry you did both. Now answer your damn phone," he growled.

Pulling it out, I glanced at the screen.

"Who is it?" His eyes fell to the screen.

In any other circumstance it wasn't any of his damn business who was calling but I knew this one was both our business. "The Madam," I whispered.

"Answer it." He pointed his finger at the phone securely tucked inside my right hand.

I blinked. Still staring at the screen, I said, "I don't want to talk to her."

"Kendra, answer the fucking phone!"

Fire burned in his eyes when I turned to look at him. He wasn't messing around and I dreaded to learn the reason Madam was calling me now. "Fine," I conceded.

Kelly watched me lift the device to my ear with dark eyes, and just as I was about to answer my call with the Madam, he snatched it out of my hand. "You may not want to talk to her, but I do."

33

Kelly

"We have a problem." Kendra's concerned eyes were fixed on mine.

"Kelly, darling, what a surprise." Madam laughed. "It's such a delight to hear your voice when I was expecting Kendra."

"Didn't you hear what I said?" I watched Kendra's hand move to her neck before pinching the skin as she continued to look on with a wrinkled brow.

"I did but you're not the person I want to be talking with." Madam's tone was cordial, always keeping things polite and friendly even in the face of adversity.

Kendra let go of her neck and reached out to take the phone. She mouthed for me to allow her to speak with the Madam, though I refused. "She doesn't want to speak with you."

Kendra's lips parted a second before her eyes went wide. "I do," she whispered.

Covering the microphone, I lowered my voice and said to Kendra, "That's not what you said before."

Kendra tipped her head back and brought her hand to her forehead.

"Then, what is it, Kelly?" Madam sighed.

Keeping my eyes on Kendra's soft features, I didn't want to discuss business matters in front of her. She didn't need to know the ins and outs of what I did, the troubles and stresses I had to deal with, or the complications that came up when I decided to work with the Madam. "I can't tell you over the phone," I muttered. "It's best that we speak in person."

"Oh, sweetie, this sounds important."

"It is."

"Where are you?"

Taking my eyes off Kendra, I said, "Not far."

"Good. Meet me at the office. And please, doll, don't make me sit around and wait."

Killing the call, I tossed Kendra her phone, turned the key, and set the wheels in motion.

Without looking at Kendra I could feel her glaring at me. "What is so important you have to speak to Madam in private?"

My eyes narrowed, and though I didn't show it, inside I was smirking. Kendra rubbed both hands over her thighs and I purposely stayed silent, letting her think the worst.

"Kelly, look," she angled her head in my direction but kept her gaze forward, "I'm sorry I ditched Maxwell. I should have told you where I was going."

Readjusting my grip on the steering wheel, I glared at her.

"You shouldn't worry. I'm completely committed to you."

I flicked my gaze in her direction just before I turned onto the street housing Madam's office.

"The man I was with, it was my uncle, Kelly."

There was a hint of pain in her voice, and the thought of him hurting her caused my muscles to flex. I didn't know who this man was or what it was he wanted, but the fact that Kendra seemed to be hiding that he was making visits with her had me concerned.

I parked the car out front and said, "Gather your things."

Kendra's eyes watered as she looked to me for some kind of response.

"You're coming inside with me."

She leaned forward and set her purse on the floor.

"Bring that with you," I said, pointing to her purse.

"Why? There is nothing inside that I'll need it for."

"Bring it." I jabbed my finger aggressively at the small bag.

She gave me a questioning look and bit her lip.

"You might not be coming back."

34

Kelly

"M r. Black," Janine greeted me as I tapped my knuckles on her desk.

"Things good?"

She nodded and smiled.

"Staying out of trouble?"

"Haven't called you, have I?"

I laughed and turned to find Kendra scowling at her. "Well, aren't you going to say hello?"

"Hey." Kendra waved at Janine.

"The Madam is expecting you." Janine's eyes flickered back to Kendra. "You too."

I closed my fingers around Kendra's arm and towed her up the stairs. She winced. "What's this about, Kelly?"

Stopping at the exact spot we'd first met, I turned to face her. Her beautiful green eyes pleaded with me to tell her what was going on. "You'll find out soon enough."

"Why do I have the feeling that I'm in some kind of trouble?" She breathed hard and her skin was hot against my touch. "Like I did something wrong?"

Raking her gorgeous—and irresistible—body over with my eyes, I thought to myself how I should have seen how difficult she would become. I should have known the problems she would present. But I didn't. And now it might be too late. "Because maybe you did."

She skirted around me and marched up the rest of the stairs. Jerome was waiting outside the office as usual, and as I passed I patted him on his shoulder. "Keep an eye on her, will you?"

Jerome shifted his eyes over to Kendra and nodded.

"I thought you said I was coming with you?" Kendra crossed her arms and cocked out her hip as she pleaded with her eyes to come along.

"I said you're coming inside. Now we're inside and you will stay with Jerome so I can meet with the Madam alone."

Kendra pursed her lips and turned her head away.

Stepping close to Jerome's ear, I whispered, "Don't let her go far."

Jerome agreed as I stepped through the door into Madam's office. I found her sitting behind her desk. She lifted her head when I shut the door behind me. "You're a minute late."

I moved to the wall and took a seat on the small couch. Stretching my arms over the back, I smiled at the Madam. "Kendra stopped me on the stairs up."

"Why did you bring her?" Her eyes blinked quickly.

I flipped my palms to the ceiling and shrugged. "Where should I begin?"

"You're not having your doubts, are you?"

I inhaled a deep breath through my nose as I thought about her question.

"Because I told you from the beginning that she could be problematic for you."

Without hesitating, I said, "She's not the problem."

"If not her," Madam set her pen down and folded her hands on top of her desk, "then what is?"

I couldn't help but notice the paperwork and images she had open on her desk. "Are those files on the Maria Greer case?" I asked, leaning forward and peering down at her desk.

Without looking, she nodded.

Pushing off the couch, I lunged one foot forward and jabbed my finger down hard on an image of Maria. "That's the problem."

Madam's spine straightened as she cocked her head to the side. Question marks flashed across her eyes and it was clear to me that she hadn't heard the news.

"Mario has refused Cobbs's counsel."

"Cobbs?" Her brows pinched, searching to recall who he was as her head titled further on her shoulders.

"The man I chose to oversee Mario's defense." I fell back into the couch and draped one arm over the back, settling in once again.

Madam cast her gaze to her desk, clearly thinking of the consequences of us losing control of Mario. "I thought you had this under control, Kelly?"

"Believe me, I thought so, too."

She leaned back, threaded her fingers together, and rested them over her stomach. Licking her lips, I watched her eyes move back and forth like she was deciding which option was the better choice on how to proceed.

"Anyway, I thought I would let you know." I sighed. "I wanted you to hear it from me first."

She nodded, still staring at the paperwork that covered her desk. "I've been going over the files—"

"And?" I arched a brow.

Her eyes flicked up to me. "I'm convinced Mario knows the details of Stone's operations."

My stomach dropped. It wasn't about getting justice for

Maria. It never was. The Madam only saw dollar signs and
Maria's murder was her way of getting at what Mario knew about
Stone and the drug operation he was conducting.

"Logistics, drop off points, points of entry," Madam's voice
grew with excitement with each point she listed off, "even the
businesses used to launder money." She lifted her eyes and fixed
them on me. They sparkled like diamonds—like the riches she
was after.

Turning my head to the window, I ran my hand through
my hair.

"Kelly, are you listening?"

I rolled my eyes back to her.

"We have to get Mario to talk."

"What do you suggest we do?"

"Convince him that Blake Stone murdered Maria." She stood
and stepped in front of the mirror. "It will work as long as the
story is told properly."

My face drooped as I frowned.

"What is it?" she asked, looking at me in the mirror's reflection. "Kelly, darling," she turned to glance over her shoulder, "you
don't look too sure of yourself."

"It's not going to work." My voice was flat and barely audible.

Her body twisted fully around, the lines on her face tying
themselves into knots with the questions swirling between
her ears.

"I can't toss the case on purpose." I glanced at her from
beneath a sunken brow.

"You're not thinking of backing out now, are you?"

Madam's eyes hardened and I recognized the look she was
giving me. I couldn't say it outright, but she could see it on my
face. "I don't like our plan, there has to be another way."

"Kelly," she took two steps forward and hovered over me, "I'm
afraid if you leave me out to dry on Stone's case, I'll be forced to
use my wild card."

Swallowing down the stone in my throat, I resented her for threatening to reveal my secret to the world. It would destroy me —my career—if it was ever revealed, and she knew it. Without saying anything more, we both knew that wouldn't be necessary. "You know I wouldn't do that."

"Good." She cheered up and spun around, taking her desk phone into her hand. Her fingers dialed a number. She turned around and rested her tailbone against the edge of her desk and kept her eyes on me when she finally got through. "Oscar, darling." She winked at me. "How are you? It's Maddy."

My eyes widened as a dark tunnel blurred my vision.

I couldn't believe it. Madam had called the DA.

The walls of the room closed in as I sat with my elbows on my knees, trying so hard to listen past my thrashing heart.

Was this her plan all along?

They were discussing Mario's case, the case I was supposed to be overseeing.

I blinked and gently cast my gaze to the floor, thinking.

The Madam was giving the DA ammunition he could use to make a full-on assault against me—and my reputation. What was she doing?

By the time I had snapped out of it, she had hung up. When the room stopped spinning I said, "What was that about?"

"Oscar will knock some sense into Mario," she said, stepping around her desk and floating down to her chair. "You know, threaten him with a bleak future without having strong representation." Her face scrunched with added thrill. "All the juicy stuff DAs do to get people to make the decisions we want them to be making." Her cackle filled the room.

Leaning back, I blew out a weighted breath. And without taking my eyes off of Madam, I knew she had more strings to pull than I ever thought possible.

"I need to know what Mario knows about Stone." She picked

up a pen. "And if you can't convince Mario to accept Cobbs's counsel, then I will."

An intensity zapped the room that wasn't there before.

"I hate to say this, Kelly," she sighed, "because you rarely let me down, but if Kendra is the reason you've failed to find a way to work with Mario, then perhaps I'll have to nullify the month-long agreement I allowed you to have with her."

"Don't be ridiculous." I waved her accusation off. "That's ludicrous."

"Then do me a favor." She set her pen down. "Send her in. I'd like to have a word with her."

My tongue swept across the seam of my lips as my heart paused in my chest.

Her brows raised. "Alone."

35

Kendra

With his hand firmly placed on the small of my back, he nudged me out the front doors of Madam's building reminding me to keep quiet until safely tucked inside his car.

Janine eyed me on the way out but I refused to stoop to her level. I had more important things on my mind than having to show her my claws.

Kelly held out his keys and unlocked his car. The horn beeped and the lights flashed before he stepped forward and reached for the handle. Opening the door for me, he held out his hand and assisted me inside. "Good thing I didn't leave my things in your car," I said, peering up at him.

He slammed the door hard enough to get my insides to jump. Then he marched around the hood of the car and jerked his door open. The entire car dipped and shook under his weight and he adjusted his seat behind the wheel with a grunt of frustration.

He wasn't in the joking mood so I wasn't going to say anything else. Silence filled the air as I looked everywhere but at him. Finally, he said, "What did Madam have to say?"

Glancing up at the red-brick building that housed Madam's office, I said, "It's nothing. Don't worry about it."

Kelly put the key in the ignition and just before I thought he was about to crank the engine over, he paused.

I didn't want to tell him what the Madam said. The thought of her taking him away from me—now, with everything going on in my life—was unbearable. I needed him. More than I was willing to admit myself. But I could still hear her words echoing between my ears. *"Kendra, doll, don't get too attached to that man. Soon I'll require more of your time for deliveries."*

"I see," Kelly said, nodding. "And you expect me to believe that?"

I cast my gaze down to my fingers playing on my lap. And even though I wasn't looking at him, I knew he was looking at me. I despised having Madam come between us. But there wasn't anything I could do about it. At least not now.

And on top of her demands, I had Kelly's too. Not to mention worrying about what my uncle would do next. Letting my head hit the headrest, feeling exhausted, I sighed. "Can we just please drive?"

Kelly didn't budge. He held his stare and I refused to look him in the eye out of fear that this conversation may very well lead to a discussion I simply didn't have the energy for. "Kelly, I'm exhausted." I closed my eyes for a second before rolling my head to him. "We can talk about this later."

His brow wrinkled and his jaw was tight. "Whatever she said, it's probably bullshit."

I rolled my eyes thinking that nearly everything that woman said was complete and utter bullshit. But what could I say? I was stuck.

"You can't break up with me, Kendra. It won't be that easy. And I won't allow it."

I gave him an arched look.

"That's what she wanted to tell you, wasn't it?" His nostrils flared. "To give you a way out."

My brow furrowed. "Excuse me for saying this, but isn't that what you were speaking to her about?"

He laughed. "This isn't a game."

I clucked my tongue, shaking my head. "Good. Because I'm not playing any games. Now, let's just drive."

"If I wanted to end this it would have been finished already." He breathed hard, hot breaths through his flared nostrils. "I don't need the Madam to make my decisions for me."

There was heat in his eye when I lifted my gaze up to his. We stared at each other, neither one of us blinking, before he shoved his fingers through my hair and pulled my face close.

My heart pounded in my chest.

He set my insides ablaze.

But there was also enough uncertainty to keep me feeling trapped.

I didn't know what he was going to do or what his intentions were. But somewhere past the fears I silently begged and pleaded for him to claim my lips as his own.

"Tell me, *Bella,* if it wasn't about our relationship, then what was it you discussed with Madam?"

I couldn't stop staring at his thick lips. The same ones I wanted to be tasting. I liked the way they moved when he spoke. How his tongue darted out from time to time to wet his lips exactly as I saw them go dry. The man was intoxicating and I needed him to see how drunk I was on him.

His other hand lifted to my neck. Gently, I felt the pads of his fingers smooth over the thick vein pulsing below my ear. My panties were wet knowing he could have me any way he wanted, yet, for whatever reason, he refused to take me until he learned the *exact* details of what it was Madam had to tell me.

"Fine," I conceded. "You want to know why Madam keeps contacting me?"

He leaned closer and I could feel his hot breath over my face. "I do," he said in a low, sultry whisper.

My heart slammed against my chest. It raced as adrenaline filled my body with the courage I needed to peel his fingers off my neck—uncurling them off the back of my skull. A small whimper escaped my chest as I reluctantly said, "There's been a man stalking me."

His eyes darkened into something dangerous. It was a new look, one I hadn't ever seen. And though I wouldn't want to see that look directed at me, I could appreciate that his anger was fixed on the secret I had just shared.

"There. Are you happy?"

His eyes twitched as he turned his head. "You should have told me."

I reached over to his lap. Taking his hand inside of mine, I squeezed.

He snapped his head back up. "What's his name?"

My eyes softened though I couldn't stop the tremor that visibly shook my entire core. This wasn't what I'd discussed with the Madam but it was better than having to explain the deliveries I was making for her. Slowly, I shook my head and a lump formed in my throat.

"I fucking knew it." Kelly slapped the steering wheel with his hand. Then he turned and gave me a disappointed look that made me want to cry.

"I didn't know what to do." Tears clouded my vision and my chin quivered.

"You come to me," he barked. "I'll deal with it. That's what you do. That's what you *should* have done."

My tongue darted over my lips as I nodded. "Except it's not what you think."

Our eyes danced as I saw assumptions quickly fill his head.

"I've been seeing this guy everywhere. He knows me and I know him." My words came out fast, like I'd been waiting for the day to finally tell Kelly everything. "He haunts me, Kelly. I can't go anywhere without having to look over my shoulder, thinking that he's just one step behind." I rambled on and as I did, my mind was processing everything at the same time, trying to come to some conclusion that would make sense of the madness that seemed to follow me wherever I went.

Then I stopped.

Kelly leaned forward and lifted his hand to my shoulder. "What is it?"

A light went off and I couldn't believe it. "Madam knew. She knew everything."

Kelly hooked his finger under my jaw and forced me to look him in the eye. He shared the same glossy look as I had as he raced to keep up with what I was saying.

"She got me all riled up." I laughed. "Made me get angry that you were representing a rapist."

Kelly looked at me like I had lost my mind and I couldn't stop from rolling through a fit of disbelieving laughter. "Kendra, baby, tell me who is stalking you."

I covered my mouth to stifle my laugh when I looked at him.

"What does he look like?"

I threw his hand off of me. "I can't believe you. I tell you this, and you think I've forgotten about the blonde you've been seeing?"

He shook his head and turned the key. The engine purred and as soon as we hit ten miles per hour above the speed limit, I rolled down the window and let the fresh air hit my face.

I felt used.

Betrayed.

And, most of all, confused.

The Madam knew about my rape—had *known* about my rape —and I had to assume that Kelly did, too. Why else would he have demanded I stay at his apartment until further notice? Or assign Maxwell to take me wherever I needed to go?

Rolling my head toward him, I said, "You knew."

Kelly down shifted and took the next turn much too fast.

I braced myself and rode it out. Then, when we hit the next straightaway, I said, "You both knew."

"Excuse me? Knew what? Kendra, listen to yourself. Words are coming out of your mouth but you're not saying anything."

My eyes narrowed. "When did she tell you?"

Kelly's foot hit the brake and slowed to turn into the hotel parking lot.

"Did she tell you before you purchased me for a month? Or did you find out after?"

The sun disappeared as soon as Kelly dove the car beneath the concrete garage and zipped to the corner where he parked in his special spot. He killed the engine, leaned over the center console, and said, "Please tell me what exactly you're talking about. Because I don't fucking know."

My chest heaved as I looked back with protruding eyes. "You knew my uncle lived in LA. So did the Madam. That's why you put Maxwell in charge of me."

"Why should I worry about your uncle?" His eyes danced with mine. "Huh? Tell me. Is he dangerous?"

"I hate him so much," I whispered, feeling my entire face scrunch up. Heat flushed through my body and my muscles quivered. The deep hatred I was feeling toward everyone I knew consumed me. I wanted to fight back, show them that I couldn't be fooled. But, most of all, I wanted to run away and start over.

"Why Kendra? Tell me why you hate him so much."

Squeezing my eyes shut, I whipped my head around with

tears filling my eyes. "Because he's the man who raped me!" I screamed.

Kelly's eyes went wide.

I watched him slowly retreat, looking at me like he didn't know who I was.

My heart ached as I wiped the tears away that were streaming down my face.

A hollowness filled my chest as I looked around, wondering what would happen to me.

I loved living in LA, was enjoying my time with Kelly, but now neither one seemed like the friend I thought I had. They were strangers in a familiar land. And it hurt, hurt so fucking bad.

I wrapped my arms around myself. I tried to bring life back to my cold, dead body. When I glanced at Kelly, his eyes were still bulging out of his head and he hadn't moved since learning my secret.

"That night I left your apartment," I began, choking back the tears as I talked, "the night of strawberry champagne and fruit..."

Kelly blinked and I knew that he was listening.

"The reason I left," I paused, unable to believe I was actually telling him this, "is because the way you touched me," the tears began pouring from my eyes, "reminded me of him."

Kelly dropped his head inside his hand, refusing to show me the pain I knew he was feeling.

I sat there crying, waiting for him to speak. An eternity seemed to pass. The tears continued to fall and I sniffed them back, hopeful that he would still want to make this work.

Several minutes passed before Kelly brought my worst fears to life.

"I can't do this, Kendra." Kelly's voice was soft, low and hidden behind his hand. "All the games, all the demands, the sex, the parties...it has to stop."

I broke into uncontrollable sobs as my stomach hardened.

When he finally looked up at me, his eyes were watery with regret. "Get out."

All the air in my lungs escaped and I couldn't breathe.

"Get out, Kendra."

I began to hyperventilate as I looked around, wondering where I was going to go.

"Get out!" He yelled.

36

Kelly

My knuckles were white on the wheel as I drove fast and reckless.

I was pissed. Kendra should have told me that she had been raped and that I was the cause of her trigger. I could have done something, maybe even have prevented her complete collapse.

The tires squealed as I whipped around a turn.

A car honked, having to slam on its brakes to avoid hitting me head-on, and I pressed my foot down on the accelerator and continued driving without so much as a second glance.

She had to leave. It was the only way. And though it hurt to see her looking back at me like I was supposed to be the one to cure her aches and pains, I couldn't let her stay.

My chest tightened and I had a sinking feeling in the pit of my stomach that I had made a mistake. But without being able to touch her—too fearful that I would set off a series of torments that would eat her from the inside out—it would be impossible for me to console her.

This was bad. Really fucking bad.

When I blinked, I could see the pain in her eyes. She cried like something I hadn't seen in a very long time. And that hardened my stomach with the memory of how I felt when Nora passed. Not even Kaycee cried that much these last few days she'd been in town. And my heart ached to see Kendra hurting as badly as she was.

But she had to leave.

I had to be alone.

What I was about to do she had no business being a part of.

The roadside was empty as I pulled to the curb. Shutting off the engine, I tossed the keys on the dash and took a minute to look around.

Mature trees cast their shadows over the dozens of tombstones that rested between the meandering paths. Between the grays and greens was the occasional array of freshly laid flowers. It seemed as if I couldn't escape this place this week. It was the focus of much of my attention and I thought that my latest visit with Nora was my last—at least for a while. But now I knew that I had nowhere better to go than here that would help me come to some kind of conclusion on how best to move forward in my life.

Saying a quick prayer, I reached for the glove compartment and took the revolver into my hand. I tucked it away inside my suit jacket pocket before gathering the orchid flowers I had brought Nora.

The moment I stepped out of the vehicle, I blew out a shaking breath and shoved a hand through my hair.

I still couldn't believe what Kendra had told me. She thought I knew about the rape but I didn't. And maybe Kendra was right about the Madam, perhaps she knew and that was part of the reason she told Kendra about me representing Mario. And if that was true,

Madam's plan worked—creating tension within our budding relationship to cast enough doubt to get us looking at each other with a skeptical eye. But that wasn't the reason I demanded she live with me, or the basis for why I assigned Maxwell to be her driver.

My vision tunneled as I worked my way through the maze of tombstones.

Each step was lighter than the last.

I deeply regretted that today was going to be a much more difficult visit than my previous visits here with Kaycee.

It was different.

Darker.

With more at stake than what I thought was possible.

But, truth be told, I'd had enough. Enough of Madam's fucking games. I was growing tired of how she controlled and manipulated her way into my relationship with Kendra. If only things would have been different—if Kendra wasn't one of Madam's girls, if we'd met under different circumstances—then maybe we wouldn't be where we found ourselves today.

Glancing down, the grass was wet on my shoes. It had been recently cut and that fresh-cut grass smell of summer filled the air. It should have been enough to fill me with hope. Instead, I was nervous and bloated with remorse.

The sun had disappeared over the horizon by the time I reached Nora's grave. The birds were singing their last songs of the day as I mumbled past a constricted throat, "You're the only one I want to be with."

Then the first tear fell.

Her name—Nora Spears— carved into stone, stared back at me as I continued mumbling through the streams of tears falling down my cheeks.

"Nora, baby, I can't let you go. I can't give you up. You're still with me. Day in and day out. You're there. Every step of the way." I pinched my nose and wiped the moisture away. "And you want to know what's worse?"

I lifted my head and turned to the street, allowing a motorcycle to whiz past before I continued.

"That I still feel that way, even with you deciding to give up on me." My eyes swelled as I choked on my own self-loathing. "My heart still longs for your love."

My fingers opened and I dropped the orchid flowers over her gravestone. They floated with grace as gravity pulled them down to earth.

"Tell me what to do, Nora. Give me a sign," I muttered as I reached inside my pocket to allow my fingers to curl around the handle of my gun. "You know about Kendra. I know you do." I tipped my head back and laughed. "You know how bad I have it for her."

A light breeze made the leaves on the trees dance just as a song bird flew over.

Taking in a deep breath, I said, "Tell me, my love—" my index finger curled around the trigger, "—should I stay or should I go?"

More tears fell and my free hand started to shake.

Everything slowed to a crawl as I pulled the gun out of my pocket and slowly angled it at my head.

My world spun and my heart thrashed between my ears.

Sweat dripped down my back as the flood down my cheeks intensified.

Staring down the barrel I cried, "We can all be together. Just the three of us. Together again."

My brows furrowed and my nostrils flared.

I sobbed as I willed my finger to squeeze the trigger.

Primal sounds escaped my body as my eyes drowned in their agony.

The moment my muscles flexed, I dropped the gun away and tipped my head back, pleading with God. "Fuck you! This is all your fault. My life wasn't supposed to be like this!" I screamed as I fell to my knees and let my head come to rest on Nora's gravestone. "God, I miss both of you." I kissed the cold rock.

I wailed into the rock until my tears ran dry. I needed an answer to what to do next. I wanted Nora to be the one to give it to me. "I really like her, Nora. She's strong. Doesn't take shit from anyone. Just like you." My face filled with a smile. "And it's getting serious between us. I need to decide."

Pushing myself back on my knees and sitting on my heels, I plucked an orchid flower off the ground and stroked the petals between my fingers.

"Nora, please, I need you to guide me in making my decision. I can only do this with you. Everything I do, I still do it for you. I can't do this without you. You know this. I'm broken without you."

My eyelids fluttered closed. And as I sat there listening, hoping Nora would respond. I found myself smiling. Warmth filled my chest with optimism. Suddenly, my shoulders felt lighter. I could breathe easier and when I heard a light flutter nearby, I opened my eyes to find a bird landing next to me.

The bird hopped around before touching an orchid flower with its beak. Then it angled its head to me and we shared a look of amazement. "Thank you," I whispered.

As soon as the words were spoken, the bird flew away.

Standing, I knew that that was Nora—her way of telling me that I must carry on without her. A minute later I was back in my car staring at my ringing cell phone, collecting my emotions. "Hey, Giselle." I cleared my throat. "What's up?"

"You need to get back to the office. And quick."

I wiped my eyes and face with my hand. "What's going on?"

"It's about Mario. He's ready to talk."

37

Kendra

As soon as I heard the knock I opened the door to find Alex waiting on the other side.

She immediately saw the anguish tearing me apart inside. It was written all over my face and I broke down crying. "Kelly left me. He left me, Alex." I couldn't hold back. She needed to know. It was the reason I'd called her in the first place.

Frowning, she took me in her arms and pulled my head down to her shoulder. My eyes puffed up and swelled as I broke down, sobbing. "It wasn't supposed to be like this. I told him the truth when I shouldn't have. The truth always gets me in trouble." I blubbered on and on in an incoherent jumbled mess that even I could hardly understand.

"Slow down, baby girl." Alex took me by my shoulders and pushed herself away so she could see my eyes. "What happened?"

Her dazzling eyes darted over my face for a second before they lifted, glancing over my shoulder. "Is he here?"

I shook my head. I knew what she was thinking. Why would I go back to his penthouse after he told me to get out of his life? But, technically, this was where I thought he would want me to go. "I had nowhere else to go." I sniffed away the tears.

Taking her by the hand, I pulled her inside.

"Can I make you some tea?" Alex offered. "Assuming he has tea."

She gave me a skeptical look and I nodded, pointing toward the kitchen cabinets to the left of the fridge.

"God, this place is amazing," Alex murmured as she took it all in. "Although having to go through a hotel lobby every time you come home is kinda weird."

I was still shell-shocked from what happened. I knew that I should be nodding or adding to the conversation by saying everything that came to mind. But I couldn't. My mind was zoning and my body was numb. It felt like I was living in a dream—an alternate reality, one in which I didn't even recognize myself.

Alex found a box of herbal tea and set it on the counter before filling the kettle. "I can't believe he wants you to stay *here* with him." She turned to look over her shoulder. "I mean, he *did* want you to stay with him." Her voice dropped to an insecure whisper as she broke eye contact and turned on the water.

My feet rooted to the floor. I hadn't moved.

I had called Alex here because she had the car—the means to get here quick—and I didn't have it in me to fight my way across the city through public transportation or even hailing a lift. Despite what Kelly did, a part of me still hoped that he wanted me here, waiting for him to return.

I blinked and when my lids opened again, Alex had moved to the bouquet of flowers Kelly had placed in a gorgeous vase on the island kitchen counter. "These are beautiful. Are these the ones he got you?"

The lump in my throat—the same one that was left over from my conversation with Kelly—grew, cutting off more of the air filling my lungs. She was right. They were beautiful. Orchids, lilies, a variety of others that brought color to the modern room. And despite their pleasant aroma, I didn't want to think of the reason Kelly had them there.

Turning my back on Alex, it was too painful to think of Kelly. I hated being inside his home where everything reminded me of all that I might lose.

I dropped onto the couch and hugged my knees to my chest, regretting having told Kelly anything. Dropping my forehead to the top of my knee, I realized that I should have taken my chances with telling him what the Madam and I were *actually* talking about. At least then he could be mad at her instead of at me.

A minute later I felt the cushion next to me sink under Alex's weight. The smells of peppermint tea filled the air and when I lifted my head, she handed me a steaming mug.

Taking a small, hot sip, Alex set her mug down and couldn't stop feeling the soft leather couch. "I love this couch." Her gaze traveled the living room. "It's all so beautiful," she said.

It was beautiful and luxurious. But it was also Kelly's. Half of the reason my belly was still tied in a tight knot was because he was here even when he wasn't.

"Now, tell me what happened." Alex bent one leg and sat on its calf, letting her other leg fall over the side. She picked up her tea and rested it on her thigh as she fixed her gaze on me.

I glanced at her, wondering where I should begin. And then, before I knew it, I was telling her everything that had happened.

Her brows squished when I told her how I thought Kelly was fed up with my antics, enough to bring me to the Madam. "I thought he was there to dump me."

"But if he didn't, then why did he bring you there?"

My shoulders shrugged. "I don't know. But Madam needed to discuss some things with me so maybe he knew that. She'd called me, after all."

"So, back up one second." Alex wrapped her lips around her mug and stole a sip. "But he did break up with you?"

I wasn't sure. "He left me," I said, still in denial of what had happened.

When Alex gave me a questioning look, I told her how Kelly and I got in an argument over what he discussed with the Madam and how he demanded he know what the Madam discussed with me. "But I can't tell him about the deliveries," I said to Alex.

She lowered her mug and let out a heavy sigh. "Because that's between you and the Madam."

I nodded. "And I know he won't like me doing it."

"So he broke up with you because you wouldn't tell him?" The wrinkles on her forehead twisted.

My words tried to keep up with my thoughts as I was talking a million miles per minute. Alex kept nodding, keeping an attentive ear on the details as I told her about my theory on how Madam knew much more about my past than I'd originally thought. "Including something that you don't even know," I said, flicking my gaze to hers.

Alex's eyes popped open.

Running my fingers through my hair, I angled my shoulders to her and said, "I wasn't completely honest with you about who my uncle was."

"Okay." She dragged out the word as if she wasn't sure she was ready to hear what I was about to drop on her. But it was important she knew.

My tongue moved over my bottom lip. "You know how I've been thinking I've been seeing my rapist?"

Her head nodded once.

I swallowed back a small sip of my tea to relieve the parched feeling I was experiencing. "It's because I have."

Her lips parted and her brows knitted. "Your uncle?"

Fear rattled my insides, knowing that if I didn't tell her this now—come clean to her about everything—that this would be the one thing that might eventually push her away, too. She was a much better friend then I was, and I couldn't lose both her and Kelly in the same night and over the same demon from my past. A chill worked its way over me as I nodded.

Alex turned her head, blinking, before touching her head. "If you knew, Kendra, why did you agree to meet with him?"

Looking away, I knew how it seemed. "He's family."

"I get that. But if he did those things to you..." Her voice trailed off.

"He's an old man now."

"Who gives a shit?"

I dropped my feet to the floor and set my mug on the coffee table. "Deep inside I want to believe that he is sorry for what he did. I want to believe that he's changed and that he's here because he wants to make things right." I paused.

"But?"

I turned and fixed my eyes on Alex. "But no matter how hard I try to forgive and forget, every time I look him in his eyes," my gaze dropped to my knees as my voice lowered, "I just want to kill him."

"Oh, hun." Alex set her mug down and wrapped her arms around me. "And you mentioned all this to Kelly?"

With my cheek against her shoulder, I nodded. "I also told him that he was the one to trigger the flashbacks."

Her cheek hit the crown of my head and she squeezed her arms around me tighter. "This isn't good."

"I don't know what to do." There were no more tears to shed. I was dry. Just hollow, like I'd lost part of my soul today.

"First thing you have to do," she unwrapped her arms from around me and stood, "is get your butt out of his place and over to mine."

Looking into her eyes, I knew that she was right. No matter how much I wanted to stay and wait to talk to Kelly, deciding to

stay here was a bad idea. Alex's place was the better—safer
—option.

Together, we had my things packed in no time, and as soon as
I zipped up my suitcase I said, "I'm ready."

Alex took a step forward and hugged me. "Everything will
work out the way it's supposed to."

"I know," I murmured as we marched to the front door.
Reaching out to turn the knob, the door swung open just as a
slender wrist caught my focus. The balled hand about to knock
on the door lowered to a waist. I couldn't believe who was
standing there on the other side.

38

Kelly

I stared out the passenger window with a pinched expression.

That same song bird's tune from last night played inside my head on repeat and I couldn't deny the clear sign that it was. I had little doubt it was Nora's way of speaking to me.

She was there.

She was listening.

I knew it was her. She wanted me to fight. Not only to survive, but thrive.

The street lights flickered as we passed beneath them.

For too long I'd lived in self-pity. Whether I wanted to admit it or not, that was the cold, hard truth. It was time to stand up and move on. Time to allow myself to open up, to learn to fully trust, and most importantly to learn to love again.

And love with the same intensity as I loved Nora.

We hit a bump and my eyes popped open.

Feelings of regret stirred inside me and there was little doubt in my mind that if I could go back in time, I would do things differently. It was those lessons I needed to remember if I was ever going to find my way to seeing the light once again.

"Hey, you all right?" Colin glanced over at me from behind the wheel.

"Yeah." I dropped my hand away from my face and quickly glanced in his direction before fixing my eyes on the road ahead. "Just thinking about the case."

"I'm sure Mario has come to his senses," Giselle's voice said from behind me.

Colin nodded.

"Why else would he request to speak with all three of us? And so urgently?" Giselle continued sharing her thoughts.

Glancing at the clock, I knew that we were calling it close. Visiting hours were nearly done for the day yet here we were, trying our best to see what news Mario desperately wanted to share. And when I should have been concentrating more on him, my mind drifted back to Kendra.

My nose was runny and my eyes gritty.

I didn't know where my relationship with Kendra would go from here. All I knew was what I saw—heard—when visiting Nora's grave. Kendra had to be my priority. I had to have her in my life.

My stomach rolled and I deeply regretted yelling at her to get out. I should have never gotten so angry with her over something she had no control over. A part of me hoped that she knew me well enough to find refuge inside my apartment, waiting for me to come back, trusting I eventually would. But I couldn't blame her if she didn't. Not with the way I'd directed my anger at her—like she was at fault for what happened.

Pulling out my cell from the inside of my suit jacket pocket, I knew we were a minute out from arriving. Scrolling through my list of contacts, I quickly found her name and I debated whether or not to press the call button or send her a quick text. I needed to hear her voice—know that she was all right. But instead I sighed and tucked it back away.

"Look, we'll set Mario straight," Colin said to me. "He has to know his options are slim."

Nodding, I struggled to decide whether or not I should share what I knew the Madam had done when placing a call to Oscar. Giselle and Colin deserved to know but, in the end, I decided to let it go, choosing to first hear what Mario had to say.

The Madam's call to the DA still didn't sit well with me and perhaps that was another reason I was quietly stuck inside my head. "I know we will," I muttered.

Giselle let her hand fall to my shoulder. Her fingers gently squeezed and my lips tugged at the corners. It was like she knew the battle I was fighting inside my head—knew the kind of day I'd had.

Crossing my arm over my chest, I patted her hand with mine.

She was putting in another excruciatingly long day and it wasn't going without notice. I still didn't like how she was putting more energy into Mario's case than working on her personal relationship. But I couldn't say anything because I was, too.

We arrived at County and as a wolf pack of three, we made our way through security, leaving all our electronics at the door. I was happy to see Mario already waiting in the visitor room, knowing that this meeting would be cut short due to running out of time.

"Nice to see you actually showed up this time," I said as we entered.

Mario looked less than amused as he looked me over.

"I suppose you should start this meeting, seeing as you're the one who called all of us in." I followed Colin's and Giselle's lead at taking a seat around the chrome metal table.

Mario's eyes squinted as he rubbed the stubble on his face.

"Okay, since you're not in the mood, I guess I'll go ahead and get us started." Not wanting to waste any more of our time I began, "This is your new lawyer, Colin Cobbs."

Mario folded his arms over his chest and angled his head to the side.

"He's the one who will ensure you walk free." I paused to gauge Mario's reaction. There was still nothing. "This isn't a game. Your time is close to up."

Colin leaned forward. "The case the DA is building against you isn't good." Slowly, Mario's squinted eyes turned to Colin. "Would you like to hear just a taste of what image they'll paint for the jury?"

Mario's tongue slid across his top teeth as he looked away.

"I'll tell you anyway." Colin lowered his eyeglasses. "They will argue that a sex-crazed immigrant lunatic was terrorizing inno-cent women's lives and Maria Greer was the unlucky one among dozens who just happened to be murdered at the hands of Mario Jimenez." He threw down image after image of domestic violence photos. Pictures of battered women's faces, all puffed up and swollen, soon filled the entire table. "And they'll connect you to all these unsolved cases."

"Mario," I said, leaning forward. "You have two options. Allow Mr. Cobbs to represent you—where he'll put together a foolproof strategy that will cast doubt in the eyes of your peers and counter the facts the DA's office is relentlessly building against you—"

He cocked one brow.

"Or work a plea deal."

He laughed.

I shared a quick glance at Giselle.

"I guess you haven't heard," Mario sneered.

"I've heard that you have refused Mr. Cobbs's counsel. I've heard nothing else since you failed to show the other day." I brought my elbows to the table and leaned forward. "Do you think this is a game?"

He shook his head and chuckled. "Too late, Mr. Black."

My brow furrowed as I held my breath to listen.

"I've already cut a deal with the DA."

"I knew this was a waste of our time." Colin pushed his chair back from the table and stood.

"Is that right?" I asked.

Mario nodded. "Earlier today. After he visited me."

Giselle glanced at me as she asked, "You visited with the DA?"

"It's over." He licked his lips and had the look of a man who had already accepted his fate. "I'm a dead man, Kelly. Either in prison or on the outside. I'm dead."

The room fell silent.

"Nothing I can say now will change that."

When the large metal door buzzed opened, I glanced at the clock and knew our time was up. I watched the guard motion me with his hands before moving to pull Mario up to his feet. Reaching across the table I grabbed Mario by the arm. "Who got to you?"

The guard pulled on his opposite arm and I pulled back, refusing to let him go. "Did Stone threaten you?"

He jerked his arm free and kept his eyes fixed on me without saying a word as he slowly walked away.

The room spun as I followed him with my eyes, watching him until he disappeared completely. Shoving a hand through my hair, I slammed my hand down on the table and cursed.

"What the hell just happened?" Cobbs asked, stunned.

"I don't know but, I'm going to find out."

39

Kendra

I gaped at her.

She was stunning.

The way her blonde hair cascaded over her shoulders and down her back in thick waves had me backing away. Her fair skin was covered in silver jewelry that reflected perfectly against her white plunging drape dress with a surplice front that opened at the midriff, perfectly highlighting her lean legs.

Without having seen her before, I knew who she was. But what had me most surprised was her intelligent eyes.

"Is Kelly home?" she asked.

A flash of jealous anger zipped up my spine. Taking a quick glance behind at the suitcase I was pulling, I reluctantly said, "No."

She cast her gaze to Alex and then back to me. "And you are?"

"Kendra." Then I debated whether or not I should also add,

Kelly's girlfriend, but decided to leave that part out because I didn't know if I was or not.

"Ah, yes." She smiled. "I've heard lots about you."

My lips parted with disbelief.

"Can I come inside?"

Alex leaned against my shoulder and whispered in my ear, "She's the one I saw Kelly with."

The woman heard Alex and countered, "It's not what you think."

I wanted to believe her. To hear her out. But with all the ups and downs of my day, my shield was still up and my defenses were ready to strike. I openly stared at her with my muscles bunching. Finally, curiosity got the best of me and I nodded and stepped aside. "I don't know where Kelly is but you're free to come inside."

She glanced at Alex, then to my suitcase.

"We were just on our way out."

She reached out and fingered my hand. "If you have a minute, I'd like to speak with you."

I glanced over my shoulder to Alex. Without a word, I knew exactly what Alex thought I should do. But despite her silent pleas for us to leave, I couldn't run. Not when I could finally get some answers to my many questions—learning why Kelly had been secretly meeting with this woman when he should have been with me.

"Preferably alone." She nodded to Alex.

I twisted around and smoothed my hand down Alex's upper arm, nodding.

"I'll be in the hallway if you need me." Alex leaned in and kissed my cheek.

"I'll be fine," I said. But we both knew that wasn't completely true. There was no telling what would happen.

Waving her inside, I couldn't deny how emotionally wrecked I was tonight. And to top it off, I now had to face off with this beautiful woman whose original intention in visiting was to see Kelly. Before reaching the kitchen, I turned around and said, "What's your name?"

Over my shoulder I saw Alex pause before stepping into the hall, wanting to learn her name as well.

"Kaycee." She smiled.

"Can I make you some tea or something?" I asked when I found my empty mug in the sink.

She kindly declined my offer. "Look, I know how awkward this all must seem to you."

Refusing to look at her, I kept my back turned and washed my mug. She had no idea how awkward this was. With the little bit I knew about her, I couldn't deny the thought that both of Kelly's lovers might now be standing in the same room. "You said you've heard lots about me?"

Slowly, I turned to find her resting her tailbone against the stool behind the island counter. "I have," she said in a friendly tone. "Once I got Kelly to open up, I couldn't get him to shut up about you."

That didn't seem like the Kelly I knew. Naturally, I remained skeptical. "Why would he do that?"

She brushed her hair away from her face as her lips tugged upward to reveal her pearly whites. "He likes you Kendra."

Dropping my gaze to the floor I thought about her words, then fixed my eyes back on her. "But aren't you two..."

She snickered, shaking her head. "Oh, no."

My brows drew together. "Then who are you?"

Her eyes lit up. "I'm his sister-in-law."

I wanted to laugh but I just felt like crying.

"Nora was my sister. Kelly was married to her," she added when I showed no understanding.

"Kelly was married?" My voice was weak, cracking with insecurity.

"I know, I can't believe it either." She laughed. "I'm in town because, well..." she cleared her throat and looked away, "it's the fifth anniversary of her death."

My neck craned toward her and that same ache in the back of my throat from earlier came back. This time it was much more intense and I felt my eyes begin to swell with tears.

Silence filled the room as neither one of us knew what to say next. I couldn't believe my ears. First, Kelly was married. Then I learned that his wife had died. "I'm sorry," I held a hand over my mouth, "he never mentioned any of it to me."

Her hand flew to her chest. "I thought you knew."

Shaking my head, I fought back the tears that threatened to spill. "We haven't been seeing each other that long."

Kaycee pushed away from the counter and moved to the living room with crossed arms. I watched her casually browse the walls, stopping to stare at photographs of Kelly, paintings and art placed throughout the room.

"He's happy, Kendra." She turned her head to meet my gaze. "And I'm certain it's because of you."

Warmth filled my insides when hearing her words but I also wondered if it was coming a little too late. I moved to stand to the side of the island counter, balancing myself with one hand on top. "Then why hasn't he mentioned any of this to me?"

She pivoted and squared her shoulders with mine. "Have you ever lost someone you loved?"

Dropping my gaze, I didn't have the heart to tell her that I'd lost my entire family but not to death. I shook my head.

"God willing," she cleared her throat to get her voice back, "I hope you never do. But if you do, then you'll know just how hard it is."

"I'm sorry for your loss." My words floated through the air like clouds on a calm day.

Suddenly, the front door opened and we both turned, expecting to see Alex.

Kelly stood there with disbelieving eyes. Doing a double take, I smiled and he blinked back.

Kaycee strode over to me and gave me a hug. "It was nice meeting you, Kendra."

"You too."

Then she turned her head and whispered in my ear, "Don't let him go. He's a good one. And I'm sure you are, too."

I nodded. "Thank you."

I watched Kaycee make her way over to Kelly. She hugged him like she did me, and I heard her tell him that she just wanted to say goodbye before leaving town. Kelly thanked her for visiting, saying how great it was to see her. Then she was gone.

When the door behind her closed, Kelly turned to me with a glimmer of danger in his eye and I knew then that this was our chance to make our break it.

There was no turning back.

If he truly wanted me, it was now or never.

40

Kelly

I knew the moment that I saw them together that Kaycee had done the hard talking for me.

Sauntering over to Kendra, I could see the nerves ticking in her neck. "Kelly, I had nowhere to go."

I closed the gap that kept me separated from her one step at a time. The way she was looking at me led me to believe that Kaycee had told her about Nora. I didn't mind. It was only a matter of time before I would have to confess my past marriage. But what she didn't know was that Nora was the reason I'd come back to her tonight.

"I was just leaving." She pointed to the suitcase propped by the door. "Alex is somewhere in the building. She can help me gather my things." When her eyes met mine, she gulped down a large breath of air. "I know you don't want to see me and I can just stay with her."

Tucking a loose strand of hair behind her ear, I quickly pulled back, hesitant to touch any more of her. My brows pinched with a painful expression as I held my hand close to her face, willing myself to not take it any further out of fear of being the one to set off another trigger.

Kendra turned her head and looked at my hand, her pupils dilated. She was as nervous as I was. And though I knew she couldn't see or hear my pounding heart, I was terrified, not knowing how best to deal with this.

I wanted to touch her. Comfort her, let her know that she was here to save me.

Everything slowed down.

The room spun.

And soon it was just us, together, breathing as one.

Finally she lifted her hand, stealing mine somewhere along the way, and brought it to her cheek.

Her face was warm in my hand, soft against the touch. Closing her eyes, she pushed more of her face into my palm. Slowly, her lips tugged into a smile and as bad as I wanted to lift my other hand and smooth it down her opposite arm, I didn't have it in me to do so.

We continued on like this for what felt like forever, suspended in time. My eyes raked over all her delicate features I loved so much. And she continued to nuzzle into my hand like a cat seeking attention.

My entire body tingled for her. I knew that whatever Kaycee had said made Kendra think twice about the man I truly was— the man I wanted to become. She knew what I knew. That she was here to take me out of the darkness and guide me into the light.

I held my breath when Kendra's eyes fluttered open. Standing on her toes, she curled her fingers over my shoulders and pulled herself up against my chest. Then she pressed her lips against mine.

My muscles were stiff as I stood there frozen, unsure if I could kiss her back.

"Kiss me, Kelly."

I was dizzy as I let my eyes dance with hers.

"It's okay, Kelly. I want you to kiss me."

She pressed her lips against mine again and without thinking, my mouth parted wide enough to allow her tongue to slide into my mouth. What started off slow and cautious quickly intensified into desperate flicks and thrusts.

My fingers clamped around her waist and she whimpered into my mouth, buckling at the knees. Hanging on for dear life, I caught her weight and pulled her tighter against my hard body.

I would never let her fall. "Kendra, baby, I needed to be alone. What I didn't need was for you to disappear forever."

She laughed and kissed me deeper. "Kaycee told me, Kelly."

My lips rounded and I blew out a heavy breath.

"Why didn't you tell me?" Her voice was sincere, filled with compassion.

I snaked my hand around her waist, raking my fingers up and down her spine as I brought my gaze above her head. "Her name was Nora. She was the most beautiful woman in the world."

Kendra kept her head tipped back, staring at my face as I talked. Her eyelids hooded over with immense pain for my loss. I could appreciate it but I didn't need her sympathy.

"She was my world." The memories that still haunted me swelled behind my eyes. "And then one day," I swallowed down the stone in my throat, "she killed herself."

Kendra's head snapped up as she gasped. Then her eyes closed just before she rested her head against my dead heart. "Oh, God, Kelly."

I closed my eyes and just wrapped her up into my arms, needing to hold onto something good. The room was silent, lifeless as we just stood there, holding each other into eternity. Then

I said in a low voice, "I loved her. More than anything. *God*, I still do."

Kendra clasped her hands behind my back and squeezed my torso as hard as she could.

My vision blurred as my eyes watered with remorse. "And there is nothing I can do to bring her back."

Kendra lifted her head, tipped her chin back, and brought her hands around front and placed each of them on both sides of my face. Then she kissed me.

Then she kissed me again.

And again.

"You're loved, Kelly."

I nodded.

"I'm here if you need me."

Her lips pressed against mine again.

"We all go through tough times. And I'm here." She smiled.

Thanking her, I said, "I want to be here for you, too."

Her eyes fluttered.

"I know we can make this work."

She bit the inside of her cheek and nodded.

"But I don't want to be the reason you're reminded of what your uncle did to you."

She wrapped me up in her arms and clung to me as if her life depended on it—which in a sense, it did.

"What he did was wrong and I will do anything to make sure he gets the justice you deserve."

She sniffled and I knew that she was crying. Then, after a silent minute, she collected her emotions and said, "I want to help you heal the hole left in your heart."

My eyes closed as relief washed over me.

Kendra flattened her hands on my chest and took one step back.

I watched her cross her arms and pinch the hem of her shirt before lifting it over her head. My heart slammed against my chest as I watched her toss it to the floor. My gaze lowered to her breasts and my cock twitched. Before I knew it, she had stepped out of her pants and was standing there in nothing but her underwear.

God, she was beautiful.

I was hard but hesitant.

And too afraid to tell her that I didn't know how to love her any other way than what she already knew. Our sex was fun and I still held onto the desire to make her submit fully to my demands. But I couldn't risk losing her along the way.

Stepping forward, she must have seen the struggle I was waging with myself, because before I knew it, she was ridding me of my clothes for me. My fingers flexed as I bit my lip, holding back the dark desires of what I wanted to be doing to her.

I wanted to spank her.

Flip her around and taste her.

Shove her to the floor and tell her to wrap her plump lips around the tip of my cock.

I wanted to tie her up and test her limits. I wanted to do all these things to her. Instead I murmured, "You tell me what you want—what you *need*—and we'll play by *your* rules."

Her eyes sparkled with a renewed hope. "Is that a demand, Counselor?"

Nodding, I smiled and crashed my lips over hers.

41

Kendra

He knew he was strong.

A powerful masculinity that I'd seen from day one.

But past his strong jaw and his broad shoulders and towering height, it was what he didn't do that showed me what he was really capable of.

I raked him over, taking all his powerful beauty in with my eyes as I reached behind my back to unclasp my bra. His dark stormy eyes watched me with a hidden courage flickering inside them. Stepping out of my panties I took two steps forward, meeting him where he stood. The heat from his body radiated off his skin and though we weren't touching, my body responded as if we were.

My stomach fluttered.

His eyes locked with mine.

Feeling my nipples perk in response to the heated gaze in his eyes, I cast my eyes down and let myself admire the planes and valleys that made up his torso. His arms were down by his sides, his hands balled into tight fists. It must have been hard for him to not reach up and touch me. I knew how passionate he was, the way he liked to tangle his fingers in my hair, dig his nails into my soft flesh, greedily marking his claim.

Slowly, I lifted my hand to his bare chest and gently rested my hand over his galloping heart. It raced as fast as mine, and he widened his stance like a Titan when I worked to remove his shirt, then his pants.

His muscles jumped against my touch and I could feel the trepidation—knowing he was the reason for my own terror—playing with his nerves. But despite his apprehension, his cock was stiff and neatly tucked away inside his briefs that stretched tightly over his thick thighs.

My body tingled with each accidental touch and his restraint was what had me wet and totally turned on. His gesture to hand over complete control was hot. I appreciated his ability to recognize that I needed this relationship to be mutually respectful. It was about trust, and I knew where we needed to go. Without saying it, I knew he knew what needed to be done as well.

Taking it slow, I circled the dark pigment around his nipple with my nail. It hardened and Kelly only watched, growing harder with each one of my touches.

We took it slow. So slow it was romantic, almost sweet.

I wanted to flick my tongue over his nipple, taste him, remind myself what he tasted like. Instead I raked my fingers over his abs before plunging my hand past the elastic band of his underwear.

He sucked in a deep breath while keeping his gaze locked with mine.

My fingers wrapped around his shaft. His skin was hot, soft and satin-like. It pulsed against my hand and I slowly began pumping him. "We'll get there, baby."

His eyes were dark—ominous with subdued pain—when he nodded.

"You're not him." My palm polished his hot helmet. "And I don't want you to be."

Kelly turned his head, taking his eyes off of me for the first time since our clothes came off, and ran a hand over his face.

Slowly, I pushed him back, guiding him to the chair in the corner. He backpedaled until his massive body crumbled into the chair. Falling on my knees, I pulled his boxer shorts free. His hardness sprang up, hitting him in the bellybutton, and it was gorgeous.

The thick vein beat with life as his cockhead flushed a deep purple. Licking my lips, I leaned forward. Taking my breasts inside each of my hands, I squeezed them around his rod.

His arm lifted, reaching for my face. I watched his fingers flex an inch away before retreating back to the armrest. He wanted to touch me but still couldn't. His pecks jumped as his chest rose, then fell. Torment billowed in the color of his eyes.

Moving up and down his length, I used my breasts—my pebbled nipples grazing his inflamed skin—to massage his member. He groaned and I kept at it.

After a few minutes of teasing him with my breasts, I stood and turned back to the bed. Bouncing my hips with each step, I climbed onto the mattress on all fours. With my ass sticking in the air, I teased him with flirting eyes as I glanced over my shoulder, giggling.

Flinging my hair over my back, I spread my ass cheeks and grazed a finger through my arousal. Then I flipped onto my back and scooted myself against the wall, perching myself up on the pillows.

Kelly lifted a hand to his mouth and sank further down in his chair, highlighting each ripple of his abs.

"Watch me," I purred.

Kelly's tongue glided over his bottom lip before getting stuck in the corner.

Spreading my legs, I licked my middle finger and slowly

brought it between my thighs. Sliding it between my moist cleft, I started to masturbate for him. "I'm thinking about your big cock," I mewed as my finger dipped inside me. "Are you thinking about me?"

My eyes were heavy with seduction but when I glanced in his direction, he was stroking himself. "I am."

"Tell me." I bit my bottom lip as I circled my swollen clit. The tingles of nerves zipped up my spine and curled my toes. "What are you thinking about?"

From root to tip he worked himself harder. "The way I know your sexy pussy feels as it glides over my dick."

His voice was the deep, husky sexiness that had set my body on fire so many times before. My hand worked harder and I began to pant.

I loved the way he watched me. It was like I was a diamond he couldn't take his eyes off of. There was no doubt in my mind he thought I was beautiful—irresistible. We had our flaws, but our need to be with each other would prevail.

Rolling a nipple between my fingers, my hips bucked off the bed as I imagined him moving inside me. He was handsome—the most beautiful man—jerking off for me. His body, a temple for me to worship. I couldn't take my eyes off him. I liked knowing that he was thinking of me—what I felt like when fucking him—when he was driving himself closer to the elusive edge of orgasm.

My knees fell further apart and my body was hot with sweat. "I'm going to come," I breathed.

Kelly's hand worked harder. His face twisted between the pellets of sweat dripping from his brow and I knew he could explode through his own release any minute, too.

"Oh, God, Kelly." My eyes closed and I felt my velvety walls close around my finger. A second finger nudged its way inside as I cried, "Come with me, baby."

"I'm there," he grunted. "Tell me when. I'm right there with you."

The room was humid with our heavy, fast breaths. Bright lights flashed behind my lids as heat spread to my limbs. And when my toes started to curl, I cried, "Now. I'm coming now."

My body shuddered through its orgasm and I could hear Kelly cursing through his. When I opened my eyes, I found him with a creased brow staring at his semen-covered knuckles still tightly gripping his pulsing shaft. Slowly, he lifted his head and he fixed his gaze on me—holding it for a moment—before standing and moving to the bed. He plopped down—lying on his back next to me—and I crawled on top of him, needing to feel him pressed against me.

Our eyes danced as I touched his face. I didn't say anything, and neither did he. We knew. Knew that no words could describe the way we felt for each other. This was real. He was real. And what we had now was only the beginning.

Taking his arm in my hand, I lifted it and placed it on my hip. He held it there still for a minute, then started to smooth it up and down my sweaty body.

We had a long way to go but we would get there, I thought as I felt him get hard again.

Pushing myself up off his chest, I straddled him. Reaching behind my back, I took him by the root and placed his cockhead at my entrance. Then I slid down on him, deciding that it was time he earned his keep.

42

Kelly

All night I held Kendra like I was afraid to lose her.

We made love late into the night. It wasn't rough. It wasn't kinky. Just straight up sex where two people were bound together in a variety of different positions that kept our heartrates up.

It had been a while since I had wanted to do something like that with a woman. I had put more heart into last night than the previous times I'd been with her. It wasn't about pushing boundaries or looking for new ways to increase the height of our sexual prowess. It was all about being there for each other, knowing that we were stronger together.

Kendra snored and I chuckled.

Holding her in my arms, I wanted my touch to be familiar, something she craved, second nature to her. Sometime after her fourth or fifth orgasm she collapsed to the bed, resting her head on my chest. Soon she fell asleep while I let my thoughts drift.

When she rolled away I adjusted myself to her, making sure that I was always there. I wanted my touch to sear into her skin until we became one. I was certain about her, didn't care about her past, and I was willing to make the commitment to ensure this worked —that *we* worked.

My sleep was light, unable to turn off my brain. I couldn't stop thinking about how if Kaycee hadn't come back for the fifth anniversary of Nora's death, I may not have brought myself around to thinking of Kendra as something more than a month-long contract. But I knew what my heart wanted—what it craved. And she was the one.

As soon as the mid-morning sunlight filled the room, Kendra stirred.

I ironed my hand up and down her arm.

She bent her knee and wrapped her leg over my waist, snuggling up against me. "Did you sleep at all?"

"Couldn't."

"Hope I didn't keep you awake. Sometimes I snore."

Tucking her hair behind her ear I said, "You were the reason."

She lifted her head up and rested the point of her chin on my sternum.

"But not because you were snoring." I smiled.

She gave me a questioning look.

"Because last night was amazing."

Kendra crawled up my body and pressed her lips against mine. They were soft, like satin, and I didn't want to ever stop kissing her.

"We can repeat that fun this morning." Her eyes sparkled with renewed passion.

I let my hand drift down her back until stopping to rest on her ass I loved so much.

"You don't have work to do, do you?"

I chuckled, thinking that there was always work to be done. Suddenly, my cell started to ring. "Speak of the devil."

Kendra frowned. "Let it go."

I kissed her before rolling her off so I could reach the night-stand. A quick glance at the screen let me know that it was Giselle. "This better be good," I answered.

"I'm downtown." She was breathing fast. "And I just received word that Stone approved our names to his visitor list."

Perking up, I twisted around to find Kendra splayed on her back with an arm draped over her forehead. Her breasts were weighed down by gravity but still soft and perky. I didn't want to leave her—especially with her naked and in my bed. But I knew that I had no choice. "That's great," I said.

"It gets better." Giselle's voice floated cheerfully through the line. "He's requested a meeting."

43

Kendra

Kelly was rolling out of bed much too quick.

My hand swatted after him but missed. His feet hit the floor and I knew that something was up. Refusing to let him go, I followed him to his closet.

Pulling a collared button-down from the hangar, he turned to me and said, "I'm sorry. But I have to run. Something big is happening at work and Giselle needs me to meet her downtown."

I strode toward him. Lifting my arms up to take his waist inside my hands, I stopped him in his tracks. "When can I see you again?"

He pushed his fingers through my thick locks and bent his neck to kiss me. It was just a gentle peck on the lips but I closed my eyes anyway. "Soon."

Reaching my hand between his legs, I cupped his groin. "Are you sure you can't stay just ten minutes?"

He groaned and plunged his tongue into my mouth. I sucked it before he pulled back. "I can't. This is important."

"More important than me?" I yanked on his limp dick.

He chuckled. "I've requested to represent a big name in hopes of making him my client. It can't wait."

I frowned, refusing to listen to his reason.

He thrust his tongue into my mouth again, swirling it against mine. I whimpered and he promised to call. "What time?" I asked.

He stepped back and shoved his arms through his shirt. Checking the time, he glanced at his gold watch. "Noon."

Reluctantly, I stepped forward and helped him button up. "If you're a minute late I'll be calling you."

He wrapped me in his strong arms and nuzzled his face against my neck. I giggled and laughed, loving how we were back to the playfulness that made him so much fun to be with. "We'll pick this up where we left off."

He pivoted on a heel and reached for his trousers. Stepping through each leg, he glanced up at me. "I'll take you for a romantic lunch. You can drink wine and then we can come back here and make love."

My heart fluttered as I folded my arms across my chest and leaned my shoulder into the doorframe. "I'd like that."

He kissed my cheek as he skirted by, heading for the bathroom. Kelly sprayed some cologne masking the smell of sex still lingering on his skin before brushing his teeth.

"I'm planning to visit Alex," I said, choosing to be transparent.

Slowly, he turned and fixed his eyes on me.

"I thought you would want to know where I'm at." I bit the inside of my cheek. "You know, in case you were wondering."

He lowered his head and marched to the bed stand, taking his cell into his hand. I watched him scroll through his screen before tapping the corner and lifting it to his ear.

A blank expression crossed my face as I wondered who he could be calling.

The conversation was quick and as soon as Kelly lowered his phone away from his ear, he looked me in the eye. "That was Maxwell. He'll take you to Alex's."

Running a hand through my hair, I chuckled. "As long as he's there for convenience and not intel."

Kelly strode toward me, taking my shoulders between his strong hands. He squeezed. "Purely convenience."

"Then I can live with that." My eyelids hooded with the way he was looking at me.

"Now, I really have to be running."

I nodded as he kissed the center of my forehead. As soon as Kelly was out the door, I messaged Alex, letting her know I was on my way. She took the day off from work, and since she rarely did that, I knew that I had to take advantage of her free time to catch up on news.

Once showered and dressed, I found Maxwell in the lobby waiting. When he saw me coming, he stood and smiled.

"You know I'm not happy with you," I said as we strode side by side out to his vehicle.

"I only do as I'm told," he assured me.

"I'm going to forget what happened," I said as I slid into the back of the vehicle, "but please, stay out of my private life."

Maxwell tipped his hat and shut the door. I didn't know if he would respect my request, especially since I knew his loyalty was to Kelly first, but I could only hope that Kelly now understood that it was important he trust me.

We mostly drove in silence to Alex's. Along the way, my mind drifted back, reliving the last twelve hours. The world was full of sunshine and when I thought of Kelly, I smiled. There was still a lot I had to work out with my uncle—and to learn about my parents—but I was feeling much more optimistic about my future than even twenty-four hours ago.

When we arrived to Alex's, Maxwell opened my door. "I'll be parked here, waiting for your return, Ms. Williams."

"Don't get too bored. It might be a while." I smiled, straightening his tie as I stepped out.

He watched me enter Alex's building and I took the elevator up with excitement growing, barely able to wait to tell Alex how amazing last night was with Kelly. As soon as I went for the door handle, the door came flying open. "You're late," Alex said.

I laughed. "Didn't realize we were under the wire."

Her eyes traveled the length of me. "I take it Kelly's return went well."

"What gave it away?"

"Your perky eyes. Smiling face. That fresh glow you only get after amazing sex."

Dropping my head, I giggled. Then I lifted it back up with eyes that smiled. "I'm sorry I asked you to leave after coming to rescue me."

She leaned in and gave me a hug. "That's what I'm here for."

My eyes closed as my chin rested on her shoulder. A fresh scent traveled up my nose as I sniffed. "Are you cleaning?"

Alex laughed. "Didn't think I knew how, did you?"

"No, I knew you did." My brows pinched, trying to understand what was going on.

She pushed my shoulders away. "And now you can help."

"Oh, no. *That* is not what I'm good at."

"You're great at everything you do." She took me by the hand and dragged me inside her apartment. It sparkled and shined with that freshly cleaned smell. "Now, come help me unpack the groceries."

My lips parted at the sight. Alex was good with food, always had plenty, but I had never seen it like this. She had taken it to a whole new level. The kitchen counters were filled with grocery bags. I gave Alex a look and she reminded me, "Nash is coming home."

"It's about damn time."

Alex covered her mouth and squealed. "And I'm planning a sexy night for our reunion." She pulled out a bottle of wine and held it up.

Snatching it out of her hand, I read the label. "Fancy." My eyebrows wiggled.

When we finished filling the fridge, Alex asked, "Did Kaycee stay long?"

"We talked for a while." I moved to the liquor cabinet, pulling out a bottle of vodka. "Then Kelly came home and she said her goodbye."

"Awkward," Alex sang.

My mind zoned, orange juice in hand, as I thought about how Kelly had been married and how he was technically a widower.

Alex's hand drifted across my shoulders before she snatched the juice bottle out of my hand. "Here, let me make it. I want one, too."

I blinked and glanced at her.

"Screwdriver. That's what you're making, right?"

Taking a deep breath, I said, "Kelly was married before."

Alex's eyes rounded as she set the container of juice down on the counter. "Wow." I could see that she was thinking. "Then who was Kaycee?"

"Sister-in-law." My eyes flicked up to hers. "Visiting."

"Visiting Kelly?"

Nodding, I added, "In town for the fifth anniversary of her sister's death."

"Shit." Alex lifted a hand and touched her neck. "That's heavy."

"You're telling me."

Popping the top off the bottle of vodka, Alex poured two glasses then mixed it with orange juice. "I wonder why we couldn't find that out." She handed me a drink after she'd stirred it. "You'd think it would be an easy internet search away."

I shrugged, taking a sip. "It doesn't matter."

Closing my eyes, I felt relaxed and at peace. Maybe it was my after-sex glow whose high I was still riding out, or perhaps it was believing that Kelly would make all the bad in my life disappear. Whatever it was, I was confident in my steps going forward. When my eyes opened, I caught Alex glaring. "What is it?"

She set her drink down and sighed. "Did you two discuss more about what your uncle did?"

"I'm not worried about my uncle."

"That's not what I asked."

"I trust Kelly." My tongue slid over my lips. "I just want to move on."

"You can't just push aside what happened to you."

"I'm better when I don't think about it."

"That's not a good approach."

Taking my drink with me, I padded to the living room and fell into the couch. "What do you want me to do?"

"Get help. To not push this to the side. I saw how much it affected you and I don't want to see you have to go through that again."

Tossing back my drink, I gulped down a mouthful. I wished people would just let this go. I knew I had lots of work to do—find ways to come to terms with the trauma I'd experienced. Kelly would seek justice and Alex would push me to seek professional help.

"I still think that you should seek professional counseling."

Then, there it was. Finishing my drink, I checked the time. It was nearly noon and I knew Kelly would be calling. Moving to the kitchen, I dug through my handbag for my cell. "Kelly, should be calling soon," I mumbled.

"You don't notice it, do you?" Alex huffed.

I glanced at her with an arched brow.

"How you always change the subject when the conversation gets real."

Staring at the time, I waited and watched for Kelly to call.

"You can't run away from this, Kendra."

The clock ticked over and Kelly still hadn't called. I hurried to the window. "I'm calling him."

Alex threw her hands down to her sides and turned her back.

The line rang a couple of times before a woman's voice answered. "Kendra, it's Giselle. Kelly's assistant."

My heart stopped. With a knitted brow I twisted my spine to find Alex staring at me with folded arms. "Is he all right?"

Alex scampered over to me and touched my arm, knowing something was wrong.

The next words out of Giselle's mouth faded the light I'd felt growing in my life. A dark tunnel closed around my vision and I felt dizzy. "I'll be right down," I murmured. Then I ended the call and looked at Alex.

"What is it?" Her neck craned.

With a parched throat I said, "Kelly's been arrested."

Continue the series in Black Obsession. Click here to start reading today!

AFTERWORD

Never miss a release. Sign up to my newsletter and stay in the know. Visit me at www.CJThomasBooks.com

ALSO BY CJ THOMAS

City by the Bay series

Ruin Me

Promise Me

Save Me

Take Me

Control Me

Tempt Me

Hollywood Dreams series

Big Willy Box Set

Beyond Tonight Box Set

On My Knees Box Set

Capture Me

Heat

Hard

A Kelly Black Affair

Black Desire

Black Demands

Black Obsession

Black Regrets

Black Promises

Black Escape

Black Surrender

High Stakes Billionaires

This is Love

Accidentally in Love

ACKNOWLEDGMENT

I want to thank all of my readers for being supportive with each new story I write. It's because of you and your willingness to WANT to read my stories that make this all possible. Mwah!

I also want to thank my editor, LNS, for bringing my stories to life and constantly providing constructive advice on how to improve my craft. The same goes to my street team and beta readers, for without you, I'm not sure I would have the confidence to continue living inside my characters' heads day after day.

And last but not least, my family for giving me the love and inspiration to keep writing.

Never miss a release date. Sign up for my Newsletter!
www.CJThomasBooks.com

CPSIA information can be obtained
at www.ICGtesting.com
Printed in the USA
LVHW051119041218
599198LV00001B/55/P

9 781549 754098